Life of the Party

A Trials of Katrina Novel

Maureen Moore

Published by Northern Amusements, Inc., LaSalle, Ontario.

This is a work of fiction. All of the characters, organizations, and events portrayed in this novel are either products of the author's imagination or are used fictitiously.

Life of the Party / Maureen Moore - 1st Edition Trade Paperback
ISBN 978-0-98128170-4

This book and others by Northern Amusements are available in electronic format. Visit our web site at www.northernamusements.com.
e-Pub version
ISBN 978-0-98128171-1
e-PDF version
ISBN 978-0-98128172-8

Cover by Ami Moore

Printed and bound in the United States.

Dedications

For Mom, with all my heart.

And for my brother Dale, for making this possible.

1 HARLEYS, HARLEYS EVERYWHERE

"Hey, little lady, aren't you gonna let me in?" growled a voice from the porch after several persistent bangs on the door.

Katrina, at 5 foot 10, was hardly little, but as she squinted up at the bulking mass before her, she felt puny. It was Harley, her landlord. How did he ever fit on his motorcycle? All that blubber must roll over the sides of the seat. It was a wonder his Harley didn't keel over and die. But she knew from her ex-boyfriend Len that there was muscle under all that fat. He'd told her stories. Scary ones. After all, Harley was the head of the Glory Riders, one of Toronto's infamous biker gangs.

"What is it?" asked Katrina, trying to keep the tremor from her voice while taking a step back. She didn't want this cretin in her house, even though he *did* own it. She glanced into the living room to gain some comfort from the sight of her roommate and best friend, Stevie, who had stood up from the couch and now gazed questioningly toward her. A whole lot of help he'd be protecting her. Stevie weighed about 90 pounds and flapped his skinny little arms like a scarecrow in the wind when he was scared. A butterfly's wings would knock him down.

There'd be no help from her other roommate, Boris, either. The sun was still shining, so he hadn't slunk out of his bedroom upstairs yet. Boris only went out at night. Doing God-knows-what. Dressed all in black. Katrina always wondered when he would flash his fangs or flutter against her window. She and Stevie had discussed carving wooden stakes and bulking up on their garlic supplies.

"That's it?" said Harley, interrupting her thoughts. "'*What is it?*' No 'Hello, how are you? How's it hangin'?'" He turned the handle on the screen door, which Katrina had forgotten to lock, as usual; people in her home town of Pipton rarely locked their doors. "We need to talk."

Katrina looked up at his scruffy beard and aviator sunglasses, so dark you could only imagine the evil glint in his eyes. "Well, uh . . ." But by the time she managed those meager words, he was already in the door.

"Where's that little pansy friend of yours?" asked Harley, taking a step toward Katrina.

Stevie ventured cautiously into the hallway, then shrank into himself when he saw that it was Harley. "Oh . . . it's you," he managed to squeal.

"You two gettin' cozy on the couch?" accused Harley, stepping forward again so that Katrina had to shuffle aside.

"No, I'm just—" began Stevie, taking a step back.

Harley laughed, interrupting him. "Don't shit yourself, kid, I'm just askin'."

He turned away from Stevie, no longer interested. He focused on Katrina. "Your rent's goin' up, darlin'."

Katrina gaped at him. "But why? When?"

"Effective immediately. Isn't that what they say?" Harley grinned, baring his hideous yellow teeth. If he'd ever visited a dentist, it wasn't in this century. He told them how much the increase was.

Katrina gasped. "I can't afford that!"

"That's insane!" added Stevie, as he slid quietly behind Katrina.

Harley just shrugged. "You guys have had it way too easy for way too long. I gave Len the rent real cheap 'cause he's a great mechanic, and he always gave me an awesome deal on his hash. But you two . . . what've you done for me lately?"

Katrina felt the urge to cry but fought it. "But I've only been here 2 months. How could you—"

"Len was here first, and the lease was under his name. Been a year now, I figure. Time for an increase." Harley grinned at their discomfort. Len never did have a lease, but no reason for them to know that. He peered toward the kitchen. "By the way, how's that dog of his?"

A howl erupted suddenly from the backyard, as if Spot, the Doberman, knew they were discussing him. Harley shook his head. "Still tying him up back there, eh? Len's not gonna like that. Not gonna like it at all."

"But Len must be halfway to South America by now," said Katrina, trying to keep the pleading note out of her voice.

Harley swiveled his head away from the kitchen and glanced down at Katrina. "The world's a small place these days, little lady. I know how to get in touch with him."

Katrina cringed. The thought of Len keeping tabs on her from thousands of miles away was terrifying. The thought of the Glory Riders doing it for him was almost enough to make her pee her pants.

"First of the month," said Harley. "That's when I expect the first increase."

"Does Boris know about this yet?" asked Katrina. "If he doesn't, *I'm* sure not telling him."

"I'll tell him," said Harley. "Let the little shithead sleep." He laughed heartily at some joke of his own. "I'm sure he's got a busy night ahead of him."

Katrina and Stevie exchanged a wary look. They didn't know what Boris did for a living, if he even *did* do something for a living, but whatever it was, it was only at night, after receiving a phone call which he never discussed with them. They were scared to ask, and he wasn't about to tell. Aside from rarely seeing him, Boris wasn't exactly one for lively conversation.

Harley stopped laughing and did the menacing thing again. "And make sure the prick gets the rent to me on time this month. I don't take kindly to this late payment shit. There could be interest involved."

"Interest!" gasped Katrina. "Now you're talking a rent hike *and* interest? I told you," she said as she glanced around at Stevie for confirmation and discovered he was quivering a foot behind her, "we can't afford it."

Harley picked at some fungus on his teeth. "Then find a way."

Stevie wobbled forward and somehow managed to defiantly lift his chin. "We'll move out!"

Harley spit a little as he laughed at Stevie. "I don't care what *you* do, dickweed, but sweet little Katrina here has to stay."

Katrina's mouth dropped as Harley continued. "You must've known Len's possessive nature. He's been keeping an eye on you all along."

"But he's thousands of miles away."

"Sure, but he's not stupid. He's got eyes everywhere."

Katrina and Stevie whirled around, suddenly suspecting cameras in the house. Harley's eyes drifted upward, and theirs followed. A camera in the ceiling?

"Boris has been keeping a watch on you. He reports to me, and I report to Len. Good little system." Harley spat out whatever it was he'd found in his teeth. "I mean, that's what friends are for, right?"

Stevie was so outraged that he temporarily forgot his fear. "You can't be serious!"

"Oh yeah," said Harley, temporarily forgetting about his teeth.

"Yeah?" said Stevie dispiritedly, with a shake to his voice and other body parts.

Harley suddenly lunged toward Stevie and slapped him hard across the face, so fast he hadn't even known it was coming, and with about as much effort as he'd use to pick his belly button.

Stevie flew backward into the wall, smacked his head, and crumpled into a heap on the cracked old linoleum floor. Katrina threw Harley a look of disdain, then crouched down to comfort her friend.

Harley watched her with a smirk. "Great bodyguard you've got there." The floor shook as he stomped toward the door. He grabbed the handle, then turned. "Just remember—if you don't pay what I'm asking, it could get a lot worse."

The door slammed and a minute later Katrina heard his Harley pipes roaring down the street as she held Stevie's lolling head in her arms. She was about to get up to grab a wet cloth for him when he muttered something she couldn't understand. Katrina leaned closer and heard him gasp, "Beer . . ."

"What?" said Katrina, "I still can't hear you."

"Katrina," he mumbled, as if with his dying breath, "must . . . have . . . *beer* . . ."

2 THE ROBIN HOODS

Harley rode over to the Glory Riders' clubhouse in East York, where he had an apartment on the second floor. He needed a shower to wash off the stink of that homo Stevie. His hand felt infested from just slapping the twerp. When Boris had told him that the little faggot had moved in, Harley knew he had to do something about it. Len wouldn't like that at all. Not that he had a clue where Len was or that he could possibly contact him, but it was the principle of the thing. Although Harley owned the house, he somehow felt that it rightfully belonged to Len. It was Len's style, not Harley's. Harley was more of a bachelor pad type of guy.

He was glad to get away from the house in Riverdale. He *hated* Riverdale. All those frigging yuppies and rug rats and baby carriages with their presumed right-of-way. If you weren't careful, you could break your neck just walking down the sidewalk. It was too fucking genteel for him. If that was the right word. He'd heard somebody use it once and asked what it meant, and he liked the way it sounded: *Genteeel.*

He'd take East York any day. That was where he'd grown up, where his dad had named him Harley because he revered the big hogs. East York was where the working-class people lived. People with fridges stocked with beer on their front porches, people who watched hockey in the garage, people who actually smoked *inside*. He could live there and feel at home, and go steal from the rich people someplace else. Harley saw himself as a kind of modern-day Robin Hood; he stole from the rich to give to the poor—himself.

The house in Riverdale had been a great deal at the time, a few years ago, when a fellow Glory Rider had to get out of town quickly and was willing to sell at rock-bottom price for cash. The guy hadn't exactly been The Happy Homemaker; the place was a pit. Harley didn't care about the décor, though—it was the neighbourhood that bugged him. Too many frigging neighbours complaining about his yard—what was the problem with a few trash cans and some Harleys chewing up the grass—and the noise? Harley liked his music loud and his bikes louder.

When Harley found out about an apartment for rent above the Glory Riders' clubhouse, he nabbed it. Who the hell would complain about noise to a bunch of bikers? Len, who was the mechanic for most of the Glory Riders and worked from the garage of their clubhouse, moved into Harley's house. Len wasn't a Glory Rider, though he'd been offered, likely because he sold great dope. He saw himself as a lone wolf, not into the group thing. Which Harley thought was stupid, 'cause he hung around with all of them most of the time anyway. But he was happy to find a renter. It'd be hard to rent to someone else; most people were a little bit pickier about flaking plaster and wayward mould and a yard that looked like a construction site. And he didn't want to sell, since the housing market was total shit right now.

Only problem with Len renting, though, was his damn dog, Spot. The noise factor again. Now the neighbours were bitching about the continuous howling from the backyard. Len had cleverly told them all to call Harley to voice their complaints. *He* was the landlord, after all, and Harley thought, *Fuck, how am I going to get out of this one?* Len told him he just didn't have enough time to spend with Spot, what with the mechanic gig and the dope-selling. If he only had someone to help him out . . .

Right away, Harley thought of Boris. He knew that Boris and his partner Ray were getting sick of each other, living and working together 24/7. He'd heard rumblings from both sides. Maybe he could stop the bitching from all ends . . .

Boris and Ray had been best friends in Montreal. In fact, Ray had been Boris's only friend. Boris had never understood why sunny Ray had gravitated toward *him*. Boris could only figure his youngest sister Tracy and her big boobs had something to do with it.

Despite Boris's hundreds of lessons over the years, he was lousy with languages and could never grasp French. Besides, he thought, why should he? He was in an English-speaking country, for Chrissakes. Fuck 'em! He couldn't get out of that town soon enough. He was dying to move to an Anglo place where people could actually understand what he was talking about and not scowl at him when he spoke his native—shit—rightful!—language.

So at 16, he and Ray had dropped out of high school, packed up their hockey bags, and left. Not that their families would miss them. They both had divorced, drunken parents who'd remarried and sprouted new little brats, then forgot their older kids existed. Tracy was about the only one either of them would miss. And pretty soon, she'd probably be popping out little monsters and forgetting all about them, too. Boris and Ray figured the grass would be greener in Toronto. Hell, it had to be—at least people there spoke English. And Ray had a small connection: good old cousin Harley.

Harley and Ray were distant cousins, having only met a few times at family reunions in their teens. But Ray had kept in touch because he was in awe of the guy. Harley was only a couple of years older, but even as a teenager, he'd already started his life's work: burglary. And by his boasting and his expensive leather jackets, Ray was sure he was damn good at it.

When Ray and Boris had shown up at Harley's door in Toronto, he had barely recognized his cousin. And he had to figure out what the hell to do with him. Ray was family, so some tiny favour was in order. He would've gladly thrown Boris out on the street, but Ray put his arm around Boris's shoulder and gave him a pleading look. Harley wondered if they were queer.

Harley had finally decided to place them as spotters at the airport. All they had to do was hang out at the check-in lines and read the tags on the luggage and find out the names, phone numbers, and addresses. Then, Harley would phone to see if anyone were home or if the house were empty while the good people enjoyed their vacation. No answer and off he went to burgle to his heart's content.

The first time they'd gone to the airport, Ray, whose memory wasn't so good, had pulled out a notebook right there and started jotting down the information while also lifting the tags for a better view. Several people waiting in line had given him suspicious looks, and Boris saw one guy waving at a security guard. They'd scurried out of there fast, and the next time they wore subtle disguises. It was fun for a while, but soon they wanted in on the *real* action.

Harley was pissed off at having to recruit new spotters, and he only worked solo, so he had no opportunities for them. But he gave them some tips anyway. He felt the weight of family responsibility, even though he hadn't seen Ray's parents in 10 years and wasn't sure they'd even give a flying fuck. Besides, these two guys would never be as good as him in a million years and were hardly competition. In fact, they hadn't even been very good spotters. Harley suspected that half the time they got the phone numbers and addresses wrong, because most of the places he called had somebody home and no signs of people away on vacation. If Ray and Boris were smarter, he might've suspected they were holding out on him and burgling the places themselves.

But brains weren't a highlight of The Dark Duo, as they liked to call themselves.

So then they were on their own. They cruised the streets at night in Ray's beat-up black van, peeping in house windows, hoping for open curtains, checking to see what goodies the homeowners had. Checking curbs for big-ticket boxes (stereos, TVs, computers) showing new purchases. Praying for open windows and garage doors. They looked for places with lots of hedges and few lights and, most importantly, no security systems. They got in and got out and somehow managed (by the skin of their teeth) not to get caught. But by the time they sold the stuff to a fence who took a huge cut, the money was less than great. And they had to go out 6 nights a week to keep the money coming in. No vacations. No sick days. No benefits. It was all starting to get Boris down.

Lately, Boris and Ray had been considering getting out. They'd come too close to getting caught too many times, and the cash just wasn't what it should be. God knows they didn't want to go straight, but it was getting harder to be a low-level burglar these days, what with security systems and cameras everywhere. They didn't have the skills to deal with that shit. It was too much work and too much risk. With the money they were making, they might as well be shoveling up ice cream at Dairy Queen to snot-nosed kids.

Though Harley had been making a neat little profit selling Len's pot to The Dark Duo (or Dim Duo, as he thought of them—talk about dopes, they didn't even have a clue what an ounce of pot was supposed to cost), he was getting sick of being the middleman and decided to introduce them to Len. After all, Harley was no dope dealer. All that damn math you had to do in your head. All that sitting around. Harley saw himself as a man on the move. And he was getting real tired of all those drunken, desperate, late-night phone calls.

It was Ray who'd really wanted to meet Len. He was the big pothead. Boris wasn't much of a smoker. He was sullen enough on his own, and weed made him worse. He just kept trying it, hoping the effect might change. Ray, on the other hand, already a disgustingly cheery guy, got even happier on the stuff. In fact, he was a regular Wake 'n' Bake. Sometimes Boris wanted to attribute Ray's lack of brains on all the dope he smoked, but then he'd have to admit to himself he wasn't that much brighter, and he barely smoked at all.

When Boris, Ray, and Harley had arrived at Len's house, they were greeted by a fearsome growl. A monstrous Doberman paced the hallway, occasionally leaping against the screen door of the porch where they stood. Ray, not a keen dog fan, backed off the porch altogether. He'd had unhappy experiences in the past, which wasn't a real plus when you were in the home burglary business.

Boris was vastly relieved when Len showed up and gently patted the dog soothingly, saying, "Chill, Spot, chill." He attached a leash to its collar and led it down the hall and motioned the others to come in. They followed Len and saw that he was tying the dog to a post in the small backyard. The dog was looking even more murderous now, and Boris thought he wouldn't want to encounter that sucker alone in the dark.

Len returned, and they did their intros and shook hands all around. His nails had permanent grime encrusted underneath, and his palms were almost black. Harley had told them that Len was the mechanic for most of the Glory Riders. And Boris thought, *Oh great, another one*. He was surrounded by them. Which wasn't good, because they scared the shit out of him, though he'd never admit that to anyone, even Ray. And *definitely* not Harley.

"Sorry about the dog," Len said gruffly. Len was a macho dude. He wore loose jeans that hung down from his sloping belly and scruffy cowboy boots that looked like they'd cost a lot of money once. The only odd thing was the pink golf shirt, one of those ones with the little lizard or whatever over the tit. It seemed pretty gay to Boris, but Len looked like the type of guy who wouldn't appreciate you making fun of his clothing choices.

"I haven't been getting him out as much I should. I've been working a lot of overtime and getting a lot of orders for the other shit, too. It'd be easier if everybody just came over here, but half the time the assholes are late and I spend all my time waiting, so I'd rather deliver to them." He sighed and picked at a greasy nail. "Jerk-offs."

"The dog's okay there . . . like that?" asked Ray with a quaver in his voice. Len looked him over with disdain, like he'd like to punch him in the gut.

"Yeah, he's happy. Can't you tell?"

Ray shut up after that and didn't say another word the entire visit.

"Thing is," continued Len, moving toward the dreary living room and motioning the others to sit on the sagging furniture, "I had a roommate who walked the dog a lot for me. But the shithead took off with half a pound of my best hydroponic."

"Fuck," said Harley, though he'd already heard all about it. He'd been quiet up till now as he watched Boris and Ray with sly amusement, fully aware of how shit-scared they were.

"No kidding," said Len. Then he smiled, displaying surprisingly good teeth. Somehow Boris had expected them to match his hands. "But I'll get the bastard." He winked at Harley. "Or our buddies will."

The dog suddenly howled from the backyard, as if imagining torture and dismemberment. Len grinned, as if joining in the vision. "Spot's a great dog. Real friendly once he gets to know you." He looked at Ray and Boris. "What I need is a roommate. Someone to help me walk the old guy."

Boris caught Len giving Harley a sidelong look, and a light bulb lit up in his brain. So this was what Harley had planned all along. He wasn't just being nice about the pot; he was doing Len a favour and setting Boris up. He shuddered thinking about what other kind of favours the Glory Riders regularly did for each other, and Spot, as if reading his thoughts, howled again.

Boris stared up at the ceiling and counted the cobwebs. He held his breath, hoping this might make him invisible. In his peripheral vision he could just make out Ray, who seemed to have melted into his chair.

"Rent's real cheap," added Harley, who didn't want to disappoint Len. His black hash and his bike's health depended on it. And what other suckers would want to live in this dump?

Boris didn't respond, because it was hard to talk and think at the same time. Living with Ray was driving him crazy. Not just the constant chipperness, but working *and* living together 24/7 with fucking Peter Pan. Jesus, a guy needed time to be alone and miserable now and then.

But did he really want to move into a house where the landlord, his roommate, and his dog *all* scared the hell out of him?

"I'm hardly ever home," added Len. "Most of the time it would be just you and Spot."

That wasn't what Boris had wanted to hear. He shifted his eyes from the ceiling and glanced over at Ray, who was staring intently at his shoes.

Harley finally caught Boris's eye and scowled at him, but Len just shrugged as he pulled a baggie of pot from his pocket. "Think about it. How 'bout we get down to business?"

A couple of weeks later, Boris and Ray had a big blowout over who ate all the pastrami and who'd sucked back the last of the beer. They grudgingly decided to remain business partners, but not roommates.

Boris called Len.

3 ROOMIES

As soon as Harley left, Katrina helped Stevie stagger into the living room, where he collapsed into the threadbare upholstery. Stevie now had a bag of frozen peas in one hand, pressed against his cheek, and a bottle of Lakeport Lager in the other. Katrina sat beside him with her own beer and tried to put a comforting arm around his shoulders, but he groaned in pain from his slump against the wall, and Katrina eased away.

"That's okay," murmured Stevie, moving closer. "It only hurts for the first 20 seconds."

Katrina smiled at him and slipped her arm back around his shoulder as she sipped her beer. She didn't really like the taste of it herself, but it seemed the drink of choice for everyone she met in Toronto, and she didn't want to stick out by ordering white wine or vodka coolers. Not that Katrina could *not* stick out. She was a stunning girl, and quite aware of it, though completely uncomfortable with it.

"When do you think he'll be going out?" whispered Stevie, peering at the ceiling.

"It's almost dark," whispered Katrina, "and the shower stopped a few minutes ago. He should be leaving soon."

"What do you have, bionic ears?"

Katrina shrugged. "Survival skills. I try to avoid him as much as possible."

Stevie shuddered. "He's so creepy. Even his name is creepy—*BORIS*."

Katrina patted his arm, eliciting a grimace, but Stevie held back the groan this time and didn't move or protest.

"Once he's gone," whispered Stevie, "we really have to talk."

Katrina was about to reply when she heard a creak at the top of the stairs, and she instinctively grabbed Stevie's hand. A moment later, Boris reached the landing and caught sight of them together on the couch. They looked like tweens caught in a heavyweight petting session.

Boris sneered as Stevie quickly slid away from Katrina and removed her arm from his shoulder. Katrina thought that strange, but figured Stevie was just cowering from Boris. Katrina barely noticed Boris's sneer, since it seemed to be a permanent fixture on his face. Like the shaggy black hair and raised furry black brows which met the bangs and gave him the appearance of a pissed-off sheepdog.

But Stevie cleared his throat and fidgeted and moved away even more, as if guilty. Why, Katrina couldn't imagine. She tried to look away from Boris. He always made her squeamish. But it was like staring at a car accident—you couldn't help but gawk.

Stevie recovered his composure and sat up straighter. "Have you talked to Harley?"

"Harley?" asked Boris, stopping midway to the kitchen. "What about?"

Katrina glared at him. "Don't tell me he hasn't told you about raising the rent?"

Boris looked surprised. "He's raising your rent?" He started to laugh.

Stevie jumped up from the couch, forgetting his pain. "You think that's funny?"

Boris was trying to quell the laughter. "He's not raising mine."

"What?!" squealed Katrina.

"Harley's my pal," said Boris, and Katrina thought she actually saw his chest pump up with pride. "And so are the Glory Riders."

"Oh, be serious," said Katrina. "You never even hang out with those guys. You don't hang out with anybody."

Boris looked strangely hurt for a second, then he shook his unruly mop of black hair and started for the kitchen door. "Doubt at your own risk," he growled.

Katrina and Stevie stared at each other in amazement, then Stevie scampered over to the living-room window to watch Boris saunter down the street. The minute Boris was well out of earshot he slumped onto the couch and finished his beer in one gulp.

"The little prick!" he exclaimed. "You'd think he owned the place!"

Katrina smiled grimly. "His friend does."

"Friend!" huffed Stevie. "More like warden."

"He's being threatened by Harley, just like us," said Katrina. "You can't really blame him."

"Oh, seriously!" snorted Stevie. "Next you'll be comparing him to Mother Theresa."

"He's not that bad," mumbled Katrina. "I mean, we hardly ever see him. That's worth *something*."

"Not that bad?" said Stevie. "The guy practically threatened us with a bunch of hooligans, for Chrissakes! Our lives are at stake!"

Katrina said, "Now you're exaggerating. And besides, Harley's the one with the hooligans, not Boris."

"Yeah, like Boris wouldn't love to see us crushed like ants." Stevie turned away to delicately belch, then leaned in closer to Katrina. "Besides, that's not all he's up to."

Katrina gulped down some beer to catch up with Stevie. "What are you talking about?"

"I think . . ." Stevie hesitated, hoping to create more suspense. Katrina took the bait; she leaned closer, holding her breath.

"I think that Boris has been erasing your phone messages."

"What?" Katrina shot up and sloshed some of her beer onto Stevie's thigh. He barely noticed; he was peering intently at Katrina.

"Think about it, Katrina—why aren't you getting any phone calls?"

"The girls from school call once in a while. And my mom just called last week, and—"

"I mean from *men*, sweetie."

Katrina gaped at him. "You can't be serious."

Stevie nodded.

"Why on earth would he do that?"

Stevie raised an eyebrow. "Why do you *think*?"

Katrina did think, hard. She remembered staring bleakly at the answering machine just a few days ago, wondering why the men she met never called. Len had been gone for a month, and she was ready and eager to start seeing other guys again. The last hot one that Katrina had met, who'd practically dragged her away from her friends at the Tipsy Fiddle in the middle of a post-work bitch session, had seemed thrilled when she gave him her number. So thrilled he'd asked her back to his place on the spot for a first date—why wait? Katrina had blushingly declined, aware of her friends' scrutiny, certain he'd call her in a day or two. Three, tops—it was always hard to judge the timing between looking like a total desperate loser and I'm-too-good-for-you-you-can-wait. But 4 days later the phone remained mute.

If she weren't so shy, she would've called *him*. But most people terrified Katrina, and the thought of calling up a near stranger was enough to make her gag. Besides, she couldn't find the guy's card. She was always losing things like that, certain she'd tossed them on a counter or a table, only to have them mysteriously disappear. Was she absentminded or just plain stupid, like so many people assumed when blinded by her looks?

When Katrina thought about it, there were at least two other guys who should've called her in the last couple of weeks but hadn't.

"Not Boris!" cried Katrina, cringing at the thought.

"I've seen him staring at you when you're not looking," Stevie said, his tone implying that he didn't want to say this, but really felt he must.

"But he's never even here!"

"Yes, he is, you just don't notice him. He *lurks*, Katrina. I've seen him lurking and ogling you."

"That's crazy."

"*He's* crazy." Stevie swigged the remains of his beer and pointed the bottle at her. "You've told me yourself he gives you the creeps."

"So does the mailman, but I don't see much of him either."

Stevie heaved himself off the couch and went to fetch two more beers. Katrina could hear him talking loudly from the kitchen.

"I think he's in love with you, and he either hangs up on these guys when they call, or he screens the answering machine and erases the messages."

Katrina took the fresh beer Stevie handed her and looked up at him in horror. She gulped some down and thought the stuff wasn't half bad once you got used to it.

Stevie bent down to look her in the eye. "That's why we have to get the hell out of here. Do you really want a live-in stalker/spy as your roommate and the Glory Riders holding you hostage?"

Katrina shook her head. "But you heard Harley. You might be able to get out of here, but I can't."

"So we do it together, without them knowing. We sneak out under cover of darkness."

In spite of the circumstances, Katrina had to suppress a giggle. "Sounds very spy novel, Stevie."

He gave her a stern look. "Don't laugh—I'm serious."

Katrina became somber. "I know."

"Look," said Stevie, "Boris will have no idea where we've gone. We'll be out of all this craziness. We'll be fine." He said this almost as if he believed it himself. To bolster their courage he added, "We'll just keep the classifieds hidden so he doesn't see them, and make sure he doesn't catch me on Craigslist. The creep really likes to look over people's shoulders."

"But the computer's in your room," pointed out Katrina.

"I wouldn't put it past him."

"Stevie," said Katrina, "this all sounds great in theory, but I don't make enough money to pay much more rent, let alone furniture and stuff."

"You'd be paying more here anyway, with Harley's damn rent hike. I've got everything we'd need in storage, and we could get a one-bedroom. It'd be cheaper."

"Right—and where do we both sleep?"

Stevie shrugged. "Lots of one bedrooms have small alcoves or something that you can turn into an extra room. Or I could have a pull-out bed in the living room."

"That wouldn't be fair. What if we just got a bigger place and got another roommate?"

"No," said Stevie, "I'm sick of roommates." He caught her look. "Except for you, of course. We get along so well. I want it to be just the two of us." He pinched Katrina's cheek, got up, and came back a minute later with the classifieds from *The Toronto Star*.

"Then I'll get a part-time job," said Katrina.

"No, no," said Stevie, "I can pay a little extra. We'll be fine in a one-bedroom, you'll see."

Katrina grabbed the "Help Wanted" section from Stevie's hands and pecked him on the cheek.

"I love you, sweetie, but we both need our space."

Stevie groaned inwardly, then started poring over the "For Rent" section.

4 SPECIAL K

When Katrina was born, one of the first things Katrina's mother noticed was her pointy little toes, which looked like they'd never be happy until they were encased in ballet slippers. So she christened Katrina with a Russian-sounding name, befitting a ballerina. As Katrina got older, she cursed her feet, which were far too clumsy for ballet, and seemed far too long and narrow for her slender frame. She was always self-conscious of them, imagining people were staring at them, laughing to themselves. Though, in fact, people had much better things to stare at on Katrina.

She was the last of five girls, which might have bothered her father. But the two middle sisters, Katie and Kelly, played baseball and hockey better than most of the boys in their school, and he was content with that. When they eventually lost interest in sports and took up with boys, he invited the boyfriends over as often as possible to help balance the testosterone and give himself a break.

Katrina's closest sister, Kandy, was only a year older than she. When she was born, Katrina's mom took one look at her and thought she looked like a piece of bubble gum, all soft and pink and pretty. She called her Candy with a K, because she wanted to keep the K thing going. She claimed she'd eaten Special K cereal through all her pregnancies, and had managed to keep her girlish figure. And since her name was Karoline, with a K, it seemed only right.

Katrina's three oldest sisters, Katie, Kelly, and Kitty, were pretty, but nothing near beautiful. They had rather bland, pleasant features that were nicely enhanced with makeup, but wouldn't stun anyone standing on their own. Katrina and Kandy, however, were a different story.

From the time Katrina and Kandy were babies they were adored for their beauty. The older sisters, of course, were jealous, and bullied them every time their parents weren't looking. Katrina and Kandy didn't go through their sisters' awkward adolescent phase, either; none of that gangly stuff for them. Their beauty forged straight through those nasty early teen years.

Karoline, Katrina's mom, had been a hairdresser in Pipton all her life, and for the past 20 years had owned her own salon, where all the girls worked growing up. The middle girls, Katie and Kelly, still worked there, though they were now married and had kids of their own. Katrina's dad, Ken, worked as a shipper-receiver at a nearby Sears. They led a comfortable, just-getting-by life in Pipton, where things were cheap, and there wasn't much to spend your money on anyway.

But it wasn't enough for Katrina's closest sister Kandy. Not suffering Katrina's shyness, she soon had enough of the small-town Pipton atmosphere, her parents' lack of money, her older sisters' bullying, and the going-nowhere aspects of her life. She secretly had photos taken and entered several beauty contests. One day she got a phone call and then a visit from a lady from Toronto. Soon she was a model in Toronto, then she was hitting New York, and soon she was hanging out with celebrities and pulling in the big bucks. Her parents were proud of her, though a little worried; the older sisters were jealous as hell and insisted she had no brains (what woman with brains would sell her face and body like that?), and Katrina was envious because she wished she had the confidence and guts to do something like that herself.

Kandy's move was an inspiration to Katrina. It occurred to her very suddenly that she, too, had to get out. They'd always been close and now Katrina felt all alone with her older bullying sisters and her mother and father who were very loving and dear but far too much older than Katrina for her to have a very close relationship with them.

At her mother's insistence, Katrina worked in the salon for a year after finishing high school. But she couldn't stand it anymore, felt she was suffocating. Katrina had to get out of that place and that town. She decided, secretly, to go to Toronto to study at an aesthetician school. She'd saved enough to pay her tuition, but rent in the big city was another matter. Her oldest sister Kitty was the only one she knew there, and Kitty had never been her biggest fan.

When Katrina shyly approached her mother with the idea, her mother tried to talk her out of it. She said there was no need for her to go to school; she could teach Katrina everything she needed to know. Katrina insisted she wanted to eventually work in Toronto, and to work in the big city she'd need to know the latest techniques. Karoline had to sadly admit she wasn't quite up to date with the newest trends. A lot of people in Pipton still thought shags and mullets were the height of fashion.

Katrina's father called her sister Kitty and suggested (more like ordered) that she take in Katrina as a boarder, since Kitty's son had just moved to college. Kitty was not thrilled with this idea. She figured she could get a little rent out of her youngest sister, sure, but that much beauty around a husband of 18 years was definitely trouble.

So Katrina headed for the Big Smoke. Kitty and her husband Jim lived in Scarborough, but not too far from the subway, so the commute wasn't totally hell. Kitty worked a lot at night as a nurse, which left Katrina a lot of time alone with Al. He was always eyeing her in a way that made her extremely uncomfortable, asking her about things that she thought were none of his business. He was vulgar without ever actually touching her or making a pass. But his actions made Katrina squirm, and she knew one day he'd lunge. She couldn't stand it anymore and knew that soon she'd have to move out.

Kosmetic Kastle was a combination aesthetic school/salon in Yorkville. Downstairs, the girls (and one girly guy) took lessons and did cheap coupon assignments on human guinea pigs. Upstairs was a real salon, named simply "K," where they would finish their schooling and, hopefully, get their certificates and, if they were in the top percentage, be granted the favour of working as true professionals with full-paying, fully fastidious customers who paid ridiculous prices and tipped almost accordingly.

Katrina met Len in her second month at Kosmetic Kastle. He'd received a free coupon in the mail, and his friends dared him to go. So, being the macho guy that he was, he went. Besides, the dare was 50 dollars, and he'd get a free manicure and pedicure. It wasn't like he'd have to get waxed or anything.

Len had smelly feet. Still, he somehow turned Katrina on. Maybe because he was kind of rough, and most of the boys back in Pipton were so nice, nonthreatening, *safe*. Except one. And, of course, Len reminded her of him.

Katrina had known Jesse slightly in high school. She'd always had the hots for him. Like Len, he had a bike. But just a little dirt bike that he buzzed around on, pretending to run Katrina over. He usually showed off to her when he was with other girls, just to rub it in. Jesse was a bad boy (or as bad as they got in Pipton), and he called Katrina a keener (which was the worst insult you could get).

Katrina had always been a good student. She was afraid to be anything but—what if the teacher asked her something in class and she didn't know the answer? She'd look like an imbecile. As if being called on in class wasn't mortifying enough!

The other thing Jesse did was mock Katrina's feet. He called her Big Foot, even though by then, she was so beautiful everyone gawked at his insolence. Katrina would do her best to saunter by as he called that out, holding her head high, wishing she could banish the blush that conveyed her true shame.

Jesse never showed much interest in Katrina, aside from the biker tactics and the foot comments. But every time he came near her, she swooned and fantasized his kiss. One night he stepped onto her porch while everyone else was out back around a campfire and told her he was going away. Then, without warning, he pulled her to him and attacked her lips. It was crude, but suggestive. It might have gone further, but his girlfriend saw him under the porch light and screamed at him to get over here this minute if he valued his life. The next week he was gone, as if he'd never existed at all. And Katrina had always wondered, what if . . .?

Then she met Len. And in a way, she had a chance to finally find out. As she massaged his feet (breathing through her mouth, which she'd quickly learned to do), she learned he was a biker, and by the way he talked, she could tell he hung out with unsavoury types. Len could be her Jesse. Besides, there was some crazy sexual attraction. Len wasn't very attractive. He was overweight and not too tall, and frankly, his clothes were a mess. But still, there it was. Totally unexplainable. And when Katrina jokingly said something about her own feet being way too big, Len looked at them and said, "No way." They were perfect, just like the rest of her, and Katrina was ready to have sex right there and then, though she'd never had it before, and wasn't sure what to do. But one look at Len told her *he* knew, and would be quite willing to share his knowledge. He did—the very next night.

For a while the sex with Len made Katrina forget her other problems. One being school. Sure, she got along with most of the other students there; a few of them were new to the city, too, and those that weren't offered to show her the ropes. They often went out for drinks after class, or cooked cheap meals for one another. No, the other girls (and one boy) were fine. It was the clients Katrina couldn't stand.

So far, she'd only tended to the cheapos downstairs, the ones with the discount coupons. And she was horrified enough by *them*. Katrina couldn't even imagine what the upstairs clientele must be like, though the teachers had told them horror stories. Katrina was used to the small-town clientele of Pipton. She knew them all; they knew her. Sometimes people were a little unpleasant, but she was always treated with respect.

At Kosmetic Kastle/K's (or KKK, as the students called it), Katrina felt like a slave, a servant girl, as if the more submissive/humiliated the clientele could make her, the better. And those were the cheap seats! Katrina knew that upstairs it would be 10 times worse, that even the nice clients, no matter how well they treated her, would always think of her as beneath them.

No, she couldn't take it anymore. She couldn't work for people like that unless *she* was the boss, and she could turn down anyone she pleased. She needed to open her own salon. But she'd need money for that and had no idea how to get it. Her part-time job at Cups Café certainly wouldn't cut it. If she quit school, she could work there full-time, but it still would be barely enough to get by, let alone save anything.

The other major problem with opening a salon was Katrina's shyness. That was nothing new, of course, but she'd thought it would be better here. She figured if only she could get away from Pipton, where everyone knew her, maybe she could go to the big city and be anonymous, create a different personality for herself. She knew gay guys did that all the time—came to Toronto to start a new life—so why couldn't she? Yes, she'd thought she could fool them all—maybe even herself. But her shyness followed her everywhere she went. It was like an unwanted acquaintance, a leech, sucking the personality out of every step she took.

5 HASHISH

Things had gone okay between Katrina and Len until he'd put too much pressure on her to move into his house with him and Boris, and rather than fight about it any more, she'd reluctantly agreed. She'd had it living with her sister and brother-in-law. And besides, she'd just quit school and knew that sooner or later they'd find out if she continued staying with them. Kitty would be on the phone to her parents in seconds. And even though Katrina had paid her own tuition, her parents would be deeply disappointed and want her to come home. They would accuse her of giving up, though Katrina thought of it as simply choosing a different path. Yeah, like they'd understand *that* concept.

But she could never afford a place on her own with Toronto's rents. She didn't know anyone who was looking for a roommate, and she certainly wasn't about to move in with a stranger. Besides, Len offered to pay a big chunk of the rent. How bad could it be?

It lasted a month. Len was crazy jealous of all of Katrina's friends, especially Stevie—even though they both thought Stevie was gay, though he never said so. Before she moved into the house, Katrina hadn't met any of Len's friends; he always said he wanted her all to himself. But once she'd moved in, she met a few of them on the rare occasions they came by. And she found out about the Glory Riders.

Len insisted they weren't criminals, though Katrina thought they sure looked like it. He said they were just regular guys who hung out in their clubhouse most of the time drinking beer and watching sports on TV when they weren't going on road trips. Sure they liked scaring people and messing with their heads, but what was the crime in that? It wasn't like they were *killers* or anything.

Katrina would've argued with Len if she'd had the nerve, but he'd always intimidated her a little. And no matter what he said, the bikers terrified her. They positively *drooled* at her when Len wasn't looking. She felt pathetically young and straight around them, like their next virgin sacrifice. Len's presence should have made her feel safe, but she always felt he was more on their side than hers. After all, Katrina had known Len for 3 months; he'd known these guys all his life. Katrina withdrew more and more into her already-overcrowded shell, and Len got more and more pissed off at trying to get her out.

Katrina wondered about the constant phone calls Len got on his cell. She figured he was just a popular guy, though he didn't get all that many visitors. When they did come (the Glory Riders, of course), Len would proudly and pointedly introduce them to Katrina, then almost immediately usher them into the back room off the kitchen, leaving her sitting in the living room by herself. Then the bikers stopped coming altogether, but Len started going out all the time at strange hours, often late at night. He claimed he had emergency repairs to do for his buddies, but Katrina was starting to have her doubts. Besides, she hated being alone in the house at night, with only Spot's howls to keep her company. Which actually frightened her more, because if he was howling, what on earth was he howling *at*?

A month after she moved in, when Len was at work and Katrina was off, she got up the nerve to check out the back room. She listened at the bottom of the stairs to make sure there was no movement from Boris's room, then crept through the kitchen to the back. Katrina had never used this room, since it was a manly spot with a couple of cupboards and a huge table with tools spread out all over the top. There were drawers underneath, lots of them. Where to begin?

The first couple of drawers held documents: taxes, insurance, passport, medical records. Len visiting a doctor? Katrina had figured that like most men, Len would sooner go permanently bald than see a doctor. When she opened the third drawer she saw what looked like a giant slab of dark chocolate, with a strange stamp on it. Definitely not Hershey's or Nestlé's, though. She sniffed it. Definitely not chocolate. It had a peculiar, pungent smell, kind of like the Turkish tobacco one of her uncles used to smoke in his pipe.

Suddenly Katrina heard laughter behind her and guiltily whirled around. She still had the strange slab beneath her nostrils.

"You gonna smoke that or eat it?" asked Boris, who stood in the doorway with an amused look.

Katrina turned beet red. She was mortified, as if she'd been caught stealing. Even worse, she had absolutely no idea what it was she might be stealing.

Boris noticed her totally clueless look and laughed again. "Haven't you ever seen a block of hash before?" He pretended to be considering this. "Hmm. Guess not. I suppose in Pipton, the most you can get is a gram at a time, wrapped in a teeny piece of foil."

"Hash?" said Katrina stupidly. The word seemed vaguely familiar, as if she'd heard it mentioned before, maybe in the café where she worked.

"Hash. Hashish." Boris put his fingers to his lips in a smoking gesture. "Hard to get in good ole T.O. Not like Montreal—they've got tons of it. I don't know where Len gets a hold of it, but he must make a killing. Not my thing, though—I'm a weed man. If I'm gonna get high, I want some wheelchair pot. I don't wanna know what I'm doing; I wanna feel fucking retarded."

That shouldn't take much, thought Katrina, as she dropped the slab of hash onto the table like an envelope full of anthrax.

Boris snorted at Katrina's trembling hands. He nodded at the hash lying on the table beside a scary-looking chainsaw, and Katrina wondered if she'd plunged into a horror movie. She'd never even seen drugs before, let alone a drug dealer. And the dealer was her boyfriend!

Boris picked up the hash and sniffed it appreciatively. "Do love the smell of it, though." He handed it to Katrina, who was forced to take it.

"I'd put that back where I found it if I were you. Don't want Len to catch you with your pretty little hands in the cookie jar."

He laughed again, and she could hear him bounding up the stairs to his room.

That night Katrina had it out with Len. She called him a druggie, a criminal—how could he do this to her? How could he *hide* this from her?

Len, in turn, accused Katrina of being too close to Stevie, of spending too much time with the little pansy, of ignoring *him*.

The screaming match continued for a good half hour until Len couldn't take it anymore. He punched the living-room wall, jumped on his Harley, and roared off into the night.

The next morning Katrina woke up alone in her bed. She looked out the window and saw that Len's Jeep was gone. She went downstairs to the back room and peered in the drawer where Len's documents had been. No passport. The drawer where the hash had been was empty. It looked like Len had flown the coop.

So that's it, she thought. Not like it was destined to last. All they had in common was sex, after all. Great, great sex. It had almost seemed like enough.

6 *LEN'S HANDIWORK*

Boris had overheard almost the entire fight between Katrina and Len. The weather was brutal that night, wind squalls and lightning and lashing rain, and he thought, fuck it, he'd rather starve than go out in *that*. Besides, if *he* was staying in, that meant everyone else in town probably was, too. A bad night for burgling all round.

When Spot first started howling from the kitchen (which was, unfortunately, right beneath Boris's room), Boris figured the storm must be getting on his nerves—even the most vile pit bulls quivered like Chihuahuas at the sound of a little thunder. Soon he'd settle down, or Len would take care of him. But The Beast just went on and on. Boris turned up the TV, but it didn't help; Spot kept wailing like his dick had been whacked off and his nuts shoved up his ass.

Finally Boris sighed and went to the door. When he opened it, he realized the reason for Spot's distress: Katrina and Len were in the living room, screaming at each other like wild animals. Boris crept down a few steps where he could hear without being seen, and listened as intently as he could with Spot still barking up a storm.

When he saw Len stomp out of the living room and slam the front door, he almost laughed out loud. Len and Katrina were quits! No way would they get back together after this! Hah! Boris almost did a little jig. It was about time Len got rid of that bitch.

A few months after Boris had moved in with Len, Katrina had started coming over now and then. Boris couldn't believe a savage like Len could get a beautiful babe like her, but maybe he had more going for him than Boris knew about. Like many inches more. Soon after that, she moved in. Boris couldn't believe it. Len didn't even ask his approval. Where was the roomie love? Len just pulled up to the house with Katrina by his side and a bunch of boxes and shit shoved in the back of the Jeep, and announced, "Here she is!" like he'd just bought himself a fine thoroughbred.

Boris and Katrina hated each other from the start. Well, maybe hate was too strong a word for that bitch. She looked too delicate to hate anybody. She looked over Boris with distaste. A very bad taste. Sure she was gorgeous, but not at all his type. He liked women with a lot more meat on their bones, a little more rough 'n' ready. Boris supposed this Katrina chick got it on with Len, since he hardly seemed the type to go celibate, but she sure looked like butter—or a dick—wouldn't melt in her mouth.

Katrina hated Spot even more than Boris did. In fact, Boris had kind of gotten used to him, and only got annoyed when the dog sniffed at his crotch or dry-humped his leg. But he could tell Katrina was terrified. Sure, she played all nicey-nice with him when Len was around, but once he left the house, she tied the dog up outside and retreated as far as she could. Hell, she looked like she ought to be on a chain herself, all cringing and quivering like that.

The morning after the fight, a phone call from Harley woke Boris from an awesome dream about dancing TVs and singing stereos, all skipping happily into the back of Ray's van. Harley told Boris that Len had spent the night at the clubhouse, pounding back all the Jack Daniels and talking to a few

Glory Riders who were off on a yearlong trip to South America. Len had drunkenly decided to join up. They were leaving tomorrow.

"So what's this got to do with me?" asked Boris, desperate to get back to his dream.

"Len says you and Katrina have to stay in the house and keep Spot around till he gets back."

"*Have* to?" grunted Boris. "What the fuck is that?"

"It's a favour to Len."

"A favour from you, you mean. What the hell do I get out of all this?"

"You all get to stay in your happy little house. Len wants you to keep an eye on Katrina and report back to me."

"What am I, a babysitter now?" Boris did his best not to squawk; Harley wouldn't take that too well. "Why doesn't Len just kick her out? I mean, the lease is under his name, right?"

"How the hell should I know?" said Harley impatiently. "The guy was practically crying last night; it was frigging embarrassing. You ask me, he's still in love with her, poor bastard."

"That wasn't love I heard last night," snorted Boris. "And you still didn't answer me—what do *I* get out of this?"

Harley paused for emphasis. Then, almost as if he were enjoying himself: "The Glory Riders leave you alone."

Christ, thought Boris, fully awake—*no chance of more dream time now* . . . He was in the shits. He hadn't met many of the Glory Riders, since he'd usually been out when they came over to see Len, but the ones he had seen looked pretty much like Harley, like little biker clones (if you could call 6 foot 6, 300 pounds *little*), and he wasn't too eager for any close encounters.

"Talk to Katrina tonight," ordered Harley. "I know your social skills aren't exactly top-notch, so I'll give you some ideas of what to say."

When Boris entered the living room that night, Katrina was forlornly watching the tiny black-and-white TV and sipping on a beer. An empty stood on the table in front of her. The beer surprised Boris. He thought all broads gobbled down vats of ice cream when they were down in the dumps. The TV show was about right, though—some chick-flick soap opera thing that would make him puke if he were ever forced to watch it.

He attempted a sympathetic smile like Harley had instructed him, but it felt plastered on his face, and he wondered if he'd ever be able to peel it off.

Katrina heard him and stared quizzically up at his smile for a second, as if wondering if he had a bad case of gas, then turned back to the TV.

"So . . ." began Boris.

"Umm," muttered Katrina.

"Len's outta here," said Boris.

"Yep." Another sip on the beer.

"For a year, Harley told me. Off to South America with some Glory Riders."

Katrina finally turned to stare at him. "Seriously?" Boris couldn't tell whether she looked relieved or hurt. She *should* be hurt. She was the dumpee, after all.

Boris dared to take a step closer and crouch beside her. "Look, you should stay here. Harley doesn't want the house empty, and I can't afford it by myself."

Katrina looked horrified by the thought, so he hurried on. "Rent's cheap, and where else are you gonna go? You can't afford first and last and furniture and all that crap on your own." Boris tried to adjust the sympathy smile to an encouraging smile, but he'd never had much practice, so he wasn't sure whether it worked. Maybe he'd try it out in the mirror sometime. "Besides, Len doesn't want you to be lonely."

"How could I possibly be lonely with you as my roommate?" snorted Katrina. "Seeing as we're such good pals and all. And anyway, if Len was so concerned, he should've thought about that *before* he made plans to tour the world."

"Just South America."

Katrina sighed. "You're right—I can't afford to move anywhere else. I guess this dump will have to do for now." She glanced glumly around the room. Boris noticed the hole in the wall for the first time.

"Len's handiwork?" he asked. Katrina nodded. "Well, at least it didn't hurt the décor any. Maybe even adds character."

Katrina didn't seem to be listening; she appeared to be deep in thought. "But the rent will be more with just the two of us—Len paid most of mine."

Figures, thought Boris. A pretty face and you can get away with anything.

"Maybe if we got a roommate," suggested Katrina. "More money *and* more company."

Boris felt a little hurt. Maybe he wasn't the coziest roommate around, but she didn't have to act like just looking at him made her want to puke. He feigned nonchalance. "Fine by me. I could use the cash, too. But I don't know anybody who'd be interested."

"Maybe I could ask around."

"Yeah, that's an idea," agreed Boris. He'd already forgotten about Katrina's little jibe. The thought of having the Glory Riders off his back thrilled him so much, he didn't care if they rented the spare room out to Jack the Ripper. "Just get someone who can pay the rent; I don't care."

Okay, so the first part had gone better than he expected. Now for Part Two—the one Harley didn't know about. Boris stood up and started for the hallway but suddenly turned. "Oh, Katrina—there's just one other thing."

"Yeah?" said Katrina, whose eyes had returned to the TV.

"Len wants you to take care of Spot."

Katrina nearly choked on her beer.

"What!?"

Boris helplessly threw up his hands. "It's his one request. He wants you two to bond."

Katrina's mouth was hanging open, a few suds dripping down her chin.

"Don't worry," grinned Boris, and this time the smile was genuine. "It's real easy. All you have to do is feed him and take him out for a walk now and then."

7 DEAR OLD SPOT

The next morning, Katrina's alarm had just gone off when she heard a rapping on the door. She grunted and opened her eyes and before she knew it, Boris had opened the door. Katrina shot up and banged her head on the wall, stunned at his presence.

"What on earth are you doing up?" she asked, grabbing the sheet to cover her pajamas.

Boris took a step forward and glanced around the room in disgust. So girly-girl. It looked like Barbie had done the decorating. Pink, for God's sake. Some people just had no taste.

"I'm here to make sure you follow up on Len's wishes. You have to feed Spot."

Katrina was wide awake now. Boris's presence in her bedroom made her shudder. "There was a whole bowl of food when I went to bed last night."

Boris smirked. "It ain't there now." He looked her over, and she somehow managed to throw on the robe on the chair beside the bed while holding the sheet around her. Not an easy feat.

"Okay, okay," Katrina said, standing up and tossing the sheet aside, but not before tripping on it and almost falling backward onto the bed. "I'll go feed him."

Boris gave her the most menacing look he could muster, which made him look like a constipated sheepdog. “And walk him.”

“Now?!” cried Katrina. “I have to go to work! I’ve never seen *you* take him out in the morning.”

Boris shrugged. “That’s because you’re asleep at 5 A.M.”

Katrina figured that could be true. The few times she’d heard him climbing the stairs to his room it had always been very late—or very early, according to your perspective. Whether he actually walked Spot was anybody’s guess. She figured he must, or Spot would’ve let the whole house hear about it.

Katrina sighed loudly. “This whole thing’s ridiculous. We should just get rid of the damn dog. Len’s probably already left for his road trip, and for all we know, he isn’t even coming back.”

Boris’s voice was gruff. “Oh, trust me—he’ll be back.”

“Jeez . . .” Katrina shook her head. “Okay, Boss, you can go to bed now. I’ll be down there in a minute. I suppose Spot can live without me for 60 more seconds.”

Boris just stood there with his arms crossed, staring at her.

Katrina threw up her hands. “Well, I’m not taking him out dressed like this!”

“I’ll be waiting downstairs.” Boris gave her one more menacing look, then left the room.

When Katrina reached the kitchen in the grungiest clothes she could find, Spot was impatiently pacing back and forth, his humongous food bowl empty, ready to roll. Boris was holding up a huge bag of dog food.

“I saved you a step,” he said, as if he’d bestowed a great favour. “I already fed The Beast.”

“Thanks,” said Katrina sarcastically.

"This is where the food's kept," said Boris, heaving the bag into the bottom of a large cupboard that Katrina had never known existed. She wasn't much of a cook, and the kitchen was pretty much a space station to her. "I didn't suppose you'd know."

Katrina felt a fleeting pang of guilt. She'd never fed Spot, since Len or Boris always did. And even when Len had asked her to walk The Beast, she'd always managed to make up excuses or beg Boris to do it out of Len's earshot. She knew Boris's feelings for her were pretty much the same as hers for him, but he always grudgingly agreed. Maybe he wasn't as bad as she thought. Or else he had a soft spot for a pretty face.

Boris took a leash from a hook on the wall and handed it to Katrina with a malicious grin. As soon as the leather was in her hands, Spot stared up at her expectantly. Katrina avoided his eyes. Could he see her fear? Smell it? She also did her best to avoid Boris, who now sat in a kitchen chair as if pumped for a really good comedy.

This wasn't helping Katrina any. Now she was even more nervous and clumsy. Hands shaking, she tried to attach the leash to Spot's collar. But he kept jerking his head around and lurching toward the door, and Boris kept laughing.

"You've got to be master of the dog!" he yelled.

Katrina wanted to give him the finger, but her hands were too busy. She settled for a "F you!" After what felt like an hour but was only 5 minutes, she had the leash attached. She hadn't started the walk yet, and already she was exhausted.

Katrina had just managed to close the door behind her before Spot was off and running. God, The Beast must weigh 200 pounds! He nearly yanked her arm off half a dozen times. It was obvious Spot knew she was a rank amateur and was taking full advantage. Katrina half-ran, was half-dragged after him, getting a chance to rest only when he paused to lift a leg against a tree. She was terrified he'd leap in front of a bus or veer into a car. There was no stopping him. But finally, after 15 minutes, he finished his prescheduled route (God knows she hadn't had anything to do with it), turned around, and headed for home. This time he merely trotted, as if cooling down after his workout. Katrina found nothing cool about it; she, who rarely even perspired, was soaked in sweat.

Spot stood patiently on the porch, waiting for her to unlock the door. She did, and he just stood there, as if awaiting instructions.

"In, Spot!" she commanded as heartily as she could manage. Spot. Only someone with Len's twisted sense of humour would name a Doberman "Spot." Whoever heard of a Doberman with spots? She'd made it through the damn walk, and all she wanted now was to get rid of this mutt, shower, and get to work. She'd probably be late as it was.

But Spot had other ideas. She pulled on his leash to get him through the door, and he resisted. Twice she tried, and twice he refused. On the third try, for some reason, he changed his mind and played along. He sauntered through the door, and Katrina let out a huge sigh. She leaned against the inside door to catch her breath and lessened her grip on the leash. Suddenly, Spot yanked on it, whipping Katrina's head around and bashing it full-on against the doorframe.

Katrina stared fuzzily at the door, wondering why it had attacked her like that. She dropped the leash, dizzy, afraid she'd pass out. Spot watched her for a second, as if to make sure he'd done his job, then he slumped to the floor and proceeded to lick his ass.

8 IS HE OR ISN'T SHE?

The next day Stevie called and offered to bring over a pizza. He figured they could munch and gossip while they watched a "Sex and the City" marathon. Katrina had already told him about her fight with Len and the sudden departure, but he wasn't up-to-date on the events that had happened since.

Katrina opened the door with a huge shiner. Luckily for her it was a Saturday, and she didn't have to work till Monday. Maybe by then the disco-light effect would be gone.

Stevie dropped the pizza box on the porch and gaped at Katrina. "Who did that to you?" he gasped.

Katrina nodded at the pizza box. "Hope you didn't order extra sauce."

"This isn't funny!" Stevie lowered his voice. "Was it Boris?"

Katrina reflected that in a way, yes, it was Boris. But she shook her head. "No—Spot."

"You mean that godforsaken beast attacked you?"

"Seems I wasn't master of the dog."

"What's that supposed to mean?" asked Stevie, gently touching her face and producing a grimace from Katrina. "Sorry."

So Katrina ushered Stevie inside to the couch after picking up the pizza, which didn't look absolutely destroyed, though a little misshapen. Keeping her voice low (there was a 99 percent chance Boris was still up in his room), she told Stevie about Len insisting she stay in the house and take care of Spot, how she didn't have anywhere else to go unless she gave it all up and moved back to Pipton, how—

"Move back to Pipton!" exclaimed Stevie. "You can't do that! What about your dream, about having your own salon?"

Katrina's shoulders drooped. "Just a dream, Stevie. I'll never be able to afford it. I can't even afford this hole, and it's probably the best deal in town."

"But why can't you afford it?" Stevie glanced around at the sagging, threadbare furniture, the blank, nicotine-stained walls, and the bare front window. "It *has* to be cheap."

"Len paid a big chunk of the rent, and with him gone . . ."

Stevie suddenly looked like someone had lit a firecracker under his ass. "It's perfect!"

"I'd like to see what's so perfect about it," mourned Katrina.

"Think about it!" exclaimed Stevie, smacking her shoulder. "You know how I hate my roommate, right? How she stomps around half-naked and invites over God-knows-what kind of creatures, spews in the sink and never cleans it up, and shaves in the bathtub and never rinses out those gross little hairs?"

Katrina nodded—she'd heard all about it a hundred times.

"So I'll move out!" Stevie shot up straight and beamed at her, like he'd discovered a cure for gout. Katrina was staring at him, not understanding, so he added, "I'll move in with you!"

"But . . . but don't you have a lease?"

"Nope. I'd have to give the bitch a little bit of notice, maybe a couple of weeks, but then she'd probably be as glad to get rid of my skinny little butt as I am to see the last of her fat ass. She's been getting pretty chummy with one of her creatures lately anyway."

"But what about Boris?" said Katrina. "I don't think he'd be too thrilled at you moving in."

"Fuck Boris!" declared Stevie. "He stuck you with Spot, didn't he?"

"Well, technically that was Len, but . . ." Katrina smiled for the first time all day. "I guess Boris will just have to suck it up."

"That's my girl!" Stevie wrapped his arms around her and patted her back. "Don't you think it's genius? We'll both save money, we'll be allies, and I can protect you from that creep Boris. What you need, sweetie, is a man to take care of you."

Katrina restrained herself from giggling into his shoulder. Stevie, the manly-man. Frankly, when she'd first met him, she hadn't known *what* he was.

They'd hit if off from the first time he'd come into Cups with a couple of the gay waiters that he worked with at Extreme!, one of those over-the-top, super-pretentious-so-trendy-you-could-spit restaurants where the servers all looked and acted as rich as the clientele.

Katrina had felt no shyness with Stevie at all. Partly because she thought he was a girl. He certainly looked like one, with his long chestnut hair and his high voice and his thin body encased in baggy clothes. No way of telling what was under those. And he didn't leer at her the way men usually did, and he knew all about hair and makeup and kept telling Katrina how fabulous she looked. And his name was Stevie. Which sounded like a guy, but could also be a girl. It could be short for Stephanie.

The next couple of times Stevie came into Cups, Katrina checked for an Adam's apple, but his shirts were always buttoned too high. Then she'd discreetly tried examining his chest to figure out whether he had breasts or not. That was no help with the tentlike shirts, so she checked out the pants. No help there, either. On their fourth meeting, Stevie had delicately scratched his crotch. Most people probably wouldn't have even noticed, but because Katrina had been observing him so keenly, she did. It was possible a girl would do something like that, but unlikely.

Next, she'd bribed a coworker, a feisty type, to spill coffee on Stevie's chest, then offer to wipe it off. The coworker had returned with the news: no titties. Stevie was either a very flat-chested, itchy woman, or he was, indeed, a man. The gayness seemed pretty sure, but he never talked about his own sex life (but he sure talked about everyone else's) or appeared to go on any dates, so it remained to be seen. Katrina, however, was quite certain.

When Stevie moved into the house with her, Katrina helped him store the last of his boxes in his room, then led him down to the living room. Instead of slumping immediately onto the couch as usual, she waved her arms around and said, "So—what do you think we can do with it?"

Stevie gazed blankly at Katrina. "Do with what?"

"The room, silly. You know, fix it up, make it look pretty."

"The only thing that would make this look pretty is about 50 posters of you spread out on the walls."

"Stevie," said Katrina, punching his shoulder, "I'm serious."

"So am I. I sure don't have a clue. I wouldn't know where to begin." He gazed around the room again. "Maybe a beer would help."

Katrina sighed. She was an expert on dressing herself fashionably for next to nothing and artfully applying makeup the rare times she used it, but had absolutely no clue about how to dress a house. She'd assumed that Stevie would, since she was sure he was a closet gay, and in books and movies all the interior decorators were gay—all the good ones, anyway.

But Stevie was still staring vacantly around the room when she returned with the beer.

Katrina sniffed and almost put her foot in it when she said, “Well, you’re not very artistic for a—” She managed to cut herself off at the last second by saying “Aries” and Stevie stared at her quizzically.

“Pisces—I told you that. And we’re not known for that anyway.”

Katrina thought, *Oh yes, you are. Why don’t you just admit it?* But she remained mum. When he wanted to come out with it he would, and till then, it was none of her business. Though she was sure dying to know.

Then it came to her: Maybe Stevie was appearing ineffectual and uninterested on purpose, so that Boris wouldn’t think he was gay. He might report that to Harley and his Glory Rider pals, and a guy didn’t want to go prancing around them in a tutu, that’s for sure.

9 LIFE OF THE PARTY

After Harley's violent visit shortly after Stevie moved in, the idea of him protecting Katrina in any way seemed ludicrous. So after some lengthy tutoring from Stevie on his computer (Katrina was definitely techno-challenged), she went onto Craigslist and checked the *Star* with a vengeance. She *had* to get another job and get them both out of Hell House.

Jobs, Katrina soon discovered, were scarce. And her timing was bad. Cups had just hired two new weekend people and couldn't give Katrina extra hours, "not unless the new ones fuck up," the manager had said, and staring at the zombie face on one of them, Katrina thought she might not have too long to wait.

But she didn't have time to wait. Unfortunately, she didn't have much experience, either. Which was ridiculous. You couldn't get experience unless you had a job, but you couldn't get a job without experience. One of those just-shoot-me Catch-22's.

She probably could've gotten some work at a low-end salon, but the idea of robotically trimming hair, applying nail polish, or—God forbid!—waxing for 8 hours a day at minimum wage at some Crappy Cuts place made her shudder.

There was a counter help job at an all-night donut shop, where she peered in the window at the rumpled men inside ogling the lone young clerk in her hideous orange outfit, as if ready to cover her in chocolate glaze and sprinkles and wolf her down. Katrina pretended to change her mind about going inside for a coffee and got the hell out of there before they realized her initial goal and ran out and forced her into that ungodly uniform.

Then there was a bartending job in a club, where the male model type stocking beer had stared at her breasts the whole time he spoke. "We could sure use your looks, honey. The other girl's a dog, but we really do need someone who at least knows how to make a Manhattan," and he shook his head sadly at Katrina's blank stare. Was that actually a drink? And did that mean there were cocktails called Miamis and Pittsburghs, too?

Her family had never been big drinkers, though her mom and dad had the occasional sherry and her four sisters had been known to get tipsy on vodka coolers. Katrina enjoyed the initial effect of alcohol: It eased her shyness, loosened her inhibitions, made her feel like a different person—until she threw up. And she always did, after three or four. It just wasn't fair. Here was an opening to the world, a way out of her shell—and all she could do was puke. She supposed it might be a good thing, stopped her from becoming a wino, but she envied her friends who could go out drinking for the night without having to run to the bathroom after the third round.

An ad in the *Star* struck her: "Outgoing? Gorgeous? Enjoy P/T evening work? Good fun! Good pay! THIS IS PERFECTLY LEGAL!"

Katrina was leery at first. It certainly sounded like an escort service or something equally sleazy. But it insisted it wasn't. Well, what the hell. Applying for the job didn't mean she had to take it. Whatever *it* was.

A few days after she e-mailed her scant little resume with the least flattering photo she could find (she didn't want to be hired for her looks alone, though God knows "outgoing" wouldn't get her anywhere), a crisp English voice phoned and asked if she were available to come late that afternoon, and she was directed to an address on Parliament Street.

Definitely the *wrong* end of Parliament. A shabby, two-story building crammed between a crusty-windowed diner and a men's hostel. Slovenly men clustered outside, yammering at each other but basically talking to themselves. The sight of Katrina quieted them, and they stared at her in bewilderment more than lust, as if wondering whether she'd dropped from the sky. Katrina scurried between them before they had time to realize they weren't hallucinating, and ran up to the second floor, grateful there were lots of stairs between them. Those men looked like a mere step or two would do them in.

All the doors on the first floor had been boarded over, as if a plague had hit, or maybe some of the men from the shelter had tried using them as a second home and finally been blocked out. Upstairs, the doors were open for business, but not much more inviting. The first office she came to read "Eagle Eye Detective Agency." Number two was "Wayward Press," whatever that was. Door number three was the jackpot, if you could call it that. The back of a pizza box was taped to the filthy, frosted glass. Scrawled in a magic marker were the words: "Stewart Windle & Associates."

Wanting to flee, but also in no hurry to return to the street and the hostel hordes, Katrina slowly gripped the doorknob, wishing she'd brought some antibacterial lotion in her small bag. Before she had a chance to turn the knob, a voice from within boomed out at her: "Don't be shy! You'll never get a job here that way! Just come on in!"

Oh God, thought Katrina, what was she *doing* here? She turned to run, but the door opened and a man a couple of inches shorter than she threw his arms wide as if at a long-lost friend, his square face shattering into a smile that broadcast his gleaming white teeth.

"You must be Trina," he said, standing there for a moment with his arms still open, and she shuddered, certain he was about to hug her. But he lowered his arms and ushered her in, as if into a sumptuous abode. The only thing sumptuous about it was the man's fine woolen suit.

"*Katrina*," she mumbled, overwhelmed by the force of his personality. Gregarious types always made her shrink. She wanted to fade into the wall, disappear into the plaster. Instead, she glanced around the office and felt as if she were back in her rented house.

The walls were a similar nicotine beige, completely bare. A door to the left led either to another office or a washroom. Two hard wooden chairs faced the single desk, which was as bare as the walls. No computer. No filing cabinets. No photos. Not even an in/out basket. Just a few papers that looked to be blank. And not another soul in the office. The man caught her staring and grinned.

"Oh, there are no others. I just put 'Associates' on the door because it looks better, don't you think?" He held out his hand. "I'm Stewart. Stewart Windle."

"Katrina," she said again, trying not to grimace at the grip. He could crack skulls with those fingers. She was suddenly aware of how alone they were. She retrieved her now-red hand and cleared her throat to tell him she'd changed her mind about the whole thing, but he was too fast.

"I know it looks tacky, luv, but it's a small business. Most of my transactions are done through personal connections or friends of friends. All I really need an office for is to hire people and pay them. It's kind of hard to interview people on the street, and I'd look like a bloody pimp if I offered to meet them in a restaurant or bar."

But *are* you a pimp? Katrina wanted to ask. Again, he seemed to read her thoughts.

"Like the ad said, the business is perfectly legit. It's called Life of the Party."

Windle sat down behind his desk and motioned Katrina to sit in a chair facing him. She sat, winced as the hard wood dug into her butt, and plastered on a smile, wondering what she was still doing here. Windle turned over one of the papers on his desk, and it was the photo that Katrina had faxed, along with her half-page résumé.

"Your picture doesn't do you justice," he said, studying her. He squinted a little, as if the sun were in his eyes, and in some ways it was.

"You have a little Latin in you, what?"

"My great-great-grandfather was Spanish, so I've been told." Her skin looked slightly sun-touched year-round, and glowed amber from within. It perfectly set off her olive green eyes and wheat-coloured hair. At least Len, and countless others, had told her as much. Which she knew was meant as a compliment, but made her feel like a canapé.

"Jolly good," he said, staring at her, leaving the words in the air for a good 2 minutes.

Katrina tried not to twitch in her seat. She averted her eyes, felt herself blushing. She felt like a display in a jewelry store—or that canapé, waiting to be snatched off the buffet table. Had he actually said "jolly good"? Did anyone really talk like that? She was a big fan of old movies, and Mr. Windle sounded just like Watson talking to Basil Rathbone in a Sherlock Holmes flick. Next he'd be saying "Righto." Was he for real? He certainly had the white skin of a certifiable Englishman, and his brown hair tinged with red had a European cut, as well as his suit. Was the joviality a little forced, or was he honest-to-God charming? Katrina finally felt his gaze leave her, and she looked up again and slowly let out her breath.

Windle looked down at the photo of her, shot in a bad light at a bad angle, miraculously unflattering considering her looks, then glanced at her one more time and shook his head, as if to say "Impossible." Then he put the photo aside and folded his hands on the desk.

"Let me tell you a little about the company, then if you're interested, we can get into your background."

What background? Katrina wanted to say, feeling, at 21, that she had barely lived, and had absolutely no past to talk about. But she stayed mum and waited. In spite of her misgivings, she really was curious.

"Life of the Party," said Windle, now staring off into the distance as if focusing on a rehearsed speech, "is a business which hires escort-type professional partygoers to enhance the quality of a party with their wit, looks, or charm—or, in a perfect world, all three. Sometimes they are there merely to enhance. Other times they are there because the host of the party has very few friends of his own, yet he desires to appear that he does."

Katrina had latched onto one of Windle's first words and barely heard the rest. She coughed delicately and then her voice croaked out, "What do you mean, *escort*?"

"Ah," said Windle, clearly expecting this. "I mean escort in the purest sense of the word. There is no sex involved here. In fact, I frown upon it."

"You do?" said Katrina, unable to control her croak and hoping Windle wouldn't notice.

"Oh, most definitely. If one were to become, let's say, *romantically* involved with the real party guests, it could blow the cover on my business, which would definitely displease the party hosts. Obviously, they don't want their real guests knowing they've hired professionals because they don't have the personality to have interesting friends of their own."

"Obviously," said Katrina, relieved that sex was not an issue, but glum knowing that parties were. Katrina was not good with parties.

Oh, she was fine at *giving* them. Not that she was the world's greatest hostess, but she loved being amongst friends, where she felt completely safe and free of strangers. She liked to sit there and listen to them all chat and not have to worry about keeping the conversation going herself. And sometimes she'd start a conversation, just by saying a word or two, then watch it go from there. She'd imagine the direction it would take, but it never did. It always took on a life of its own, darting all over the place, depending on the whims of its creators.

Going to parties, however, was a nightmare for Katrina. For one thing, she didn't know everybody, like she did at her own parties. And you were always expected to mingle. Katrina was happiest when she hit it off with a couple of people and was able to hang with them all night. But strangers would always approach her, drawn by her beauty, and expect to chit-chat. Katrina always froze. She could do a "how are you?" and "where do you work?" but after that, she generally ran out of things to talk about and felt like a fool standing there with nothing to say. After a couple of minutes of awkwardness, she'd usually mumble some excuse and slither away, certain she'd bored the other person to death, when, in fact, they were usually so stunned by her beauty that they wouldn't have noticed a word she said anyway.

"I came up with the idea," said Windle, not noticing Katrina's trepidation, "when this friend of mine—well, an acquaintance, really, he's too boring to be a friend—was giving a party, and asked if I knew any interesting people I could invite along to liven things up. I thought, sure I could help him out—but why not make some money while I was at it? After all, I know a lot of people like him—unfortunately—and the idea seemed like a gold mine."

"So you've been doing this for a while?" said Katrina.

"About 5 months. And I have a few employees, but business is booming, so I find I need several more."

He stared at her again, and she felt some input was needed. After all, interviews were supposed to be a give-and-take situation, show your enthusiasm and all that, so she asked, "And these employees—what exactly do they do?"

"Mingle. Talk to the other guests. Or, in your case, just look beautiful."

"Just look beautiful?" said Katrina doubtfully.

"Well, of course, you have to talk to the others a little bit. Act like a regular guest. There are always other PESTS there, but you won't know who they are."

"PESTS?"

Windle laughed. "That's what you call yourselves. PESTS, as in Party Guests. Though you're actually not a real guest, but a fake one."

"We don't know who the others are?"

"Well, if you did, you might be tempted to chit-chat with each other, and that's not the idea at all."

"But wouldn't the real guests wonder why they'd never met the PESTS before?" asked Katrina.

Windle shook his head. "You say you're an out-of-town friend of the host. Just pick a town you're familiar with, in case they want to strike up a conversation."

"I *am* from out of town," said Katrina. "I'm from Pipton."

"Hmm," mused Windle, "that might be *too* small. If someone else was from there, they might have heard of you. Pick something bigger."

"But I've never lived anywhere else."

Windle sighed. "Then say you live in the country, luv—with the horses and cows and whatnot."

Katrina shook her head. "But I don't know anything about that sort of thing."

Windle scrutinized her again, making her squirm in her chair. "I don't really think they'll be too concerned about what you're actually saying."

Katrina felt a flush of anger. She knew she was beautiful, had been told by everyone she'd ever met since she could remember. But she couldn't really enjoy her beauty because of her loathsome shyness. Most people never noticed that she was smart or funny because she was too shy to show them anything about herself. So instead, she portrayed an aura of aloofness, or even worse, stupidity. Only with good friends and family did she feel comfortable enough to show her real self. So no one like this Windle guy ever saw it. And no one at these stupid parties would, either. What was the point? She'd go there and be beautiful. She'd be one of those pointless women whose self-worth revolved around their looks, and when that was gone, then what?

She wanted to stand up then and leave this silly Englishman who saw exactly what everyone else did, but before she could, he seemed to sense her hesitation, and so he told her what the pay was per party, and she plunked right down again.

"You're *sure* there's no sex involved?" she blurted, and Windle laughed.

"These people are quite well off, believe me. The money's nothing to them."

"So basically they're buying friends."

"Something like that." He leaned forward. "Interested?"

"How about a test run?" asked Katrina.

Windle grinned. "No obligation, luv. I'll set you up for a party . . . let's see . . ." He took a little black book from his inside jacket pocket and scanned the pages. "Tomorrow night, if that's all right. About eight o'clock."

"Don't you want to know anything about me?" Katrina asked, amazed at the ease of the interview.

"I have your phone number and e-mail; that's good enough for me. Unless you have a cell phone number you'd like to add."

"Oh no," said Katrina. "I'm sure I'm the only person in Toronto without one."

Stewart gave her a charming smile. "Believe me, you're better off without one. They're a pain in the ass."

If only I could afford one, mused Katrina, thinking of Boris listening in on her messages.

"Where do I go?" she asked. "What should I wear?"

"I'll call you tomorrow and tell you everything you need to know." Windle glanced at his watch. "Oh dear, this has run rather longer than I'd planned. I have another appointment in a couple of minutes."

Katrina stood up and cringed as he once again offered his hand. This time, his shake was softer, though, as if he were fearful of scaring her off. "I'll speak to you tomorrow, Katrina—and I look forward to seeing you when you come to collect your pay."

"You mean you won't be at the party yourself?" asked Katrina with some trepidation. She barely knew him, but at least one familiar face would be a comfort.

"Oh, I rarely go to the parties; I just organize them." Windle smiled at her like a patronizing father and stood up, waiting for her to go.

"And this is where I collect the money?" asked Katrina, wishing she could hide the tremor in her voice. "Back *here*?"

"I know it's not the most charming of neighbourhoods," said Windle, shaking his head with regret. "But it's where the money is."

10 A PILE OF CLOTHES

As Katrina stepped out of Windle's office, shaky from the interview but thrilled at the prospect of a good-paying job, she was so preoccupied that she tripped right over a pile of clothes stretched out on the floor. Where had *that* come from? The hallway had been empty earlier. She cursed, then glanced back at the offending object. Her first thought was that one of the hostel guys from next door had slunk up the stairs.

Remembering the curious glint in some of their eyes at the sight of her, Katrina quickly picked herself up, intent on the nearby stairs. But a strong hand grabbed her ankle, causing her to sprawl again, and a gruff voice ordered, "Not so fast."

The pile of clothes sat up. Katrina was astonished to see a woman emerge from the many layers, her long, straight black hair nearly covering her face. She yawned, flipped the hair free of her eyes, and asked "What time is it?"

Katrina glanced at her watch very quickly, careful to keep an eye on this person. "Six twenty-five."

"You kicked me in the ribs."

"Sorry about that. I thought you were a homeless guy."

"You always go around kicking homeless guys?"

"No," protested Katrina, aware of how that must have sounded. "Not a homeless guy, a pile of clothes . . . no, not clothes. I . . . I didn't see you there. You weren't there when I went in. I didn't—"

"You took long enough," grunted the black-haired woman, eyeing Katrina accusingly. "I was beginning to wonder whether it was a job interview or a game of chess."

Katrina stared at the lump on the floor, wondering how she ever expected to get a job looking like that, then pulled herself together and cleared her throat. "It wasn't that long. He didn't even ask me any questions."

"He didn't?" Now the woman looked suspicious. "Is this whole thing on the up-and-up? I applied for an ad like this before one time, and it ended up being for private lap dancing. I didn't stick around for the audition."

"Oh, it's nothing like that," said Katrina, looking harder at the woman. At first she'd thought she was a street person. But now it was apparent she'd simply had a bad day. She was in dire need of a comb and an iron. Not to mention a makeup kit. "And the interview's real easy," Katrina added, still guilty over the kick in the ribs.

The woman looked over Katrina knowingly, then her eyes turned to slits and her voice cold. "It would be—for *you*."

Katrina had received this attitude from other women all her life, especially from her own sisters. She was in no mood for it now. Working all day at Cups, then rushing over here and enduring the tension of the interview had worn her out; she just wanted to get home to a hot bath.

"I have to go," she said coolly. "Sorry about the kick." She brushed herself off and started down the hall.

"Hey, wait!" called the woman, stepping away from the office door so as not to be heard. Katrina rolled her eyes and hesitated on the top step.

"I didn't mean to be a bitch. It's just been a helluva day . . . a helluva week." When Katrina turned, she was taken aback to find the woman only a foot away from her. The stranger smiled for the first time, and a beam of energy burst from her face. Suddenly, instead of looking like a street person, she looked like a Broadway star. "Hate to burn any bridges. We could be working together."

"Maybe," said Katrina, still annoyed at the earlier bitchiness. "But not really."

"What's that supposed to mean?" asked the woman, stepping closer.

"Some kind of company policy. Windle will explain."

The woman realized her closeness to Katrina and took a step back. She glanced toward the office and its pizza box sign. "What's this guy like? Is he okay?"

"Very friendly," said Katrina, realizing for the first time that she'd actually liked Windle, found him amusing in spite of the maybe-phony charm and the initial over-friendliness. Her inquisitor looked her over again slowly, like a fish filet on sale at the market; it looked good, but could she be sure it wouldn't give her food poisoning? Katrina braced herself for the bitch look, but apparently the woman thought better of it. Instead, she laughed like she'd just heard a great joke in her head.

"Sorry, I have a natural urge to be a bitch to you because you're just so goddamn gorgeous—but at the same time, I love looking at you, too. Maybe my butch writing partner's starting to wear off on me."

Katrina stared at the woman, unnerved by her frankness. Strange women never told her she was beautiful, only women she'd known for a while, once they were friends. And even then, it often came with a little dig, something to soften the compliment, like "If I had your looks" or "Everything must be so easy for you."

"Actually," continued the woman thoughtfully, "I think she's wearing me down. My writing partner, I mean. We've been working on this frigging play for *weeks*, and it's still not clicking. Today, I felt like something was finally coming together, then I had to stop it all to come here." She sighed. "Then, after rushing here like a fiend, I found out I was *early*. I was going to knock on the door on the chance I could go in and get the interview over with, then I heard voices inside, and I knew he was interviewing someone else." She leaned closer to Katrina, as if sharing a secret. "I even tried to listen in, but I couldn't hear too well, and I was afraid if I got too close to that damn door someone would see me through the frosted glass."

The woman rummaged in a small bag that matched the duffel and tote she'd left on the floor by the door and pulled something out. "Gum?" she asked. Katrina shook her head, and the woman popped a piece in her mouth, talking as she chewed. "So I decided to sit in the hall and go over my script, but I was so frigging exhausted I guess I fell asleep." She paused for breath.

"They could put a chair or two out here; it wouldn't kill them." She dug under her jacket, adjusted her bra, and sighed with relief. "Goddamn underwire. Wonder Bra, my ass. More like 'I wonder why I'm wearing this frigging thing.'" With barely a pause she continued, "I've been doing rewrites on this play, which I'm also rehearsing 2 nights a week, and trying to raise money to put the thing on, as well as trying to find a place to stage it. I had the community centre by my place pretty well sewed up, but then they started balking at the content, like I might be performing satanic rituals in there or something.

"Then there's the other play I'm writing, this one on my own, 'cause that dyke bitch is driving me nuts, and I'm bartending 3 days a week, afternoons, but it's slow now 'cause you know how great the weather's been, and who wants to sit in a dark bar in the middle of the day when it's hot and sunny out? So obviously, I need some extra cash. I don't want to go looking for another bartending or waitressing job, though. It's too much hassle finding something you like, and I swear to God if I spend too much time in that business, I'll end up hating people and start putting rat poison in their martinis or something . . ."

The woman stopped suddenly for a deep breath, and Katrina felt she needed one herself. Then it dawned on her: She hadn't even had time to feel shy with the stranger. As the woman babbled on, never standing still, always shifting her weight to a different leg, or searching for something in her bag, or adjusting her underwear, Katrina kept tuned to the conversation, but she was also thinking how much she was enjoying listening to this strange woman. It occurred to her she really hadn't had much female companionship since she'd moved to Toronto. In school, she'd hung out with a group of girls, but she hadn't been really close to any of them. They were the type you exchanged gossip with and talked together about movies and TV shows, but you wouldn't want to divulge too much about yourself, or everyone in the school would know it in 10 minutes.

But this woman talking now, whose name Katrina didn't even know, had a warmth and intensity that drew Katrina like a magnet. She was incredibly outgoing, but not overwhelming. God, how Katrina envied her. To wake up every day and march out into the world fearless, ready to tackle any stranger!

". . . so what do you think?" asked the woman expectantly.

Katrina gaped at her, sadly aware she'd missed her last few sentences. The woman sighed and shook her head. "You got low blood pressure or something? You look kind of out of it. Anyway, I have no shame; I'll repeat myself: It's about a lesbian vampire cult that sucks the blood out of men and turns them into women. I wanted to make it about straight women—I figured the audience would be bigger—but the dyke I'm writing it with wouldn't hear of it."

Katrina debated whether to break the news or not, but the hell with it. "You know," she said, "I think that's been done."

"What!"

"Off Broadway, or Off-Off Broadway, with guys in drag or something. I'm sure I read about it somewhere. Anyway, it sounds familiar."

"Really?" exclaimed the woman, tugging on a thick lock of hair. "Shit!" She thought it over for a second. "Guys in drag, you say? So there's guys dressed as girls who hate guys and love other girls?"

Katrina had to think about it for a second, then she nodded. The other woman shook her head.

"Fucking nuts." For a moment she looked despondent, but Katrina could see the wheels turning and that megawatt smile returned. "Well, like they say, everything's been done at least once. It's how you do it that counts." She squeezed Katrina's shoulder, and Katrina didn't even shrink, like she usually would. "Thanks, you've been a big help."

Katrina doubted that, but she shrugged and shyly smiled. "Good luck with it."

The woman stared at Katrina's face for a long moment, as if enjoying a particularly fine sunset. Then she emerged from her spell and shouted, "Shit! I'm going to be late for my interview!" She held out her hand. "Cathy."

"Katrina."

Cathy laughed. "Same name, but a million miles apart!" She reached into her small bag, pulled out a pen and notepad and scribbled down her name and phone number. "Give me a call, find out how I did." She reached back in the bag, applied some lip gloss, and smacked her lips together. "How do I look?"

"Great."

"Liar. If I looked like you, I'd get the job for sure . . . whatever it is."

"You'll be pleasantly surprised," Katrina said, unable to help but smile. "I think it's right up your alley."

"You don't give away much, do you?" said Cathy quizzically, and she blew her a kiss then turned and ran down the hall.

Katrina watched Cathy knock on the door, then saw it open and heard Windle's voice boom out, "You must be Katie!" She turned and trudged down the stairs, in no hurry to reach the street and its motley occupants. Katrina wondered if Cathy really meant for her, a complete stranger, to call. Nah. She was the type who probably handed out her number 20 times a day. In an hour she would've forgotten who Katrina was. Katrina somehow felt sad at that, as if she'd lost a friend. It was like meeting someone on vacation that you truly clicked with, only to discover they had to leave the next day.

Katrina suddenly realized how much she missed a girlfriend in her life. Her sister Kandy had always been her best friend, but she hadn't seen her in almost a year, and only rarely spoke to her on the phone. And Stevie, as much as she loved him, wasn't really a girl.

Katrina sighed as she started down the stairs. Too bad about this Cathy girl. She'd probably never see her again.

11 SWINDLE

"Stewart Windle?" said Stevie incredulously, studying the card Katrina handed him.

She'd been dying to tell Stevie about Life of the Party, but he'd been at work when she got home from her interview last night and had still been sleeping when she went to work this morning. Stupidly, she'd forgotten to give Stewart her work number, and he hadn't asked, so she raced home from Cups to see if he'd left her a message. If Boris hadn't got to it first, that is.

The message light was blinking, and Katrina was just about to check it when Stevie came in the door with several bags of groceries. She helped him haul the bags into the kitchen, then quickly told him about her interview the day before. She handed Stevie Stewart's card, then she played the message.

"Katrina, darling," boomed Stewart's voice, "S. Windle here. The party is definitely on for tonight. A taxi will pick you up at your place at 7:30. Attire yourself in something cocktail-dress sexy. Think Audrey Hepburn meets Sophia Loren. Your password at the door will be 'PEST.' Any problems, let me know. TTFN."

"TTFN?" said Katrina, baffled. All these anagrams these days were getting to be too much. Didn't anyone have enough time to just say the whole thing?

"Ta-ta-for-now," said Stevie. "It's a Brit thing." He stared at Stewart's card and tapped it against his hand. "Stewart Windle!" He laughed. "S. Windle. Don't you get it? *Swindle!* That name *can't* be for real!"

"Oh yes, it is," said Boris, and they both whirled to see him standing in the hallway, a thoughtful expression on his sheepdog face. Neither Katrina nor Stevie had realized he was even in the house. He must have been lurking on the stairs.

"How do you know?" asked Stevie suspiciously.

Boris shrugged. "I've heard the name is all. In Montreal." He turned to Katrina. "How did you say this guy knows the people having the parties?"

"She didn't," said Stevie, furious to think Boris had been eavesdropping all along.

"How have you heard about him?" asked Katrina. "What did he do there?"

Boris paused for a second, then shrugged. "Not sure. Real estate, investment banking . . . something like that."

Katrina sighed. That was a lot of help. "The people having the parties are friends of his—at least the guy tonight is."

"That so?" said Boris thoughtfully. "Weird idea. But it's got potential."

"So you're an expert on parties now?" said Stevie, stepping closer. "I thought you just hung out with hooligans and threatened to beat people up." He glared at Boris, his fists clenched. If his fear didn't overshadow his anger by about 10-to-1, he'd have taken a swing at the guy.

But Boris just smirked, grabbed a Coke from the fridge, and shambled up to his room. Katrina and Stevie turned to stare at each other.

"What the fuck?" said Stevie.

"Beats me," said Katrina. "I'd even forgotten Boris *was* from Montreal."

"I thought you said this Swindle guy was English."

"Windle," corrected Katrina. "And they do have English people in Montreal, Stevie."

"Not many, I'll bet. They probably throw them all in prison until they're fluent in French." He looked at the business card again. "He had a cruddy little office, you say?"

"He claims the business is legit."

"Sure—that's what all the crooks say." Stevie frowned, and his voice rose two notches. "I wish I'd known about this earlier. I could've taken the night off work and gone with you."

"Hardly," said Katrina. "We're prescreened—we even have passwords. I couldn't just stroll in with some strange man."

"The strange men are what I'm worried about," admitted Stevie.

"I'll be fine," said Katrina, wishing she meant it. "Besides, there's a girl I met at the interview yesterday who might be going with me." She had no idea whether Cathy even had the job; in fact, she had forgotten about having her phone number till this moment. But she said it to assuage Stevie. His voice got high and whiny when he worried, and she couldn't take much more of the nails-on-chalkboard effect.

"Call her and find out for me, would you? I'd feel a lot better if I knew there was someone else there with you."

"I will," Katrina promised. She leaned forward and kissed him on the cheek. "You'd better get to work. And I have to run up and take a shower and make myself beautiful. Wish me luck."

"Luck," said Stevie, giving her a hug. "But there's no hope in hell you'll ever make yourself beautiful."

Katrina smacked his shoulder, which was still sore from Harley's slap, and he winced and watched her run up the stairs. If it weren't such short notice, he would've played detective or asked a friend to follow her to the party. If Boris weren't such a spying rat, he would've asked *him*. But there was nothing he could do about it now. He crossed his fingers, which he knew was a childish superstition and worth diddly-squat, but it comforted him. He unpacked the groceries, hoping the best for Katrina, and wishing they had squeakier floorboards in the house. Boris's sneaking around was starting to get on his nerves.

Boris crept cautiously down the stairway a few minutes later and peered into the kitchen. After making certain he was alone, he picked up Windle's business card which Stevie had dropped on the dining table and studied it carefully. Scratching his chin, he picked up the phone.

"Hey," he said to the chirp on the other end. Ray sounded like he'd smoked at least two doobies; his cheeriness was repulsive. "You remember an English dude name of Stewart Windle from Montreal?"

"S. Windle?" asked Ray. "Sure I do. You used to talk about him all the time. 'The best!' you'd say, 'The guy's frigging amazing!' I thought he was your hero."

"No," said Boris sarcastically, "he's not my fucking hero."

"But you know him?" said Ray.

"No, I only heard about him. And I saw him once."

"Oh," said Ray, not sure where this was going and not inclined to think about it too much. Boris's grumpiness was ruining his high.

"But I hear he's in Toronto now," said Boris, "and I'm wondering what he's up to."

"What's this all about?" asked Ray.

"I just thought he might be able to throw a little business our way," said Boris. "But I need a background check. Nothing major, just the basics. Would Harley be able to help us out?"

"I don't see why you can't talk to Harley," said Ray petulantly.

"He likes you better than me."

Ray just grunted; he couldn't argue with that. Anyone in his right mind liked *him* better than Boris.

"Just do me the favour, all right?" demanded Boris.

"You're gonna owe him big-time," said Ray.

"I'll handle it."

Ray sighed. "I'll tell him to call you when he gets the info."

"Just a little background check is all," reminded Boris.

"Sure," spluttered Ray as he chomped on something. "Hey, are we on for tonight?"

"I'm not sure yet. I might have something else to check out."

"Whatever," said Ray, hanging up.

Katrina was in her bathrobe headed for the shower when she remembered her promise to Stevie. She stepped back in her room, rummaged through her purse, and found the pink notepaper with Cathy's number. She picked up the phone and heard Boris saying, "Just a little background check is all." Katrina stared at the receiver. Background check? Was Boris checking up on *her*? Had he figured out her and Stevie's plan? Maybe he'd been talking to one of Len's friends; he was going to have her followed, and then . . .

Ridiculous, she told herself. Insane. Stevie's suspicions about Life of the Party had rubbed off on her, made her paranoid. Sure, Boris was Harley's minion, his mole. But he didn't pick up the phone and have people whacked. He didn't . . . She heard him coming up the stairs. Quickly, she hung up the phone, jumped up, and closed her door. When she heard his bedroom door close, she waited a moment for her heart to stop jangling, then she picked up the phone again and dialed.

A rough, guttural voice answered, more a bark than a hello. Katrina checked the pink slip of paper and was about to hang up when another voice took over.

"Hello? Hello?"

"Cathy?" asked Katrina doubtfully.

"Yeah, that was Helga, don't mind her; she's not good on the phone. Who's this?"

"My name's Katrina. I met you outside Mr. Windle's office yesterday. You were—"

"Oh yeah, yeah, hold on a second, will you?"

Katrina could hear Cathy whispering something to Helga, whoever she was. Then she remembered Cathy mentioning her lesbian writing partner. Was there more to it than just business? Did they live together? Maybe she shouldn't have called. Katrina was used to hanging around gay men. All Stevie's waiter friends hung out at Cups all the time and were like sisters to her, though less bitchy than her own. But she'd never known any lesbians, and they scared her a little. The odd one she saw in Cups or behind the counter at the health food store (she assumed they were lesbians; they certainly didn't look like they were trying to attract any man) always glared at her accusingly, as if she were defying feminism with her beauty.

"Sorry about that," said Cathy. "Helga's a nosy little bitch. She always wants to know who I'm talking to."

"You two . . . *live* together?" asked Katrina, not certain how to tactfully ask the question.

"Oh God, no!" laughed Cathy, almost in hysterics. "I mean, she lives here sometimes. Half the people I know crash here sometimes. It's a big loft, lots of space. As long as they throw in some money for food and toilet paper I don't give a rat's ass. But Helga . . . God, no! I like my men as much as the next red-blooded woman."

Cathy paused for a second, and Katrina could hear her unwrapping some gum. When she spoke again, it was a little more difficult to understand her through the chewing.

"Speaking of men, what do you think about that Windle guy? Is he cute or what? I mean, his accent seems kind of fake, but I think he's perfectly charming, and so boyish in an adult, wolfish kind of way. But, of course, I'm sure he's more interested in *you*. Not like I looked like a million bucks yesterday or anything. In fact, I'm sure I looked like I'd been dragged through a sewer. I'll look better next time I see him though, I can tell you that."

"You mean you got the job?" asked Katrina, surprised she was so happy to hear it.

"Yeah, I'm going to my first party tonight."

"Me too!" Katrina hesitated. "Wait! You think it's the same one? A cab's picking me up. I don't know the address."

"Yeah," said Cathy, "I'm not crazy about that part of it. I hope they don't blindfold us when we get in the car."

Katrina, horrified, sputtered, "You're not—"

"I'm *joking*," said Cathy, and when Katrina didn't respond she asked, "Hey, are you okay?"

"Just a little tense," said Katrina, thinking of Boris and his background check, wondering if he (or one of The Glory Riders) was listening in on her conversation right now. The phone could be bugged, for all she knew.

"Well, it has to be the same party," continued Cathy. "You saw his office. The guy's operation's not that big. Oh, and remember, when we see each other tonight we have to pretend we don't know each other." She suddenly laughed with delight. "And when you see me tonight, you probably won't."

"Won't what?" asked Katrina, confused.

"Know me, kiddo. Windle warned me I'd have to look the part. Full hair and makeup. But hey, I'm an actress. It's all part of the show."

"I thought you were a writer," said Katrina, a little overwhelmed by the verbal onslaught.

"*And* a director *and* a producer . . . Hell, Kat, I do it all." Cathy laughed at that. "Hell, cat . . . Hellcat, get it? I'm surprised no one's ever said it to me before. Look, I hate to interrupt, but I've got a lot of work to do on the face. I'll see you around eight, at our mystery destination. And remember, you don't know me."

The phone rang while Katrina was in the shower. She heard Boris running downstairs to answer it. She knew he didn't have a phone in his room, and obviously, he didn't have a cell phone; maybe he couldn't afford one, either. Not that she'd ever been in Boris's room. He'd installed a lock on it as if it were stocked with rare artifacts. She had no idea what was in there and didn't want to know. Thankfully, he never went into her room to answer the phone, at least not when she was home, and she'd never had to tell him not to. Insensitive though he was, he seemed to understand that she wouldn't take kindly to that.

"Harley here," Boris heard as he recovered his breath. He'd heard Katrina in the shower but didn't want to take the chance she'd scramble out and get to the phone before he did. If she'd been out, he would have used the phone in her room, in spite of all the stuffed animals and girly shit that made him want to gag. But she'd have a hissy fit if she ever caught him in there, and living with her was enough of a pain in the ass without that.

"How're your little roomies doing? Shitting in their pants, I hope." Harley chuckled, then continued, not waiting for an answer. "You're lucky my buddy from Montreal just happened to be home." He talked fast, wanting to get this over with. He thought it beneath himself to supply a former employee and current informant with information at a moment's notice, but he liked people to owe him favours, so what the hell.

"The guy's well known in Montreal circles, but he's from Toronto. Claims to be an investment banker or something, but my friend hears he's a big-time con artist. His family's loaded. His father's some big-shot lawyer. The guy went to private school with a bunch of other little rich kids, pretended to be English."

"*Pretended*?" said Boris, somehow deflated by this news. He'd only seen Stewart Windle once in person, at a fake fundraiser in Montreal which Boris had crashed just to see the Swindler, as he secretly called him, in action. A friend had pointed him out, and Boris had been surprised at how boyish and respectable the man looked. No wonder he could con so many people! They hadn't actually met. Boris had watched and listened from a few feet away, hiding himself behind a potted palm. He would've sworn, hearing the guy, that he was an English duke or earl or something, definitely the real deal.

"Yep," said Harley. "His family lived there for a while, but they moved back here when he was like 5 or something. Kept the accent to impress people, I guess."

"No shit?" said Boris, still thinking back to the fundraiser, saving the agouti of Costa Rica, which was apparently some kind of cat-sized rat. The real rat was Windle; all the proceeds went directly into his own pocket.

"Well, thanks, man. That was fast. I didn't know you were so well-connected with the Frogs."

"I wish I was as well connected as this Swindle guy."

"Windle," corrected Boris.

"You owe me for this, Boris," said Harley in his most ominous voice. "What's it all about, anyway?"

No way was Boris letting the prick in on this action. Before Harley could ask him anything else, he hung up.

When Katrina had finished dressing she went downstairs to wait for the cab. She was surprised—no, astonished—to find Boris sitting in the living room. The only rooms Boris ever used in the house were his bedroom, the bathroom, and the kitchen. The most time he spent anywhere near the living room seemed to be while lurking in the adjacent hallway.

"Who called?" she asked, trying to appear casual as she sat in a chair facing the window.

"Just a friend of mine," said Boris shiftily, and Katrina wondered once again why she'd never spent the extra bucks for call display. For all she knew, the call could have been Windle, calling back to change plans, or one of the men she'd met in the last month, giving it another try.

"You must be kind of nervous about this whole party thing, eh?" said Boris idly.

"Hmm," said Katrina, wondering why he'd picked right now to make conversation for the first time she'd known him, and wishing he'd just go away.

"Guess you won't know anyone there. Unless your boss is there—you'd know him."

"No, he doesn't go, he just organizes everything."

Boris was silent for a moment, and Katrina thought he was even worse at small talk than she was. She shifted in her chair and peered out the window.

"When's your cab getting here?" he finally asked, as if it were the best thing he could come up with.

"Any minute now." *And not a second too soon,* thought Katrina.

"I could go with you if you want. I know you're kind of nervous and everything. You don't really know what you're getting into . . ."

God, thought Katrina, *maybe he's more clever than I thought*. Spying on her by acting as bodyguard—ingenious.

"Thanks, but like I told Stevie, I can't show up with some strange man. I'm supposed to be on my own. That's the whole idea."

"Oh, I wouldn't have to go in. I could just go with you in the cab then watch and make sure everything's okay before you go inside."

The thought of being alone with Boris in an even more intimate space than this one made Katrina's whole body shiver—and not in a good way, either. She covered the goose bumps she saw Boris staring at by saying, "Chilly tonight." If Boris wasn't spying on her, then why was he suddenly acting so sweet and concerned? As in *interested*.

Katrina saw a cab pull up outside and leapt off the chair.

"I've got to go."

"You sure I can't—?"

"*No!*" shouted Katrina, rushing out the front door.

"Don't worry about Spot!" Boris called after her. "You can walk him when you get home!"

Boris watched her scamper into the cab and grinned to himself. He picked up Windle's business card from the kitchen table, checked the address, and went to get his coat.

12 SHAKEDOWN

Boris would have ordinarily called up Ray and asked him to pick him up in his black van, but Ray was already annoyed at having to bug Harley earlier, and besides, Boris wanted to do this one on his own. In case things didn't work out. He'd never given anyone a shakedown before and wasn't sure of the etiquette. And for all he knew, Windle wouldn't even be at his office this late.

He stepped off the Carlton streetcar just as it was getting dark and headed south. A bunch of old rummies were hanging out on a stoop beside Windle's building. They barely glanced at Boris. He looked up and saw a light in a second-floor window. He did his best to lose his usual slouch and stand up straight—it was important tonight to look taller and bigger. There could be real money in this if he played his cards right.

When Boris had overheard Katrina telling Stevie tonight about Life of the Party, he felt like Christmas had come early. The whole scheme sounded suspicious, and with Windle's reputation in Montreal, there had to be more to it than met the eye. It had to be a cover for something, some kind of setup. Blackmail? Extortion? Drug dealing? Even if it weren't, Boris was sure he and Ray could make a killing if only they could become PESTS, too. Hell, he might not even tell Ray about it. Do it on the side, claim he was doing something else on Life of the Party nights. Of course, he kind of needed Ray's van, unless he went in and just stole small stuff, jewelry, and cash. But it would be so easy to go in as a PEST, leave a side door open when no one was looking, go back later and clean the place out. Park the van close by, a quick in and out . . . *nice*.

There were no locks or buzzers on the outside of Windle's building. Of course, it wasn't residential. The first floor was boarded up. Boris crept up to the second floor, saw only one light at the end of the hallway, and tiptoed toward it.

He would've liked to peep in first, peeping was his forte, but the frosted glass made that impossible. So he took a deep breath and swung the door open, amazed it wasn't locked at this time of night, in this neighbourhood. Hell, anyone could get in. Even himself, he thought with an inward chuckle.

Windle sat at a bare desk rifling through a little black book. He looked as boyish and innocent as Boris remembered, even when he narrowed his eyes at the intruder and said, "I think you're in the wrong office, son."

"Oh I don't think so," said Boris, stepping toward the desk and looming over it, something he'd seen in a movie once. He felt a bit like Humphrey Bogart, except his hands were shaking, so he stuck them in his pockets. Which put him off balance, and he staggered a bit and had to grab for the desk to right himself. He tried a Bogey smile, mouth closed, and muttered, "I hear you've got a job opening."

"What's that you say?" said Windle, leaning forward. "Speak up, I can't hear you."

"A job opening," repeated Boris, ticked off at being made to feel like a plebe. "Life of the Party. I hear you're hiring fake guests. Or PESTS, I think they're called."

Windle sat back and folded his hands together, as if ending an interview. He looked a little too smug for Boris's taste. "Sorry, chum, you're too late. I've hired everyone I need."

"Pity," said Boris, trying for nonchalance. "Isn't that what you so-called English guys say all the time? 'Pity'?"

Windle took the little black book from the desk and tucked it in his jacket pocket. He gave Boris a searing look. "How did you come upon my address, young man?"

"Let's just say I heard it through the grapevine," said Boris, and then, "Hey, you got a smoke?" He rarely smoked, but in old movies in situations like this they were always offering each other cigarettes. Gentlemanly goodwill and all that.

"If by 'smoke' you mean a cigarette, no," said Windle. "I smoke only a pipe, and I've run out of tobacco."

"A pipe! Jolly good," said Boris, covering his annoyance. "Well, I'll live. Anyway, like I was saying . . . I heard about your little business and I thought, perfect. This is my kind of gig. Free food, all the booze I can drink, beautiful babes. It's like being at one of those fancy all-inclusive resorts, only I don't pay you, *you* pay *me*."

"I see," said Windle, twiddling his thumbs as if seriously thinking about hiring Boris. "And would you have any *other* interest in this little venture of mine?"

"Shit," said Boris with a grin, "what else would a guy need?"

Windle shrugged. "It just occurs to me that a fellow like yourself might be more interested in, say, the contents of the house itself rather than the party." He smiled knowingly at Boris. "Am I correct?"

"What?" said Boris, playing dumb. "You mean, like I'm an interior decorator or something? You calling me a fag?"

"A fag is a cigarette, my dear boy. No, what I'm saying is, possibly you'd be more interested in taking things *out* of the house than putting yourself *in*."

Boris shook his head woefully. "You really shouldn't put ideas in a guy's head like that, Windle." He paused. "Or can I call you Stewart?"

Stewart Windle was looking Boris over thoughtfully now. His eyes narrowed again. "You look familiar. Have I seen you somewhere before, or is this truly my first splendid introduction?"

"I used to live in Montreal," said Boris. He pulled a cigarette from his pocket, lit one, then offered one to Windle, who shook his head, a bit bewildered. Boris waved the cigarette. "Thought I'd see if you had one first. You *are* the host, and you know what these little bastards cost these days." He blew out smoke and then said, "Back in Montreal, I used to go to fundraisers once in a while."

"Ah," said Windle, leaning back in his chair with a grin, as if immensely enjoying himself. "The agouti! I remember you now, lurking behind the ferns. I think you actually picked up the pot at one point so you could move without being seen. Lucky you didn't put your back out."

Boris's mouth gaped open, and Windle couldn't help but laugh. "I like to keep my eyes open. I've found it pays off."

"How did you—" gasped Boris, but Windle cut him off.

"Potted plants don't usually walk across the floor on their own. And shrubs don't usually have fingers pointing at me from across the room."

"Well . . ." said Boris, smoking, playing for time. He was too stunned to think of anything to say. He could have sworn he'd been invisible that night. Of course, he was 15 at the time, and his older hooligan friend who'd told him about the gig—and the infamous Stewart Windle—hadn't been much older. Or smarter.

"Well, *I* like to do research," he finally managed as self-importantly as possible. "I find it pays off. And I hear you're pretty well connected, dude. Got a lot of rich friends in this town." He looked for a place to stub out his cigarette, saw no sign of an ashtray, and threw the butt onto the wooden floor, grinding it under his black boot. Windle watched with distaste but said nothing. "Which makes me wonder," said Boris, "why you went to Montreal in the first place."

For the first time, Stewart shifted in his chair. "What's the expression? You don't shit in your own backyard."

Boris decided enough beating around the bush. He leaned forward, his face close to Windle's, and wondered if the guy was wearing makeup. His skin was so smooth. Pansy little pseudo-Brit.

"The thing I'm getting at is, maybe your friends who are giving these parties, who are hiring you to supply them with phony guests . . . PESTS . . . well, maybe they wouldn't be so happy to know about your background. It might make them kind of antsy, if you know what I mean. Them being rich and high class and all."

Windle leaned back as if Boris's breath offended him and shrugged. "Maybe they already know about my background."

"I don't think so," said Boris, wondering if he should've popped a breath mint before he left. "I think you're scared shitless about the thought of them finding out."

"We seem," said Windle slowly, "to be spending a lot of time talking about shit. Why don't we get down to brass tacks. What is it you want, exactly, Mr. . . .?"

"Boris."

"Boris what?"

"I don't believe in last names. Only old English farts like you give a shit about that crap."

Windle nodded as if Boris had a point.

"I want a job as a PEST, of course. I told you that when I walked in the door; you just don't listen."

Windle flashed his huge gleaming teeth, and Boris thought if he didn't already know the guy was a fake, he'd know now. Real Brits didn't have teeth like that. "Sorry to offend," said Windle, "but I thought you were joking."

Boris shook his head as menacingly as possible. Unfortunately, this caused his heavy black bangs to fall further over his face, increasing the angry sheepdog look. He looked like a Disney caricature.

Windle quickly covered a smirk and asked, "Did you even read the ad? 'Gorgeous? Outgoing?' Do you think these adjectives in any way apply to you?"

Boris was a little hurt. He wasn't the best-looking guy on the block by a long shot, but he'd never considered himself ugly. And he was kind of quiet, but certainly no wallflower. "Look, I know your past. I know you're a scam artist, a thief. I heard about you all over Montreal."

"I'm sure what you heard were mere rumours. And anyway, it's all ancient history now. I'm in a new town with a fresh start. I plan to make a go of this business, go straight with it. And I have no interest whatsoever in associating with young hustlers."

"Go straight, my ass," scoffed Boris. "I'll bet those joints get robbed a day or two after your PESTS go in there. Shit, I'll bet your PESTS case the joints for you."

"Goodness," said Windle mockingly, "I wish I'd thought of that."

"See!" said Boris proudly, unaware of Windle's sarcasm. "*I* did. The deal is, I go in the places, check things out, maybe leave a door or window open here or there and who's the wiser?"

"Oh perfect," said Windle. "So my friends call the police, who figure either I or one of my PESTS is responsible. That's certainly good for repeat business." He suddenly leaned over the desk, nearly bumping his head into Boris's stomach, causing Boris to lean back and lose his balance. He caught himself on the metal coat rack and straightened.

Windle went on, his face growing red. "Let me tell you this, my dear Boris, I came up with the idea for this company, and it's a damn good idea. I get to associate with the rich clients and the fun and beautiful staff. There are no large expenditures except for the rent of this unfortunate little office. I can pay the staff cash, no questions asked, and avoid all taxes. It's the perfect setup and, aside from the always-tiresome tax bit, thoroughly legitimate. And *you* have the nerve to come along and try to stop me?"

"Yeah," muttered Boris, letting go of the coat rack and trying to look cocky. "Something like that."

Windle fell back in his chair and snorted. "You're out of your mind."

Boris leaned forward and wondered again if that was Windle's natural blush or Revlon's. "And I still say you're scared shitless of your friends finding out about you. I know for a fact you were one of the best in Montreal—burglary, credit cards, fundraising scams, pyramid schemes, you name it. You had a great reputation. Nothing high tech, just good timing and brains and light fingers—"

"And lots of luck," cut in Windle. "*If* all that were true, and I'm not saying it is. The thing about a good thief, son, is that he's like a good gambler—he has the sense to get out while the getting is good."

"So you got out. Why come back here? It's not like you can con the rich people here—they're all your friends. Why here? Why now?"

It was the question of the here and now that caused Windle to give in to Boris. He would never let the crass young man know it, but it wasn't fear of his friends discovering his past that terrified him. It was his father.

Stewart really had been born and raised in England—till he was 5. He didn't remember anything about it, but he'd kept the accent. He was an only child, and his parents thought it was cute. He got kidded about it a lot at school, but he refused to give in; he wanted to be different. And the accent certainly helped in his chosen profession. It made him sound more exotic, more polished. It made it a lot easier to swindle people.

Not that Windle had planned things that way. His father was a lawyer, and had insisted Stewart become the same, carry on the tradition since he had no siblings to do it. Stewart went to the University of Toronto with the full intention of studying law, but somehow carousing and womanizing got in the way. When his father saw his deplorable grades he insisted Stewart buckle down. The thought of buckling down once he'd had a taste of the other fun to be had out in the great wide world, combined with a horror of being cooped up in an office all day actually working, was enough to cause Stewart to flee.

His parents didn't know anyone in Montreal, and he'd always been good with French in school, so it seemed a logical choice. He quickly became bilingual. What he couldn't do quickly was find a job. Not that he really wanted one. But there was the matter of food and rent and bar-hopping, and no one was offering to pay for those. There was always the gigolo route, he supposed, but he was afraid it might ruin his taste for real sex. And old women were bad enough, but old men? Even young men? *Any* men at all? The very thought made Stewart's pale skin paler.

In a pub one night (pubs were Stewart's favourite, being British and all), he ran into a drunken Irishman who talked in great detail about some of the cons he'd pulled. Windle saw wonderful opportunities opening up to him. He became fast friends with the Irishman (after assuring him he was much more Canadian than English) and sucked his brain for every morsel of criminal knowledge. They even became partners for a while—until the Irishman ripped Windle off. Thus, he learned the hard way never to trust another con man, and from then on worked strictly on his own.

From the beginning, Stewart told his father he was running a respectable business, though one time he couldn't remember what he'd said that business was. He'd been sure he'd mentioned investment banking, but his father had looked at him strangely and said, "I thought you were in real estate." He was more careful after that. Especially when his parents came to Montreal to visit. Luckily, they only made it twice in 10 years, his father being very busy with his career and his mother, her social charities. Stewart managed to avoid showing them an office. Instead he plied them with fine food and liquor and entertained them with a female friend whom he paid a lot of money to pose as his long-time girlfriend. With a respectable career, of course—one they made sure to both remember.

After 10 years in Montreal, things had started to get a little too hot. Stewart had begun to run into the same people, too often, who looked too familiar. He'd briefly considered doing cons in Toronto. But the people he'd be scamming would run in the same circles as his parents. And Windle was terrified of his father, not to mention the possibility that he could somehow find a loophole in the trust Windle's grandfather had left him, to be collected at the age 35. That had always seemed like a decrepit old age to Stewart—till now. He had just turned 32. Soon he could live off his trust fund for the rest of his life. He wouldn't be superrich, but that was fine with him, as long as he didn't have to work for a living. If Life of the Party went well, he might even continue to run it. He'd just hire more people to do the drudgery. He'd be the big boss without actually doing anything. It would be good for his social life and even better for his ego.

Still, there was his father. Since he'd moved back into town 5 months ago, Stewart had been avoiding him. He knew he couldn't fake a career here on his father's home turf; he'd have to announce that he was switching careers altogether. He'd have to—egads—go straight. And now, when he'd come up with the idea for Life of the Party after seeing so many of his old nerdy friends from high school with more money than social skills, and thought he could actually make a success of it, this young hooligan Boris had to come along and threaten everything.

So naturally, thinking of his father and his trust fund, Stewart succumbed.

"I can hardly send you to a party looking like *that*," he said, sniffing at Boris's black leather jacket and jeans.

"I don't see nothin' wrong with this," grumbled Boris. "Basic black. I thought it could go anywhere."

"You'd have to go home and change first," said Stewart, "and you're already late."

"So give me your suit," commanded Boris.

Stewart shook his head. "Now you're going too far."

"You want me talking to your friends or not?"

Stewart sighed and took off his jacket. At the last moment he remembered his little black book and slipped it out of the pocket. "I don't know about this," he said. "I already told Lawrence how many people I was sending."

"Lawrence!" said Boris, impressed. "Pretty buddy-buddy, aren't you?"

"We went to school together."

"Whatever," said Boris. He pointed at Stewart's lower body. "C'mon, gimme the pants."

"You're *not* getting my shirt," insisted Stewart, taking off the pants.

"Nice boxers," said Boris, "but the legs could use a little work. No, my black shirt'll have to do, whether you like it or not. I don't wanna get that close to your English BO."

"Some of us *do* take baths, you know."

Boris snorted. "That ain't what I heard." He put the pants on and strutted across the office like a supermodel on a catwalk. "Now, call your buddy and tell him you got a new guy comin' over. Tell him I was *detained*." He grinned, enjoying the expensive suit, wishing this crappy little office had a mirror. He winked at Stewart, who stood there looking quite silly in his boxers and dress shirt and socks.

"But tell your buddy Larry that I'm worth the wait."

13 WORK OR PLEASURE?

A sublimely beautiful man stood at the door of the Rosedale mansion checking invitations as Katrina's cab pulled up. She automatically reached in her purse to pay, but the driver shook his head. She took a deep breath and wondered what the hell she was doing here. The only thing she knew about tonight was that some guy named Lawrence was the host. She didn't know how old he was, what he did for a living, and even whether this party of his was for work or pleasure. And for all she knew, she could be walking into a raging orgy.

After waiting for a couple of women ahead of her to flash their invitations and chat to the doorman—who didn't look overly interested in their enormous chests—Katrina stepped forward and whispered, "PEST."

"Huh?" The doorman frowned at her with the cluelessness of a bad actor without a script.

"PEST!" repeated Katrina, louder.

The doorman stared at her like she was whacko, which was how she was beginning to feel. Even worse, she could feel several people waiting impatiently behind her.

"I'm from Life of the Party," she finally whispered desperately.

"Oh," said the doorman, flashing his perfect teeth. "Why didn't you say so?"

"I was told PEST was the password," said Katrina, annoyed.

"Shit, we changed it a couple of months ago. Everyone sounded like they were hissing at us all the time; way too confusing." He looked her over appreciatively, though without an ounce of lust. "You're new, aren't you? I've worked at all of Lawrence's parties, and I never noticed you before."

"How many has he had?"

"This is number five. Believe me, you'll enjoy it."

"Enjoy what?" asked Katrina, getting worried.

"Everything," said the doorman, giving her a bewildered look. "What's not to like?" He motioned inside. "Lawrence should be in the entrance hall. He likes to greet his guests right away. Get a feel for them, you know." He grinned quickly at Katrina, then turned to the new arrivals behind her. Katrina shuddered, wondering how much "feeling" was actually going on here.

The vestibule was huge, and in spite of the early hour, packed with people. The full reality struck Katrina then: She didn't know a soul. She was tempted to run out the front door, but it was jammed with people coming in. Maybe there was a way out the back. She'd never been to a party before where she didn't know *anyone*. What about Cathy—where was she? Katrina knew she wasn't supposed to talk to her, but the sight of her would at least be reassuring. Cathy wouldn't be the least bit scared. Maybe the fearlessness would rub off on her.

A waiter hovered nearby with a tray of champagne, and Katrina was tempted to grab at least two glasses. But her hands were shaking so badly from nerves that she was afraid to pick up anything that dainty. When another waiter came by with a tray of food, Katrina grabbed two smoked salmon canapés. They weren't exactly sturdy, but they were manageable and gave her something to do with her hands. She hadn't thought to wear a cocktail dress with pockets, if there were such a thing.

She was biting into her first cracker when a man a few feet away moved to let a pretty partygoer pass, and the woman at the centre of a circle of five other people, obviously regaling them all, came into view. She looked slightly familiar, and Katrina wondered how she'd know anyone in such a place. She looked again. Could it be . . .? No, the woman she'd met outside Stewart's office 2 days ago had been, well, she hated to even think the word, but *dumpy* was the only one that really applied. The woman entertaining the men a few feet away was no great beauty, but she had a pretty face, if overly made up, and terrific cleavage. The rest of her seemed a bit overly stuffed into a tight Lycra dress, but the effect was ballsy rather than desperate, as if to say, "Take me as I am. I don't give a shit if I'm no toothpick!" And the hair was long and black and glistening, as if she had a stylist standing by with spray and a comb. No, that couldn't be Cathy.

And then Katrina heard her voice.

One of the men Cathy was telling her story to turned to grab some champagne from a passing waiter. But his eye caught something else and he froze, staring at the most beautiful specimen he'd ever seen. The man beside him caught his gaping look and turned as well. Before Cathy knew it, everyone had turned away from her and was staring, her story forgotten. She knew it was a good one, for she'd kept these men laughing for 10 minutes now, despite all the distractions, like the hordes of cute, young, busty girls that seemed to keep arriving nonstop—what was with all the bimbos at this party? Whatever had caught their attention just now had to be good. Cathy was feeling a pang of jealousy and an urge to make a really bitchy comment when she lifted her head to see what all the commotion was about. And there, a few feet away, looking like the most beautiful, forlorn orphan Cathy could ever imagine, was Katrina.

She had a piece of smoked salmon dangling from her lip, and she still didn't look silly. She seemed to be staring at something, and it finally occurred to Cathy that Katrina was staring at *her*. She was just standing there, petrified; she could have been made out of wax. *Shit*, thought Cathy, peeved—if she had that girl's looks, she'd have every man in the room twisted around her finger by now. But then it dawned on her: The poor kid was frozen with fear. Cathy remembered how quiet she'd been outside Windle's office and realized immediately she was incredibly shy. What on earth was she doing taking a job like this? Oh, of course—that cute bastard Windle would have been all over her. He'd hired her for her looks alone and did not worry about throwing her to the wolves.

Katrina's first instinct was to run over to Cathy, a safe haven, but then she remembered Stewart's warnings about the PESTS not knowing each other. *But how would he know?* she thought—*he's not here*. She was considering going over there anyway when she heard a spastic grunt from at least a foot overhead, and she craned her head to see what it was.

Lawrence Marshall had spotted Katrina as he was being introduced to two Rack 'n' Roll girls, and he knew immediately she was not one of them. She was exquisitely beautiful and classy. Besides, her breasts, though lovely, were nowhere near big enough for her to hustle beer at the popular businessmen's watering hole. In spite of the cheap quality of her very engaging dress, she looked like she owned the place. Perhaps it was the tilt of her head. Lawrence stood 6 foot 7, though he stooped to atone for it.

"How do you do?" he said, certain she wasn't from one of the escort agencies he frequented, either. At first he'd hired a lot of those girls for his parties, but they tended to get antsy. Lawrence used only reputable agencies, and most of the girls were expecting to go out on a date. When they got to his parties and saw people jumping in and out of the hot tub and running around half naked, they invariably assumed that more than a date was expected of them. This girl had that same look of apprehension, but he was sure he knew where she came from.

"Life of the Party, I presume?" He'd lowered his voice so others nearby wouldn't hear him. Not that many at this party were actual *friends*, but he didn't need them to know he was paying people in that capacity. His parties had started to catch on, and there were plenty of legitimate guests these days. Lawrence's old school friend Stewart Windle had recently expanded his business, and renting PESTS from him was a lot more comfortable than going through an escort agency and looking like some lonely, desperate pervert. Which he most certainly was not.

He held out his hand. "Lawrence Marshall."

Katrina, whose left hand was holding a canapé, and whose right was sliding another into her mouth, was unsure what to do. She crammed the entire cracker in, wiped her right hand on her left arm, and offered it to Lawrence. He twitched his nostrils in what looked like a nose scowl. She had no way of knowing that the Windles, Stewart Sr. and Jr., had made fun of that mannerism for years, having lived down the street from the Marshalls the entire time the boys attended high school. They called it his rabid rabbit look. Lawrence was unaware of their mockery. He was also unaware that Windle Sr. couldn't stand him, thought him an obsequious, sniveling twit, in spite of the pains Lawrence had taken over the years to befriend the man, seeing as he, too, was a lawyer.

Katrina, mortified, introduced herself, hoping he wouldn't take her hand. She'd be too embarrassed. He glanced at it, brushed the fingers lightly for the least amount of bacterial contact, and smiled down at her.

"I trust you'll make yourself at home. There's a swimming pool and hot tub out back. No need to worry about a suit." This was accompanied by a leer. "If you get tired of the canapés—" here Katrina reddened noticeably— "there's a full buffet in the drawing room. And if you want to get cozy, the library and den are just the thing."

Katrina nodded mutely, attempting to chew the cracker with as little fanfare as possible. Unfortunately, some of it had lodged in her throat, and it was as dry as dirt, even by cracker standards. She'd give anything for a glass of champagne.

"Help yourself to anything you like," Lawrence was saying, as she felt her face going from red to blue with the effort to breathe. "And make sure to mingle."

Katrina started to nod, but she could contain herself no longer. She coughed with the force of a freight train and a chunk of salmon flew out of her mouth onto the shoulder of a nearby guest. Thankfully, the man didn't notice. Lawrence stared at the phlegmlike object for a moment then pretended not to, either.

"Before you go, Katrina—what's your cover?"

"Cover?" she croaked, trying to regain her voice.

"Where are you from, and how do I know you?" He winked, and it was more frightening than if he'd stripped down to a Speedo.

"Cover," repeated Katrina. "Yes. I, uh . . . oh! The country. Yes, I live on a farm in the country. You know, the horses, the sheep, the . . . whatnot."

Lawrence had a dubious look. "And I would know you . . . how?"

"A cousin?" suggested Katrina, and at Lawrence's scowl she realized she should've thought this out a little better. Quickly she added, "The farm! You used to ride horses up there."

He was shaking his head. "I don't ride, Katrina."

"Do you eat berries?"

"Excuse me?"

"Berries. When you were younger you used to stop by and buy berries on your way to the cottage?"

"A fascinating theory, but some of my oldest friends are here tonight, and we used to go up to the cottage together. If we'd stopped for berries and *you* were there, they would have remembered."

"Oh," said Katrina, stumped. What else had Stewart told her to say? If only she'd been less nervous and had paid more attention at the interview.

Lawrence lifted his head, thinking, and Katrina could see directly into his twitching nostrils. They were like little gerbils with lives of their own, and she half expected to hear them squeal. Finally he stopped squinting and a tiny smile crossed his face.

"I shall say we were lovers."

Katrina, horrified, jerked back and teetered slightly on her high heels before managing to right herself. Lawrence's stoop lessened slightly, as if a manly surge of pride had lifted it. Katrina looked around frantically for Cathy.

Seeing Katrina all desperate and teetering, Cathy excused herself from the men still gawking at her—not that they noticed. "I know that woman," she said, which got their attention. "I must say hello. Knowing Larry, she probably needs rescuing."

Cathy stepped forward just as Lawrence whispered something in Katrina's ear, then left her to greet some newcomers, his stooped head bobbing above the crowd. A voice beside her surprised her by saying, "Women like that seldom need rescuing. *We* need rescuing from *them*."

Cathy glanced up to see a rangy man who seemed to have appeared out of nowhere. He was dark and tall and handsome and wore a beautifully tailored navy suit and a crisp white shirt. She didn't know men outside of Hollywood were capable of looking so suave anymore.

"Well, don't *you* sound bitter," she said, studying his face and deciding she liked it. His black hair, though slicked back for the occasion, fell slightly over one eye, giving him a rakish look. His mouth was slightly lopsided, and she couldn't tell whether he was smirking or smiling. Or putting her on.

"I have three sisters just like her," sighed the man wearily. "Trust me, I've seen their effects on men."

"You sound like you're not too crazy about your sisters."

"Love 'em to death. But I feel sorry for the men who fall for them."

Cathy glanced back at Katrina, who was coughing daintily into her hand. "How do you know she's anything like them? You don't even know her, do you?"

He looked at Katrina objectively, without an ounce of ogling or gaping, then shrugged and turned back to Cathy. "Believe it or not, that kind of beauty can get a bit boring when you're around it every day."

Cathy shook her head at him. "You're cute, sweetie, but you're really kind of weird," and went to save Katrina.

In the few seconds Cathy had been speaking to Weirdo, four or five men had closed in on Katrina, and a couple of women. All had sauntered toward her as if by accident, not wanting to look obvious, the way you would approach a celebrity—act calm, do not panic, appear normal, and try your best not to stare—but how could you not?

"Sorry, folks," said Cathy, pushing aside the crowd, "but I haven't seen this girl in absolutely *ages*. I have to steal her away for a second."

"Hey, come back here!" cried one of the men.

"I didn't catch your name!" yelled another.

Cathy whisked Katrina away. She seemed embarrassed by all this attention, which Cathy would have died for. Katrina croaked, "Cathy, what about the rule? We're not supposed to know each other!"

"I am a bit pissed off you recognized me so easily," said Cathy, her nose in the air, "after the way I looked outside Windle's office. Do I look that bad?"

"You look wonderful!" gasped Katrina, meaning it.

"Coming from you, that's the best compliment I've ever heard." Cathy looked over Katrina's clinging, navy midthigh dress. There were no visible bulges, only voluptuous curves. "Did you have to make yourself look quite so fabulous? You could've given the other women here a chance, you know."

"At what?" said Katrina blankly.

"The men, stupid. Have you seen some of these guys? Gorgeous. Though how a guy like that nerd Lawrence knows them . . . must be clients or coworkers is all I can figure."

"Cathy, we're not allowed to date the guests!"

"I can look, can't I?"

Without even knowing what she was doing, Cathy dragged Katrina into the drawing room and close to the bar. Nose like a bloodhound, her mother always said. She noticed Katrina's hand on her arm was trembling, and when she looked into her face, it was ashen, despite the natural tawniness. "Jesus, you look like you just met my ex-mother-in-law. What you need is a drink."

"I'm too shaky," muttered Katrina. "I don't think I could hold a glass."

"I'll get you something sturdy." She led Katrina to the bar, in fact, practically positioned her against it, and ordered them both a double scotch.

"I don't know about this," said Katrina. "I've never had hard liquor."

Cathy rolled her eyes. "Okay, we'll dress it up a little." She motioned to the bartender before he could pour the scotch. "Two crantinis instead. Up." She grinned at Katrina. "Can't be wasting time on ice." She noticed Katrina was gawking at the martini glasses the bartender was pulling out and sighed. "Hey, barkeep, could you put those in rocks glasses instead? We wouldn't want to look girly."

The bartender, who looked pretty girly himself, gave her a strange look but did as she said. As he shook the drinks he couldn't help but stare at Katrina. She noticed and looked glumly away.

"Down the hatch," said Cathy, handing a drink to Katrina. She took a long sip of hers and smacked her lips. "Beats the hell out of that cheap champagne."

"I wouldn't know, I'm not much of a drinker," said Katrina, downing her crantini in one gulp.

"Yeah," said Cathy. "I can see that." She motioned to the bartender for another round.

Katrina stared down at the bar. "I've never been so miserable in my life."

"So why on earth did you come here?"

"The money was so great, and Stewart said I—"

"Stewart, huh? What are you guys, intimate?"

"No, I just—"

"Look," said Cathy, straightening, "I can understand your distress, you not being a naturally outgoing type and all. But I'm not here to babysit or hold your hand."

"I never—"

"All you've gotta do is stand there and look beautiful. You'll have them eating out of your hand."

The bartender set two more drinks in front of them. Cathy picked hers up and slid the other in front of Katrina. "Drink that. It'll help make you more sociable. I gotta go."

"But Cathy, please don't—"

"Seriously, I gotta go. Don't look now, but Dr. Frankenstein is in the corner, glaring at us. And as you reminded me 10 times already, there *are* rules. Good luck."

Cathy slipped away from the bar and into the throng, which was getting pretty wild. As Katrina watched, she sidled up to a man in a familiar-looking suit and patted him on the shoulder. She grimaced slightly, her hand coming away with a piece of smoked salmon. The man frowned, but Cathy laughed lightly and popped the fish in her mouth. Then she led the man into the crowd, and Katrina lost her altogether.

14 A DOUBLE-HEADER

Katrina sipped slowly at her second crantini, vaguely aware that a small group of men had huddled around her. They were asking her questions and babbling at her, something about being high-school buddies of Larry's, and she wondered who on earth Larry was. In the midst of one of their questions she caught the bartender's attention and waved her drink at him, slopping some onto the bar. "What's in these things anyway?" she asked, wondering why it was suddenly so hard to talk.

"Vodka," replied the bartender, as if she'd asked him what country they were in. Then he grinned and added, "Three ounces."

Katrina gaped at him and felt her face go green. The bartender, who'd been around, wasted no time and nodded to the left. "Down the hall."

Katrina lurched off her stool and crumpled into one of the men. He offered to help, but she suddenly sprinted as if the coach had shot the starter gun, and he shrugged and turned back to his buddies. "Chick like that should stick to white wine," he grumbled.

"Or Shirley Temples," added his buddy, and they all laughed.

Katrina stopped sprinting when her stomach's lurching became too much, but she walked as fast as she could, in a zigzag motion, banging against both strangers and walls for support. It seemed to take forever, but soon she found what appeared to be a washroom, and she stumbled toward its door, only to be interrupted by an affronted "Hey, not so fast, sister!" and various other shouts of protest. At least six young buxom girls were lined up chatting, glaring at Katrina.

"Please," she pleaded, afraid if she talked too much she'd spew out of control. The women just glared some more, shook their heads, and continued their conversations, though this time, they seemed to be whispering and staring at her, then giggling.

Katrina was mortified. This was worse than first grade, when she peed in her chair in school because she was too shy to put up her hand and ask to use the bathroom. She fled, this time as much from the evil cliquish treatment as the need to vomit.

Soon she found herself at a set of stairs. They were narrow, probably the servants' staircase, and she started up. She considered throwing up right there, as soon as she climbed enough steps to be out of view, but no luck. Pressed against the wall above her was a couple in heat, tearing off each other's clothes like they were auditioning for some soft-core. Katrina backed slowly down the steps, embarrassed, her face turning from green to red. Then she remembered the awful girls in the other bathroom. She took a breath and ran up the stairs, pressing against the wall opposite the couple.

The man had taken his lips away from the woman to catch a breath. He spotted Katrina and said, "Hey, wanna join in?"

And the woman turned and with a sly smile added, "Oh yeah."

Katrina trembled and ran ahead, not seeing their gaze following her, nor their heightened passion when they went to round two. She reached the stairwell and found herself in a narrow hallway. Turning to the right, she found herself in a different world, a corridor half the width of her house, with doors sprouting up all over the place.

Thank God, an open door . . . a bathroom! She ran for it, thrilled there was no lineup, knowing she could barely last another minute, the crantinis roiling in her stomach, and then . . .

There was a man in there, standing in front of the mirror, wiping at his shirt. Which appeared to be soaked with blood. Katrina was really ready to spew now, but her innate politeness kept her from barging in. She tried to control her breathing, looked closer, and realized the man was holding a glass of white wine and pouring it on his shirt. Finally, the man noticed her and held up the glass in greeting.

"I suppose this looks stupid, but I read somewhere that white wine can get rid of red wine stains. Have you ever heard of that?"

Katrina just shook her head and swallowed hard.

"One of those Rack 'n' Roll girls did this to me. Why they would even serve red wine at a party like this is beyond me. You just know it's going to be a disaster." He poured a little more white wine on his shirt, dabbed at it, and shook his head. "I think this shirt is history."

"Excuse me," muttered Katrina.

The man glanced up.

"I really need to use . . ." She indicated the toilet.

"Oh, sorry. You know I tried three other bathrooms before this one. I don't know what those girls do in there. No, actually, I do know. They stand in front of the mirror and primp and fix their makeup and don't care how long anyone else has to wait."

Katrina tried her best to look understanding and lurched closer to the toilet.

"I suppose you'll be needing the mirror, too. Just like my sisters. And those others." He dabbed disconsolately at his shirt and sighed. "There's a lot more of them than before. The first two parties I attended, there were only one or two. I mean, they look good, maybe a little on the skanky side, but really, what are you going to talk about?"

"Excuse me," cut in Katrina, desperate now, "but I really need to—" And she lunged forward, trying to brush past the man, aiming for the toilet, but he'd just been talking far too long and she couldn't hold it anymore. She was 2 feet short of her goal; she spewed all over his pants.

The man had tried to step back, but it didn't save him. He cringed and glanced down then shook his head. "A doubleheader," he said flatly. "A helluva day."

In the master bedroom beside the bathroom, Boris recognized Katrina's voice and could tell from her few words that she was shit-faced. He hoped she didn't get any stupid ideas and come wandering into the bedroom. He'd been avoiding her all night. Not that it had been hard. He'd spotted her shortly after whispering "Life of the Party" to the fag-ass doorman, which was kind of cool, 'cause he'd felt like he was in a spy flick as he entered the parlour, or whatever the fuck you called it, that was the size of a hockey arena and packed with chicks with huge knockers. Was he in the Playboy Mansion or what?

He'd seen Katrina right away, surrounded mostly by nerdy-looking suits, but also a few good-looking chicks that he wouldn't mind seeing Katrina getting it on with, though he figured she was too straight for that. Katrina was too surrounded to see anybody, and Boris stayed on the move, trying not to be noticed.

He'd managed to avoid the host, Lawrence, too. At one point he heard one of the suits come up and say, "Larry!" and pat a geeky tall guy on the back, and Boris had quickly stepped behind a potted palm, thinking, *Fuck Windle, I can hide behind these things just fine*.

He'd noticed the security system as soon as he entered the house. But he did a double take when he also noticed the thing was torn out of the wall, just dangling there, helpless. Holy shit, what luck! If only he'd told his partner about this gig after all. Ray could've driven the van over later that night after Boris conveniently left a window open, and they would've been rich. But Boris knew from past experience that Ray would be in a snit for not calling him and would refuse to come over, even if he begged. Boris would just have to grab what he could stuff into his pockets tonight and come back with Ray another time. He sure hoped all of Stewart's friends were as security-screwed as this guy was. His life as a PEST was looking damn profitable.

He'd found the master bedroom easily and was relieved to see not many guests had made it up to the second floor; most were content with the pool and hot tub below. The door to the bedroom itself was locked, but whaddayaknow, the door to the adjoining bathroom was open. Closing the bathroom door behind him, it was easy to jimmy the lock to the bedroom and slip in.

Boris was pleasantly surprised. He'd expected some watches and fancy cuff links (jerks like this Larry guy still wore shit like that), but what he hadn't expected was the wads of cash. In shoe boxes in the bottom of the closet, no less! Was this guy an imbecile? And what was he doing with all this dough? Did he play the horses? Sell dope? Boris rifled quickly through shelves and drawers, hoping to find some pot or coke, but there was nothing more of interest to be found. So he stashed the wads of cash in his socks, shoved a few cuff links in his jacket pocket for good measure, and headed for the bathroom door.

And heard a knock from the hallway. Boris had just enough time to shut the door to the master bedroom before a second knock sounded, and he heard the bathroom door open, a man humming. Shit. Now Boris would have to wait. Well, at least it was a man. If it was a woman, he'd have to wait forever. He didn't know what they did in bathrooms, but whatever it was, they did a lot of it.

And damned if a woman didn't show up 10 seconds later. Katrina! Christ! Of all the people. Boris was wondering if it would be completely stupid to go out through the master bedroom door. What were the chances of being seen by people wandering by and wondering what the hell he was doing in there? Then he heard Katrina puking. Could she do it a little louder, for Chrissakes? The whole neighbourhood would be here in a minute, calling 911.

Boris sighed and sat down on a leather chair to wait. And noticed that the chair he was sitting on was a deep forest green leather, though the one directly across from it was a light rose. Not a good match at all. Burgundy would've been okay, but rose? Who did this guy's decorating? And why was all the furniture shoved against the walls, like he was about to have a hoedown? No sense of coziness at all. Dismayed, Boris got up and started to move the furniture around.

15 PRINCE CHARMING

Katrina stared dizzily at the carpet and was relieved that everything seemed to have hit the man's pants. Not that that was good, but at least she hadn't destroyed anything of Lawrence's. But this man must be a friend of Lawrence's and naturally, being pissed off, would tell him for sure.

"Please don't tell Lawrence about this," she blurted. "I'll get in trouble."

"What are you, his little sister?"

Katrina was still bent over double. She stayed that way a second, breathing hard, unsure whether there was more to come. The man took a step back just in case. "No, it's just . . . he can't know . . . he can't ever know."

Oh God, she thought. She somehow had to get this man to keep his mouth shut, because if Windle ever found out about her getting plastered and puking on a guest, that'd be the end of her PEST career—and all that lovely money. And her hopes of getting Stevie and herself out of Hell House.

"Look," she said, finally straightening. She wiped her mouth with the back of her hand and smeared lipstick over half her face. She wondered why the man was looking at her funny—aside from her puking on his pants, that is. "If you don't tell anyone about this, I'll wash your pants and we'll be even. Deal?"

The man stared down at his sodden pants. "I think they're pretty much history—like my shirt. Besides, they're dry clean only."

Katrina snorted, then hiccupped. "They all say that, just so the dry cleaners will get the business. I won't get them wet, just damp." She lowered her voice conspiratorially and leaned closer. "They'll be fine, trust me."

The man stepped back from her rancid breath, then laughed. "That's a very kind offer, but what do I wear while you're washing them?"

Katrina teetered a bit and thought about that for a moment. "Ah!" She pointed at the man's face and nodded knowingly. "You could go swimming. Lawrence said you didn't need a suit."

She started to make swimming motions with her arms, which put her completely off balance. The man grabbed her just in time and steadied her, then broke out laughing.

"Are you always this funny, or just when you're wasted?"

Katrina leaned against the sink and beamed. "My dad always says I'm funny."

"Well, I hope I don't remind you of your dad," said the man, acting horrified.

"God, no!" said Katrina. Then, realizing he wasn't serious, she smiled blearily and motioned to his pants. "Give 'em up."

The man chuckled and started to unbutton his pants, as if it were perfectly normal to undress himself in front of a strange woman in a stranger's bathroom.

"You're not shy, are you?" Katrina pouted. "Not like me."

"Three sisters," said the man, as if that explained everything. "And you don't seem shy to me," he added, as he caught Katrina gazing down at his legs and boxers.

Katrina blushed and took the pants he gingerly offered. The smell of them nearly made her spew again, but she got them in the sink, breathing through her mouth all the while. As she dampened them and rubbed them with a little liquid soap (she didn't have a clue what she was doing, but couldn't tell *him* that), she sensed him staring at her.

"What?" she said, turning to him.

He scratched his head. "It's just that I saw you earlier tonight, and I said to someone . . ." He swept some hair off his forehead, and Katrina looked at him expectantly. "I just said something stupid about beautiful women, about how you're all . . . Anyway, it wasn't true."

"I'm not sure what you're talking about, but—Whoa!"

"What is it?" asked the man with concern.

Katrina turned back to the sink; she couldn't very well tell this man that he'd just sprouted a second head. She tried squinting, which someone had told her to do if such a situation ever arose, then looked back up at him.

"Hey, you're one person again! That really works!"

"What?" asked the man. He narrowed his eyes. "Can you see all right?"

"Fine now," said Katrina, still squinting. "You know, you have a nice face—when it's just one, that is."

The man looked completely baffled, but he held out his hand. "I'm Jonathan."

Katrina's hands were busy wringing out his pants. Instead of a shake, she gave him a little bow. "That's a nice name," she mumbled, suddenly feeling extremely tired. "Like a prince or something."

Jonathan grinned. "Hardly. And you?"

Katrina yawned, handed him the wet, wrinkly pants, and said, "Me? I'm . . ." The room started to whirl. "I'm . . . sleepy."

Katrina slumped against the counter so suddenly that Jonathan didn't even have time to catch her. "Hey, what're you doing?" he cried, as her head swiveled around and her eyes half shut.

Katrina gave him a dreamy smile, even though he had two heads again. "Little nap is all."

Jonathan glanced around the room—no water glass. "What you need is water . . . and maybe some coffee. Stay right there."

Katrina wasn't going anywhere. She slid slowly down to the floor and crumpled onto the plush carpet. She saw her Prince Charming's feet dash away as she curled herself into a snug little ball and promptly fell asleep.

16 TURNING INTO PUMPKINS

Boris waited a good 45 seconds before peeping into the bathroom. He knew it would be smarter to wait longer, in case that Jonathan dude suddenly came back, but he was starting to worry he'd get stuck here all night. And all he needed was to be one of the last people to leave. That would make him stick out like a sore thumb to his host. Then he'd be one of the first people Lawrence would remember when he discovered the next day (or even later that night) that he'd been robbed blind.

Katrina was curled up like a kitten beside the sink, eyes closed, hopefully passed out. Boris tiptoed past. He was almost through the door and on his way to freedom when a buxom young thing tried to shove past him.

"Do ya mind?" she practically shouted. "I gotta go."

Could this broad be a little louder? thought Boris. *She'll wake up Katrina and blow my cover*. He blocked her way, her chest bouncing into his, which wasn't such a bad thing, and he forced himself to make a gruesome face, even though he was leering inside. "I wouldn't go in there if I were you. Somebody had way too many martinis, if you know what I mean."

The Rack 'n' Roll girl wrinkled her nose in disgust and whirled into the hall. Boris ran after her toward the main staircase. "Hey, I'm available! What's your number, baby?"

Cathy had found several attentive men to fetch her drinks as she made her way around the house, singing for her supper. When she did a job, she liked to do it well, and she was in her element here, schmoozing and chatting and making up stories about herself. It was almost better than being in a play. And she was actually getting paid.

So it was some time before she found herself back at the bar. She'd assumed Katrina would still be there, too paralyzed to move. Surprised at her absence, she asked the bartender about her. He told her how Katrina had run, green, for the bathroom, and his look was a little chastising, as if Cathy had led her down the Road to Hell.

She turned her back on the snide young man (too bad he was so cute) and started a search. Three different bathrooms and always the same bitchy response from the Rack 'n' Roll girls: a tilting of the nose and a swing of the hair. If their brains and hearts were as big as their hooters, they could rule the world. Hell, thought Cathy, who was she kidding? They already *did* rule the world.

She found the servants' stairs and encountered the same couple that Katrina had earlier. They separated for a moment and leered at her. *Not bad looking*, thought Cathy. If she weren't in such a hurry . . .

A man rushing down the stairs distracted her. He was wearing only a stained white shirt and boxer shorts. At most parties that would seem a little strange, but at this one, Cathy just assumed he was headed for the hot tub, possibly to multitask: clean himself and his shirt at the same time. It was only after he'd passed that Cathy realized he was the weird guy who'd made the comments about beautiful women earlier. Probably had an assignation with an ugly girl. *Yeah, right*. Cathy snorted to herself and continued up the stairs.

The bathroom was halfway down the hall and miraculously empty, except for Katrina curled up on the floor, fast asleep.

“Jesus,” muttered Cathy, “I told you to relax, not go into a coma.” She noticed a man’s navy jacket on a towel hook, and socks and shoes on the floor. “What the hell have you been doing in here?”

Katrina stirred. “Jonathan, is that you?” Her eyelids fluttered.

“Who the fuck is Jonathan?”

“My prince.”

“Well, say good night, sweet princess. Jesus, it reeks in here. Which half of the royal couple puked in here, anyway?” Cathy started breathing through her mouth so she wouldn’t hurl, too. Of course, that made it difficult to talk. “Listen, we’ve got to get you out of here before your host sees you like this.” Cathy prodded Katrina with her foot until her eyes opened, then she leaned over and lifted her up.

“This must be the first time in my life I’m glad another woman is skinnier than me.”

“But what about Jonathan?” muttered Katrina. “He’s bringing me some coffee.”

“A quadruple espresso wouldn’t help you now, sweets.” Cathy put Katrina’s arm around her shoulder and started for the door. “Let’s get you to a cab before they start turning into pumpkins.”

17 ASLEEP BESIDE ANOTHER WOMAN

Stevie knocked on Katrina's bedroom door late the next morning as soon as he got up. He knew she usually slept in on her days off from Cups, and she'd probably be in. When she didn't answer he gently opened the door.

And was shocked to see Katrina asleep beside another woman.

Cathy hadn't meant to stay overnight. She hadn't even meant to share a cab. She'd managed to slip a wobbly Katrina past that pervert-nerd Lawrence, who was busy with a bunch of Rack 'n' Roll girls in wet T-shirts. But by the time the doorman found them a taxi, Katrina was asleep and wouldn't wake up. So Cathy had rifled through her purse, found her address neatly written on the first page of her phone book, and escorted her home.

Stevie stared at the strange creature in the bed. She was awake, covers thrown off, wearing only a polka-dot bra and panties over her ample frame. A mass of wild black hair nearly covered her face. She was scanning a *WHEN* magazine. Seeing Stevie, she didn't flinch or try to cover herself. She just glanced at Katrina and put her fingers to her lips.

"What the . . ." sputtered Stevie in spite of the warning. Katrina was under the covers, facing Cathy. She lowered the sheet, opened her eyes, and jerked up, horrified. Quickly, she yanked the covers back over her head.

"It's okay, sweets," said Cathy, patting Katrina's shoulder. "I brought you home last night, don't you remember?" Katrina's eyes peered out from the covers just enough to stare at Cathy like a terrified bunny. Cathy chuckled. "No, I guess not."

She turned to look at the person by the door. Was that a man or a woman? The voice was high and the hair long. The sweat suit could be covering anything. Cathy hadn't talked to Katrina enough the night before to know anything about her living arrangements. Hell, when she thought about it, she didn't know anything about Katrina, period. She could be a mental outpatient for all she knew.

"What the hell happened?" cried Stevie, rushing to Katrina's side, where she noticed him for the first time. When he knelt beside the bed and took her clammy hand, she stopped shivering a little.

"She had a little too much to drink," explained Cathy, setting aside the magazine and sitting up. "I was afraid she might choke on her own puke so I stayed up and watched her."

"Well, I could've done that," huffed Stevie. He looked accusingly at Cathy. "And why was she drinking so much in the first place?" He gasped. "She didn't drink *liquor*, did she?"

"Crantinis," said Katrina with a wan smile. "Tasty." The smile evaporated. "At first."

"I'm sure," sniffed Stevie.

"You weren't home when we got here," stated Cathy in the same accusing tone. What was with this guy? Girl? Whatever? Why did it sound so possessive? Of course, if it was a gay man that would explain a lot. She knew from her own gay friends that you didn't mess with *their* girls. And if it was another girl . . . well, she could have a crush.

"I got stuck with the closing shift at the restaurant." He stroked Katrina's hand. "Hon, I'm so sorry. How was the party?"

"Awful," said Katrina, wincing. She remembered Cathy's presence in the bed beside her and slid away a little. Then she closed her eyes with a dreamy smile. "But I met my prince."

"What?" Stevie dropped her hand.

"The man of my dreams, my soul mate."

Stevie looked inquiringly at Cathy. She shrugged. "Don't ask me. I wasn't around for the Great Romance." She suddenly remembered her manners and held out her hand. "I'm Cathy, by the way. A fellow PEST."

"I figured that." He/she brushed its fingertips against Cathy's hand so lightly that it almost tickled. "I'm Stevie, Katrina's roommate."

"Stevie?" repeated Cathy. Shit, that didn't help at all.

Katrina opened her eyes slightly and went on talking as if they hadn't said anything. "He never once mentioned my looks—"

"I've had that, too," cut in Cathy, "only it's usually out of tactfulness."

"He seemed to see inside of me," continued Katrina.

"Was he a psychic?" asked Stevie, alarmed. "Were you guys doing tarot cards or something?"

"No, he just . . . *got* me, you know? No man's ever done that before." Katrina laughed weakly. "He even told me I was funny."

"Now *that* I get all the time," said Cathy.

"But who was he?" asked Stevie, studying Katrina's hand as if he might see into it, too.

Katrina opened her eyes fully and sighed. "I have no idea. All I know is his name is Jonathan."

"So he was one of the guests," said Stevie.

"No," snapped Cathy, "he was the cleaning woman."

"Just asking. After all, she *was* drinking."

"He didn't look like a cleaning woman," said Katrina, still groggy from the booze. "Not that I know what a cleaning woman looks like."

Stevie leaned forward and stroked Katrina's hair and glared at Cathy, who was patting her shoulder again. This woman had a lot of nerve. Katrina must have known her all of 2 whole days and she was acting like her long-lost sister. "Well, it's a nice fantasy, hon, but it's not likely you'll ever see the guy again. I mean, it'd be like looking for a needle in a haystack."

"You never know," said Cathy, annoyed with this Stevie person. What was he/she so jealous about? You'd think Cathy had ravished Katrina the night before, instead of taking her home and cleaning her up and saving her ass. "If this Jonathan guy was at last night's party, he might show up at some of the other parties too. Windle—the guy who runs Life of the Party—told me a lot of the hosts he hires us for are old friends of his from school. So they probably all know each other—I bet it's one tight little circle."

She caught Stevie's nasty look and tried not to smile. She'd never fought over another woman before. She squeezed Katrina's shoulder, more to bug Stevie than anything. "So keep your hopes up, sweetie. Maybe you'll meet him again at the next party."

"I threw up on him," said Katrina morosely. "I doubt he'll ever want to see me again."

Stevie winced. "*That* could put a damper on things."

"But I washed his pants," said Katrina proudly.

"Well, *that* makes it all better," said Cathy.

"You washed his pants?" repeated Stevie, horrified. "Then what the hell was he wearing?"

"Relax," said Cathy, "most of the people there were half-naked."

"*What!*" Stevie looked ready to start flapping his arms.

"There was a pool and a hot tub," said Katrina matter-of-factly. "And Lawrence said we didn't have to bother with bathing suits."

“Katrina,” said Stevie sharply, “I don’t know if I want you going to any more of these things.”

“Then how will I find Jonathan?” Katrina stared at him with such determination that he took a step back and softened his tone.

“Look, Katrina, I’m sure the whole thing was very romantic, and it’s a nice little memory to get you through the cold winter nights. But think about it: If the guy was at that kind of party, he’s obviously some big shot, and you don’t exactly run in the same circles.”

Cathy was about to protest when she heard a nearby door slam shut, then a banging in the hall. She turned to the open door to see a shaggy-haired man in black shorts struggling with a table against the wall, apparently trying to replace it after he’d knocked it over.

“Our other roommate, Boris,” whispered Stevie.

“Looks like he had a rough night, too,” whispered Cathy.

Stevie sniffed. “Boris only *does* nights.”

Cathy turned to Katrina, who seemed to have forgotten her homophobia and accepted Cathy as friend rather than rapist; she didn’t slide over this time. “Tell me, sweets, why did you join Life of the Party? It’s obviously not your line of work.”

“I warned her not to—” started Stevie.

Katrina held up her hand. She peeked into the hall to make sure Boris had made it back into his room, then lowered her voice and told Cathy about their suspicions of Boris checking her phone calls and spying for Harley, and of Harley threatening them because of Len.

“And,” added Katrina, as if this were the worst of it, “Boris is making me look after Spot!”

“Is Spot the horrific thing I heard howling while I was lugging Katrina up the stairs last night?” asked Cathy.

“He slapped me!” cried Stevie, his lower lip trembling.

"Spot the dog slapped you?" said Cathy, confused.

"No—Harley!"

"Oh my," said Cathy sarcastically. "Such brutality!"

"It's not funny," said Katrina. "You haven't seen this guy; he's huge. And he's the head of the Glory Riders!"

"The Glory Riders!" gasped Cathy. A pause, then: "Who the hell are the Glory Riders?"

18 GORGEOUS CREATURES

Even though the day after the party was a Saturday, Jonathan had to go into work. He was pissed off because his boss, his oldest sister Jillian, wasn't working even though the small modeling agency, Faces, belonged to her.

Jonathan was the office manager. Which really translated to assistant/gofer. He'd only taken the job because Jillian's former manager had run off with one of their few straight male models when he went on a photo shoot in Bora Bora. She'd sent a postcard saying "Gone Native"—end of discussion. Jillian was swamped and couldn't find anyone else on the spur of the moment, and since Jonathan was between jobs/careers/schools, he'd reluctantly agreed.

Jonathan had bummed around Asia for a year after high school, unsure what he wanted to do. When he got back, he started studying business administration, because he felt he should do something serious, but found himself bored almost comatose. A friend got him a short-lived job in retail, selling overpriced clothes to exceedingly rich ladies. They were usually more interested in him than the designers' products. Jonathan, whose idea of a hot date was smoking Thai stick and shooting the shit with sarong-clad, 20-year-old tourists, was horrified. These women didn't want to have fun, they wanted to conquer. He fled before the family jewels could be snatched and devoured.

Next, he tried a course as a legal clerk, but that was even drier than the business course, the words coming out of the teachers' mouths only so much gibberish. When Jillian's offer to work at Faces came up, he thought, what the hell, maybe he'd find his niche.

It wasn't a bad job, though his sister could've been a little more generous with the salary. And unlike his sister the boss, who spent weekends at her cottage in Haliburton, Jonathan had to work weekends whenever things went haywire. Like today. One of the models about to do a major print ad had suddenly sprouted a herpes nightmare on her lower lip. And another model's boyfriend had called hysterically, saying she'd taken Ecstasy 2 nights ago and still hadn't come down. No way could she do the shampoo commercial she was scheduled for. She'd probably drown.

Jonathan dealt with the emergencies quickly and efficiently, knowing that had Jillian been here, she would've called a state of emergency. She was a tad high-strung. Of course, her 20-year-older husband had been struck by lightning on a golf course right in front of her eyes just over a year ago, and that could have something to do with it, though Jonathan thought that the money and the business hubby left behind should have soothed her somewhat. He didn't understand why she hadn't sold the company and taken off to travel the world, like he would have done. Sometimes he wished he'd never come back from Thailand—had just stayed and turned into a beach bum. The real world so far just wasn't doing it for him.

Though Jillian freaked out over days like this, Jonathan found them quite funny. The entire business was hilarious. All these gorgeous women willing to sell their souls for a photo in a magazine. All this beauty around him every day and most of it as empty as a bulimic's belly. Jonathan's three older sisters were all stunning, so he was used to being around beauty. Being around models all day didn't faze him. Sometimes he even got tired of it. When they discovered he was unimpressed with their looks, they felt challenged and tried to snag him, just as the rich, older women in the clothing store had.

Was it something about him, he wondered, that women always felt the need to score? To possess? Most of these gorgeous models did nothing for him. They were about as exciting as the courses in legalese and business admin he'd taken. But the girl last night . . . now *she* was different. She wasn't out to conquer or possess. Her sole goal, it seemed, had been to puke. And she'd done it very well. He smiled as he thought about his pants, one of the two dressy, expensive pairs he owned, which the dry cleaner had wrinkled his nose at when he brought them in this morning.

No, there was something about her. She was so unassuming. Even though, when he'd first seen her in Lawrence's foyer surrounded by men, he'd thought, *Here we go, another one, just like all the rest.* But she wasn't. It was as if she didn't even know she was beautiful. Or was embarrassed by it. Of course, she'd been blotto. How he'd love to see her sober. How he'd love to see her, period.

He couldn't believe she'd taken off on him last night. He'd gone to the bar and asked for a coffee, and the bartender looked at him like he'd asked for a first-class ticket to Mars. He'd finally been directed to the kitchen, where the caterers were busy stacking dirty plates and quaffing leftover wine. They informed him they'd just thrown out the last of the coffee and no longer bothered bringing a cappuccino machine to these events. When a topless Rack 'n' Roll girl scurried through the kitchen, chased by a dripping-wet man clutching a martini glass, Jonathan could see why.

He'd returned to the master bath with a bottle of Evian, the best he could do. On his way out of the kitchen he'd passed a shaggy-haired man with bushy eyebrows who was slinking toward the servants' exit. *Creepy looking*, thought Jonathan with a shudder. Didn't look like a friend of Lawrence's.

Probably a party crasher. Or a burglar. Jonathan snorted at that. Wouldn't it be a hoot if old Larry got robbed? He'd love to see him trying to explain his party to the cops. *Yes, Officer, and all these gorgeous guys and girls came to my party just to see me. It's my charm and good looks, you see . . .*

The girl was gone. No sign of her, no note. Worst of all, no name. He should've expected something like this, considering her drunken condition. But he'd felt such a click with her, like they really had something in common. So unlike the other beautiful girls he knew (aside from his sisters, and even they acted quite alien at times).

Jonathan lost interest in the party after that. On his way out he sought out Lawrence. He described the Mystery Woman and asked her name.

"Ah," said Lawrence, his nostrils quivering above Jonathan's head, "I think I know who you mean. Gorgeous creature." He looked down at Jonathan with a funny look on his face that he couldn't quite decipher. "And you find her attractive, do you?"

"Very," said Jonathan. "And it'd help if I knew her name."

"Well, if she didn't want to give you her name, I don't think it's any of my—"

"She wanted to, she just didn't get around to it."

Lawrence eyed Jonathan, as if wondering if he were telling the truth. He squinted his eyes in concentration, and a funny *harrumphing* sound issued from his throat. "I'm terrible with names, so I usually have little mind tricks I employ to remember." He opened his eyes and shook his head. "Unfortunately, tonight, with the amount of people here . . ." He smirked, and his nostrils flared ". . . especially all the women . . . well, I was a little overwhelmed."

"Try," urged Jonathan.

Lawrence squinted his eyes again and twitched his nostrils. He smiled and opened his lids. "Carol! No, wait a minute, not Carol . . . Kelly!" Jonathan stared him down. "No, not Kelly . . . *Cathy*!"

"You're sure?"

"Well . . . almost."

"And this Cathy, how do you know—"

Jonathan was cut off by a gaggle of girls who surged around Lawrence. He was swept into their midst as if he'd scored the winning touchdown. Jonathan sighed and left.

Jonathan's musings of the night before were interrupted by the ringing phone. Another hysterical model, no doubt. He picked up the receiver, but his thoughts were still on his mystery woman.

Cathy. She hadn't looked like a Cathy to him. Cathy sounded so *ordinary*. And what was she doing at the party? Surely she wasn't a friend of Lawrence's. Or a Rack 'n' Roll girl. Or an escort. What did that leave? Who on earth was she?

19 TOO GOOD TO BE TRUE

At that moment Cathy, the real Cathy, was watching Katrina poke at the fried eggs on her plate and wondering when she'd just give up and hand them over to her. She admitted eggs probably hadn't been the best choice for someone in Katrina's condition, but the fridge options were sparse. Everyone in this house must survive on fast food; the only real staple in the fridge was beer.

Stevie, bless his/her heart, had been reluctant to leave Katrina alone with Cathy, but had a brunch date with friends that couldn't be broken. This didn't sadden Cathy. The person's presence was downright annoying. In fact, she stayed longer than she'd planned just to be annoying herself. Hell, this was longer than she usually stayed over after sex with a man. Maybe she and Katrina should start seriously dating.

"Kat," began Cathy, watching Katrina struggle with a piece of toast as if it were her mortal enemy. "You don't mind if I call you Kat, do you? It fits, you know, with the green eyes and all."

Katrina shook her head and tried to swallow. Cathy drank some more coffee and longed for a Bloody Caesar. Unfortunately, this house had never heard of a well-stocked bar. Or *any* bar, for that matter. "This Stevie person," she continued, "tell me—is that a man or a woman?"

Katrina finally got some toast down and giggled, which nearly made her choke. When she had things under control she shook her head. "I thought I was the only one. Thank God!"

"The only what?"

"The only person who didn't know. I mean, about Stevie."

"Well," said Cathy, "just look at him . . . her—that could be anything. And he/she's also awfully possessive."

"He's a *guy*," said Katrina.

Cathy leaned back and hooted. Katrina stared at her, perplexed.

"Well, it's pretty obvious," said Cathy.

"What is?" said Katrina.

"The guy's in love with you!"

"Oh come on!" gasped Katrina, dropping her toast.

Cathy snorted. "The whole time we were in your room he was glaring at me as if I was about to deflower his bride."

"Oh seriously," said Katrina. "We're best friends. And besides, it's obvious he's gay."

Cathy shook her head. "I wouldn't bet on it."

"Just look at him!" cried Katrina. "How could he not be?"

"Because he never stops staring at you. I mean, I know you're gorgeous, but if there was a choice between you and another man—and there was, when that Boris creep came out in the hall in his shorts, showing off what I must admit aren't bad legs—well, your little Stevie didn't look twice. Even if he didn't like the guy, that wouldn't stop him from staring. I'm in the theatre; I know my gay men, believe me."

"Totally not true," insisted Katrina. "If anyone's in love with me, it's Boris. He's the one who's been erasing my messages."

Cathy opened her mouth to protest some more, but Katrina stood and started clearing the dishes. Cathy was about to claim her eggs when Katrina shoveled them into the garbage. *Damn.*

"You must have things to do," said Katrina stiffly as she poured dish liquid into the sink, "seeing how busy you are with your plays and all."

Ah, the good old brush-off, thought Cathy. Now she really did feel like a one-night stand. "Say," she said, deciding it was clearly time to change the subject, "you never did tell me. What did this Jonathan guy last night look like?"

"Tall, dark, and handsome," said Katrina, her face softening, temporarily forgetting about good old Stevie.

"Come on, you can do better than that—that's such a cliché."

"But he was!"

"What was he wearing?"

"A navy suit, white shirt."

"Did you notice the label when you took off his pants?"

"I didn't take off his pants!" protested Katrina.

"When you washed them, then?"

Katrina shook her head and turned on the tap. "What difference does it make?"

"Just wanted to know if he was really rich or not."

"He was at Lawrence's party, wasn't he?"

"So were we," pointed out Cathy. She paused, then asked, "Did he have a stain on his shirt?"

Katrina nearly dropped a plate she was holding. "How did you know?"

"I think I met him—before the stain, that is."

"No way!" Katrina grabbed Cathy's arm. "Well, what did you talk about? What did he say?"

Cathy shrugged. "Nothing important. I stopped the conversation to go save you. He didn't seem all that interesting anyway. Kind of a jerk, really."

"Impossible," said Katrina. "My guy was really sweet. He couldn't be a jerk if he tried."

Cathy took over washing the dishes that Katrina had suddenly forgotten existed. "Tell me—what attracted you so much to this guy?"

Katrina stared at the ceiling, barely noticing the cobwebs and kitchen grease, then looked back at Cathy. "I think he reminded me of an uncle of mine."

"Terrific," said Cathy, "now it sounds like a father thing. You got a crush on him, too?"

"It wasn't like that at all," said Katrina. "This uncle of mine was a lot younger than my father, the dashing type, you know? He traveled a lot, and I didn't see him much. He imported fabrics or clothes, something like that. He was always beautifully dressed, looked like he belonged in one of those glamorous old movies. Like Cary Grant or something."

"Cary Grant was full of charm," said Cathy. "The guy I talked to was full of something else."

Katrina ignored her. "He looked like he should be in one of those old photos—you know, the ones with rich people in exotic ports, riding on camels or playing polo."

"Sounds rather dashing," said Cathy in an English accent as she rinsed off the dishes.

"Oh, he was! You'd never know he was my dad's brother—my dad's idea of high fashion is worn-out cords and acrylic sweaters." Katrina sighed, remembering. "Uncle Tyler would breeze into town and dazzle everybody. He flitted in and out and gave us exotic presents and told fantastic stories, and he was the most exciting thing I ever saw."

"Phew," said Cathy, "I want to meet this guy."

"I haven't seen him in ages. A few years ago he left and never came back. We never did find out what happened to him."

"He sounds too good to be true. Kind of like your prince."

Katrina haughtily lifted her chin. "What's that supposed to mean?"

Cathy put the last of the dishes in the drying rack and shrugged. "Just that you were drunk and things might've seemed a little . . . I don't know . . . *dreamier* than they really were."

Katrina turned on Cathy, and her eyes flashed. "Look, I might've been drunk, but I know what I saw . . . and felt. Jonathan was sweet, and funny, and charming. Not in a phony way, though. Charming in an effortless, reassuring way. Like he's not charming you to get something, but to make you feel at ease."

Katrina exhaled, embarrassed by her uncharacteristic fervour. "I'm just trying to explain how I feel."

Cathy put up her hands. "Okay—I think I got it."

"So what do I do now? Stevie said it would be like looking for a needle in a haystack."

"Not exactly," said Cathy. "You already have a huge head start."

Katrina stared at her expectantly. "And what would that be?"

Cathy put her hands on her hips and stared at Katrina as if she were completely dense. "You go and ask Windle, of course."

Katrina gaped. "You know that's against the rules!"

Cathy laughed and swatted Katrina with a dish towel. "Fuck the rules! You want to find the guy, right?"

20 A NEEDLE IN A HAYSTACK

Stewart's building on Parliament Street looked even more desolate than the last time Katrina had been there. Since this was Saturday and the area wasn't exactly a prime shopping district, the only people around were the hostel men, and most of them were inside since it had begun to drizzle.

Katrina had hesitated when Cathy handed her the phone and told her to call Windle, claiming she barely knew the man.

"You barely know Jonathan either," replied Cathy, "and you're ready to chase him all over town."

So Katrina had reluctantly called, but Stewart wasn't in. His machine said he'd be back in the office after two. Katrina, disappointed but relieved, told Cathy.

"Guess you'll have to go down there," said Cathy.

"Come with me," pleaded Katrina.

Cathy shook her head. "Nothing I'd like better than an excuse to see Windle—something about that guy just does it for me, and it's not just the fake English accent. But I've got a rehearsal this afternoon, for what it's worth. Half the cast probably won't show up anyway. Hell, if I were them, I wouldn't either, not with this piece of crap the dyke's got me writing. Look, I'll call you later to see how things went."

Cathy leaned closer. "You know, you still look a little green. You should pop some Advil or some Alka-Seltzer or something."

"Sure," said Katrina absently, dreading the visit to Windle.

"Me," continued Cathy, "I'm going home and smoking a huge spliff. I'm not feeling so shit-hot myself."

***

Stewart bellowed "It's open!" at Katrina's knock, and she hesitantly entered the stark office. Stewart was on the phone. He pulled his little black book from his jacket pocket and placed it on his otherwise empty desk.

"No, you don't have to know how to play pool," he was saying. "It's not that kind of pool. A pool *party*, luv—the kind where you frolic in the water and flirt with buff young men. Haven't you ever seen a beer commercial?"

He glanced with little interest at the door, but when he saw it was Katrina, his eyes lit up and he sat up straighter. Even here by himself on a Saturday he was dressed immaculately in suit and tie. Katrina wondered if he was holding more interviews.

"That's right," he said, after listening for a moment, all the while roving his eyes over Katrina. "They'll pick you up about quarter to four. No, all you need's a nice bikini . . . You lost the top? How did you . . ." He rolled his eyes, incredulous. "No, I'm sure they wouldn't mind if you went topless . . . All right then, ta-ta for now."

Stewart hung up and let out a low whistle. "Lovely girl, but not the sharpest knife in the drawer." He stood up and leaned over to shake Katrina's hand. "Katrina, what a pleasure! You're looking exquisite. Have a seat, luv."

Katrina stood there for a second as if she hadn't heard him. She was so nervous she tried to clear her throat, but there was no saliva to clear it with. Finally, she edged toward a chair and slowly lowered her body. She landed on the very edge of the chair and nearly fell off. Adjusting her butt to the back of the chair, she was now too slumped back.

Stewart patiently watched and pretended not to notice her discomfort. "Now, what brings you here on such a miserable day?"

Katrina stared down at her fingers and realized they were twisted together in a pretzel-like knot. She tried to relax them but they were trembling, so she wrapped them up again.

"I hope you're not here to collect your pay, Katrina. It usually takes a few days for me to get my money from the party hosts. If you'll come back on Tuesday, I should have it by then."

"It's not the money," croaked Katrina.

"Sorry?" said Windle, leaning closer.

"I was wondering . . ."

"Yes?"

"I was hoping. . ."

"Hmm?"

"There was a man at the party, and I just have to find out who he is and how to get in touch with him, and it's been driving me crazy, and I know it's against the rules, but I just have to know . . ."

Katrina stopped and took a breath. There. It was out. She looked hopefully at Stewart, who threw his head back and exhaled like a principal once again faced with the most wayward child in school. He picked up his little black book. Katrina's hopes shot up. But when he started flipping pages as if he were absently shuffling a deck of cards, she became despondent again. This was all crazy. What was she doing here, making a fool of herself? She tried to avoid embarrassing situations at all times, went out of her way every hour of the day, and here she was humiliating herself, her face burning hot enough to roast marshmallows.

"Dear Katrina," said Stewart slowly, with tremendous regret, "we went over this. And you just said it yourself—fraternizing with the guests is against the rules."

"But he liked me, I'm sure of it," said Katrina. "He really, really liked me."

Stewart shook his head and stared beyond Katrina, and she knew what was coming, just as it had at her interview. "None of the guests are supposed to know there are ringers. If you were to become romantically involved with a real party guest, it could blow the cover on my business, which would definitely displease the party hosts. Obviously they don't want their real guests knowing they've hired professionals because they don't have the personality to have interesting friends of their own. And even if by some miraculous chance you *could* find this person . . ."

"His name's Jonathan," blurted Katrina.

"Jonathan." Stewart gave her a thin smile. "Jonathan. I don't personally know any Jonathans, not anyone that's a friend of mine or Larry's, anyway."

"Maybe you could give me Lawrence's number. I could phone him and find out who he is."

Stewart slapped his little black book on the desk and roared, "Definitely not!" Katrina jumped at this, and he looked a bit remorseful, so he softened his tone and added, "You have to understand, luv, I can't have my PESTS . . . well—*pestering* the party hosts. It's simply not good for business."

"I wouldn't pester him," insisted Katrina. "I'd ask him nicely. It would only take a minute." She hesitated. "I'm sure Lawrence liked me."

"Oh, I *know* he did. He told me last night when I called to see how everything was going. Liked you very much. Though I must say, he sounded somewhat in his cups." Stewart winked, which unnerved Katrina, as if she wasn't enough of a mess as it was. "Said you were one of the highlights of the party. He was just sorry you slipped out without saying goodbye."

Katrina hadn't thought her face could get hotter, but it went up by about 10 degrees. She must look like a sunstroke victim by now. Stewart leaned forward.

"You must have left early, because it was only midnight when I called. But that's not the point. I don't insist you stay all night. But I'd appreciate if you'd say good night to the hosts from now on, Katrina. Some of them have very huge egos, not to mention they're spending a lot of money, and they expect their PESTS to grovel at their feet."

Katrina held her breath, certain he would ask an explanation for her sudden departure. But he switched back to the previous subject.

"Now here's something to think about, luv. Even if you did find this Jonathan fellow somehow—and you're certainly not finding him with my or Larry's help—you couldn't admit to him who you really are, could you? Not if you cared to continue working for Life of the Party. You'd have to use your fake persona, pretending however you already said that you knew Lawrence, putting up a front." He leaned forward with a disarming smile. "Do you really think you'd be very good at that, Katrina? Being as shy as you are?"

Katrina jerked back as if slapped. She hated it when people pointed out that she was shy. She always felt they'd discovered some deep dark secret about her, that her fatal flaw had been revealed. She wanted to deny everything. Right—like it was hard to figure out she was shy in the first place.

Katrina forced herself to straighten and stare Windle in the eye. She might be stuck with her shyness, but she could at least look determined and bold. Besides, another idea was coming to her . . .

As if he'd seen the wheels turning in her head, Stewart said, "And don't even *think* about going to Lawrence's house and bothering him. He wouldn't take kindly to it, and neither would I. I'm afraid I would have to dismiss you. And I would really hate to do that, especially after Lawrence's glowing report."

Katrina forgot about her boldness and slumped back into her chair. Stewart took pity on her.

"I'll tell you what. There's another party tomorrow at my friend Randy's. An earlier thing, it being Sunday and all. A pool party, about four. Maybe your friend Jonathan will be there."

Katrina's eyes flickered with hope. Stewart smiled, but it was icy, and he had a wily look. "Of course, this Jonathan could be an escort, for all we know."

"Escort?" repeated Katrina, horrified.

Stewart nodded. "I know Lawrence has used them in the past. Not for the sordid ways you might think, but for extra bodies at his parties. Before I came along with Life of the Party to save the day, of course."

Katrina found her fingers turning into pretzels again. "But you're not saying he . . . he could be a *gigolo*?"

Stewart shrugged. "It's not unheard of. Some escorts are only escorts, but others . . ." His tone implied the worst. "You say he was good looking and well dressed?" Katrina nodded. "And he's not one of my friends. And we have to admit that Lawrence doesn't have many friends of his own. So anyone that I don't know from that party was probably either an escort, a Rack 'n' Roll person, or a Rack 'n' Roll friend."

"Maybe he works at Rack 'n' Roll." Katrina hated how desperate her voice sounded.

Stewart smiled patronizingly. "Did you notice large breasts on this person?"

"They must have *some* men working there," insisted Katrina.

"Perhaps busboys," said Stewart imperiously.

Katrina sagged in her chair.

"Did your Jonathan look like a busboy to you?" asked Stewart, with a tone that implied she could never be interested in such a lowly creature.

Katrina shook her head forlornly. She had to admit, all the busboys she'd seen in Toronto seemed to be Sri Lankan men or gangly teenage boys. Jonathan certainly didn't fit either description.

Stewart watched her carefully then smiled to himself. When she looked back up at him, he was thumbing through his book, checking an address. The phone rang, and he set the book down.

"Larry! How are you doing this fine day . . . well, that's understandable. You were a bit tipsy when I called last night . . . yes, about midnight . . . No? Well, that's neither here nor there. What can I do for you? . . . Tomorrow? Fine, how's sixish, Ye Olde Pub? . . . Come now, it's not that bad . . . Okay, ta-ta for now."

Stewart hung up with a smile, shaking his head. "He needs a little hair of the dog, is what he needs." He looked up at Katrina. "Where were we?"

"The pool party?"

"Ah, yes." He picked up his little black book again and flipped through it. "My suggestion is, work the party tomorrow. Even if you don't find your prince—and if you do, I suggest you're so discreet that even I don't know about it—you'll be able to collect twice the pay when you come see me next week. Sounds fair, doesn't it?"

21 BIG BLONDES AND MOVIE STAR MEN

Lawrence had woken up extremely groggy and slightly nauseous. He glanced at his bedside table to check the time on his watch, but the table wasn't there. Neither was his bed. Finally he'd realized he was lying on a lawn chair beside his pool. His watch was still on his wrist and read one o'clock. He might have gone back to sleep, but a slight drizzle urged him out of his chair.

Why hadn't he heard the cleaning crew? He glanced around and saw that all the glasses and ashtrays were gone. The cleaners must have tiptoed around him. Lawrence had a hazy memory of refilling his drink as the sun was coming up, a couple of Rack 'n' Roll girls frolicking topless in the pool, then . . . he must have passed out. Usually he didn't drink that much, but he always got carried away during his parties, he was so excited.

When Stewart Windle had told Lawrence about Life of the Party, a light went on in Lawrence's head. For years he'd watched sixties' movies with their wild soirees and wished he could step inside the screen and pick up a cocktail shaker. Now *those* were parties: big blondes and movie star men, women dancing on tables and sprawled over pianos, not a sober person in sight. Nothing at all like the dry functions Lawrence occasionally attended as a corporate lawyer for a big downtown firm—dull, dull, dull.

In the beginning, Stewart hadn't had enough PESTS to actually fill a party, so Lawrence had to hire some women from the escort agencies he knew as well. When they didn't work out, he started inviting the waitresses from Rack 'n' Roll, which specialized in big-breasted women serving men equally large business lunches. Lawrence went there sometimes with out-of-town clients, but more often on his own after work, so he could chat up the girls. Not that he chatted much or drank a lot, but he knew how to tip. And when they found out where he lived and that his high-school and university acquaintances would be at the parties (drawn by all the beautiful babes), they were more than willing to attend.

Lawrence had to admit his schoolmates were a bit problematic. Sure, they had money, but their looks and social skills left a lot to be desired. They certainly weren't Tony Curtises or George Peppards.

Opportunity finally arose through a gay legal clerk at work. He'd been giving Lawrence the eye for some time, not so much because he liked the looks of Lawrence, but because Lawrence kept looking at *him*. So Lawrence, with a great deal of awkwardness, invited him out to lunch one day and explained about the parties: He was opposed to totally queer abandon, but if Kent was interested in great food and free drinks, a pool and a hot tub, he was quite welcome. So long as he brought some good-looking friends along, of course. No strings, Lawrence emphasized with some embarrassment; he just wanted them for their looks, to enhance the party. Not that Lawrence was gay, God forbid. But there was nothing wrong with appreciating a handsome man.

He'd been having the parties once a month for 5 months now. To Lawrence's surprise and delight, they'd become a hit. So many friends of the girls from Rack 'n' Roll started coming that he no longer had to hire the escorts, though he still hired several PESTS at each party. Most of them were total extroverts and could get things hopping in no time. Kent's friends had told their friends, and the gay legion had grown. Lawrence wasn't sure how he felt about that. He liked having all these handsome men around, but some of his old school pals had started to make snide comments about it. He might have to cut down on that contingent.

Lawrence had started the parties because for years he'd been going slowly insane. Well, perhaps not insane, just desperately mad. Both his parents had died in a plane crash when he was 10, and he'd been raised by his English grandmother. She was incredibly strict, though a terrific baker. Her cookies had cemented Lawrence's relationship with Stewart, who'd lived down the block. Stewart used to come over all the time after school for Gran's delicacies. At least until they got a little older and Lawrence turned into a true nerd and Stewart didn't want to be quite so close anymore. Lawrence suspected that many of Stewart's English mannerisms came from Gran. He also missed Gran's baking. Her cookies were better than any he'd ever tasted. Unfortunately, her mind was somewhat fuddled these days, and she didn't remember how to bake anything anymore. She would possibly risk the lives of everyone around her if she tried.

Lawrence had Gran stashed up on the third floor, where it was harder for her to get down. He had considered giving in to her pleas and putting her on the first floor, which would be much more practical. But then he'd be relegated to the second and third floors, which didn't have a kitchen, and he'd have to share all his meals with the woman. Not to mention her snooping every time he opened the door.

Gran was constantly trying to get downstairs to see Lawrence, in spite of her arthritis. And she expected him to visit her on the third floor all the time, as if he had no life of his own. Which he didn't, really. He went to work. He came home. He ate, he took care of his grandmother. Then crossword puzzles, reading, the odd (actually embarrassingly frequent) sex hot lines.

Gran, though practically infirm and senile, had the ears of an owl and could hear any company Lawrence brought over. The last time he had an honest-to-God woman (well, an escort, but a woman, nonetheless), his date had gotten a little too tipsy and too loud, and Gran was hanging over the banister in no time, screeching. Lawrence had run up to her, afraid (and half hoping) she'd fall over. His date, in the meantime, had fled.

Lawrence had debated for some time what to do with Gran when he had his parties. He'd shipped her out to her sister's for the first one, but she bitched so much it hadn't been worth it. That was when the valium came to mind. A couple of little pills smashed into her mashed potatoes at supper and she'd shut up real good. No yammering that a guest might hear. He look like a momma's boy, for Chrissakes, which he most certainly was not.

Gran's other major fault was her penchant for wandering. Though she moved at a stoned snail's pace, she insisted on going out. Lawrence used to try to go with her, but she wouldn't have it. He worked 5 days a week. What was she supposed to do—wait till he got home to go to the store? As if she couldn't have anything she wanted delivered. But there it was: Gran logic. The Old and the Restless. My Kingdom for a Rest Home.

The problem was, Gran could never remember the code to the security system and got so annoyed with the thing that she ripped it out of the wall one day in a great angry adrenaline rush. Lawrence finally gave up and left it, dangling and helpless. He got revenge in his daydreams, picturing Gran wandering over the bridge from Rosedale to Bloor Street. Leaning a little too far over the railing for a better view, a little slip and . . . *SPLAT!*

Lawrence had found real revenge by accident. One day Gran had lost an earring in her room and insisted that Lawrence find it. Impatiently, he'd scoured the floor and her jewelry box, after first checking that she wasn't actually wearing the thing. He was about to give up and remind her that she had 500 other pairs of earrings, enough already, when he decided to check the bed. Gran's back was turned when Lawrence felt under the comforter and the sheets, then for some odd reason decided to slip his hand under the mattress.

And there it was—Gran's stash. Apparently, she didn't believe in banks; she must've been hoarding tons of cash for years. Lawrence checked to make sure she hadn't seen him, then stood up and announced that the earring was nowhere to be found. Later, when she went to the bathroom (which took a very long time, what with her obvious toilet issues), he stole a wad of cash just for the thrill of it and to spite the old hag.

After he'd done it once, he couldn't control himself. It was like a thrilling game—the fear of being caught, the excitement of forbidden fruit. He didn't need or even really want the money—he just kept stashing it in his closet. He knew the money wasn't safe there, but on the other hand, it wasn't really his, so what did it matter? And if Gran did catch him, what would she do—arrest him? No, if she ever found out it was missing, he'd simply return it and insist she'd imagined the whole thing.

22 HER NAME WAS CATHY

Lawrence staggered from the patio into the kitchen, still a bit off balance, and slopped some milk into a glass. The cleaners had left a pot of coffee on, but the smell of it made his stomach recoil. He hadn't been in the pool or the hot tub the night before, he'd only watched from the sidelines, and he badly needed a shower. His head throbbing, he stumbled up to his room. The door was locked. Oh, right—he'd done that the night before, to dissuade any visitors. He entered through the master bathroom instead. He'd left that open in case of emergencies. As he lifted his hand to open the door to his room, he stopped. Odd . . . the door was ajar.

Shaking his head, Lawrence started for the closet to fetch his robe. But something else was off. What was it? The furniture! It was arranged differently than usual. It was . . . *cozy*. The chairs all faced each other in those cute little conversational huddles which were so favoured in the decorating world. Could he have done that last night in his drunken stupor? No, he didn't even remember being up here. The only reason he'd come up to his own room during one of his parties would be if he got lucky with one of the Rack 'n' Roll girls. And he really doubted that would ever happen.

Completely befuddled, Lawrence shambled over to his closet. He reached inside for his robe, then bent down for his slippers. What now?

Something else was off-kilter. His shoes—something about his shoes. One of the shoe boxes at the bottom of the closet was slightly open. With his heart actually beating for the first time that day, Lawrence lifted the cover. The money was gone. He opened another. Empty. And another. Four boxes full of cash, all missing. Lawrence staggered to the bathroom and threw up.

The ringing of the doorbell brought Lawrence's head out of the toilet, where it had been hanging in a stupor. *Christ, who could that be?* Nobody he knew came over without calling first. Sadly, aside from his parties, nobody came over at all.

As he deliberated, it rang again. And again. Lord, that was hurting his head. He was dying to ingest several Advil and brush the grime off his teeth, but the derelict wouldn't stop. He'd just have to answer it and send whoever it was on their way.

Jonathan stepped backward on the porch and stared up at the windows, trying to discern any movement inside. Lawrence's house looked a lot less inviting in the grey light of a drizzly day than it had the night before. The flickering torches had been removed, the handsome doorman was gone, and the massive oak front doors looked fortresslike, unyielding. After several minutes, Jonathan was surprised when Lawrence opened the door himself. And even more surprised by his appearance.

Lawrence's hair, which had been in a careful comb-over for the party, now stuck out in startled wisps, as if surprised they'd been set free. He wore his suit from the night before, now badly rumpled and minus the jacket, and there appeared to be small flecks of old food on the front of his shirt. Vomit, by the looks of it. Still, he stared down at Jonathan in an imperious fashion and made no move to let him in. "What are *you* doing here?" he asked, squinting, his nostrils quivering. "You know you're not supposed to—"

"Sorry to barge in on you like this," said Jonathan, leaning against the door before Lawrence could close it. "But I didn't have your number, and it's not in the book."

Lawrence gave him a snide look. "You could've asked—"

"Yeah, right," said Jonathan, cutting him off. "Like that would help."

"Help with what?" asked Lawrence.

"The girl I asked you about last night. You said her name was Cathy."

"Cathy?" Lawrence stood there thinking a moment, the nostrils working hard.

"The beautiful blonde with the green eyes."

"Ah . . . yes."

"So?" nudged Jonathan. Lawrence just loomed there, dense. Exasperated, Jonathan stepped forward and was immediately sorry: Lawrence's breath smelled as if he'd fed on dead animals in the night with Jagermeister chasers. Normally Jonathan would say something, or at least offer a mint. But offending Lawrence wouldn't help get any information out of the guy.

"Who is she?" he asked, doing his best to breathe through his mouth.

"I already told you her name."

"I need more. Who is she?"

"I hardly think it's any of your—"

Jonathan stepped forward menacingly, and Lawrence took a step back. He was a good 6 inches taller than Jonathan, but a tiny punch would probably knock his beanpole body down. "I need to know."

Lawrence's hand fluttered for the door. Jonathan brushed it aside and strode past Lawrence, through the foyer and toward the stairs.

"What on earth are you doing?" cried Lawrence.

"She was at your party, you must know her," Jonathan called back, running up the steps. "If you won't help me, I'll help myself."

"What are you talking about?" panted Lawrence, trying to keep up but failing miserably; his hangover made him ache like an arthritic old man. He finally reached the top of the stairs and spotted Jonathan down the hall, entering the master bathroom.

"Hey!" he yelled, though it came out pretty feeble. "What are you doing in there?"

"This is where I met her last night . . . Cathy, or whatever her name is."

Lawrence caught up to Jonathan and tried to catch his breath. "This floor's off limits during parties."

"Sorry, I didn't know the rules. All your Nipples 'n' Tits girls were hogging the other bathrooms."

"Nipples and . . ." Lawrence at first looked outraged and confused, but he finally got it. Stuffily he corrected, "Rack 'n' Roll girls. And they're perfectly nice young ladies."

Jonathan shrugged. "Whatever." He searched the floor and opened the cabinets, Lawrence watching him.

"I still don't understand what the two of you were doing up here," he said. "You didn't go in my bedroom, did you?"

"Lawrence," said Jonathan disapprovingly, "it was a first date."

"I found the door ajar this morning."

"So someone was curious. Happens all the time at parties. If you don't want something snooped on, you should lock the doors."

"Yes, if only I'd thought of that," huffed Lawrence.

Jonathan sank to his knees and checked out the floor under the sink. "I thought maybe if she dropped something, you know, out of her purse or something, maybe I could find a clue."

"It won't do you any good," said Lawrence. "The cleaning crew's already been in. If they'd found anything, they would have handed it over to me."

Jonathan wanted to explain that he *needed* to come up here to the bathroom, that he'd hoped to get a sense of Cathy, get back a feeling of the night before. Maybe it would jog his memory. But the nerdy Lawrence would never understand such sentiment.

"You're wasting your time," Lawrence said now, nostrils in full gear. "She's married."

"Married?" said Jonathan, astounded. "I didn't see a ring on her finger."

Lawrence leered and seemed to be getting a hold of himself for the first time. "Haven't you heard about the type of woman who takes her ring off when she goes to a party?"

"She didn't strike me as that type."

Lawrence shrugged. "Suit yourself."

Jonathan stepped forward menacingly, and Lawrence threw up his scrawny arms. "Okay, okay. A friend of mine sent her over; you know, as a kind of party favour."

"What? You mean like a hooker?"

Lawrence looked deeply offended. "Do I look like someone who hires hookers?"

Jonathan didn't want to answer that one, because Lawrence looked like the first guy on the block to hire a hooker. *Oh God, what if Cathy was a really beautiful high-class call girl? Paid by Lawrence to pleasure his wealthy friends and business contacts. She'd make the old boys' club real happy.*

When Jonathan didn't answer him, Lawrence muttered, "She's my lover." At Jonathan's look of disbelief he added, "She *was* my lover."

Jonathan stared up at Lawrence. *Why on earth would a girl like Cathy have sex with a guy like Lawrence? Of course, there was no accounting for taste. Still . . . Shit, maybe she really was a hooker.*

"Now let me get this straight, Larry, 'cause I'm getting awfully confused. Which one is it—is she married, a hooker, or your lover?"

"All of the above."

"She's your married hooker lover?"

Lawrence took a moment to digest that, then nodded.

Jonathan grabbed the collar of Lawrence's vomitous shirt. "You're full of shit."

Lawrence shrugged as nonchalantly as he could, considering he could barely breathe. "Perhaps."

Jonathan stared up at the quivering nostrils, wishing he could give them a lie-detector test. All this nonsense of Lawrence's had been no help at all, but he couldn't think of any way to get more information out of him, short of beating him up. And that wouldn't do Jonathan any good at all. The bathroom wasn't telling him anything, either; it was as if Cathy had never even been here.

"Thanks a lot," he said, letting go of the shirt and feeling some crumbly bits on his fingers. He felt the urge to gag and quickly washed his hands.

From behind him Lawrence asked in a slightly quavering voice, "You sure you never went in my room?"

Jonathan turned to him and dried his hands. "Why would I?"

Lawrence stared at him intently and suddenly asked, "You like interior decorating?"

"What?"

"You know—arranging furniture and stuff."

Jonathan stared at him for a moment, then shook his head and strode out. Lawrence slumped against the sink and frowned into the bedroom at the chairs, so happily nestled together.

23 PIZZA PIZZA

After Katrina saw Windle, she wandered north on Parliament till the crack dealers and the hostel dwellers dwindled. As she walked, she thought about Stewart getting together with Lawrence tomorrow night. Lawrence was single and seemed to live alone. Which meant his house would be unoccupied for a while. She popped into a little café and used the phone inside to call Stevie.

There was no answer. Stevie must have left for work already or had gone to Cups for a latte, and Boris was probably brooding in his room or still asleep. She hated to leave a message that Boris would overhear, but she really needed to get hold of Stevie.

"Hey, Stevie, it's me, Katrina. I've got another job tomorrow, an afternoon pool party, but I really need to see you after that. You're not working tomorrow, are you? Look, it's really important, so wake me up tonight after work when you get home, no matter how late it is."

Boris, in the kitchen fixing a sandwich, listened to the message and grinned. He knew what afternoon pool parties were like, everyone boozing it up in the sun. They'd all be loaded, and he'd have ample opportunity to scout things out. With any luck, the moron of a host would be as stupid as Lawrence and leave some goodies lying around in his bedroom, ripe for the picking. Boris put down his pastrami on rye and called Stewart.

"Yes?" said Stewart, who didn't like to identify himself on the phone, probably for good reason. There must be lots of people in Montreal still looking for him. And they'd really like a nice piece of him if they ever found out where he was.

"Hey, Windle, it's your old pal, Boris, remember me?"

"I'd rather forget."

"I hear you're doing a pool party tomorrow."

"You do have your sources, don't you?"

"I'd really like to work it."

"Look, Boris, I told you I'd do what I can, but this guy, the host, he's a real cheap bugger. I couldn't possibly get him to hire anyone else."

"So cancel another guy."

"There only are two other guys; the host wants all women at his party."

"So why two guys at all?"

"One of my rules," said Stewart. "I insist on having at least two male PESTS at every party, just in case."

"In case?"

"In case anything untoward happens."

"Untoward? What the hell's that?"

"Improper."

"Ah, I getcha. You don't want the guys getting all drunk and horny and going at it."

"Something like that, yes."

Boris laughed. "So I can be the knight in shining armour. Get rid of one of those other guys and hire me. I'll take care of everything."

"I'm sure you will," said Stewart with a sigh before giving Boris directions.

***

Katrina stepped out of the café, wondering what to do with herself. She used to have the occasional date on Saturday night, even though she despised dating, all that dreaded chit-chat and good night kissing. But since her messages had mysteriously stopped coming, things had been dry. Sometimes she'd go to a movie, but Saturdays were the worst for that—all couples. She always felt like a total loser, standing in line alone. Dinner was just as bad. Everyone in the restaurant staring at her, wondering what was wrong with her. She hadn't seen any of her old friends from school in weeks, and anyway, they weren't the type to call up on the spur of the moment. And Stevie usually worked Saturdays. Which didn't leave her with much to do. She didn't even want to go home till it got dark, in case Boris might be there. He'd creeped her out last night with all that friendliness, offering to go to the party with her—or possibly spy on her. Nope, home at the moment wasn't an option.

Katrina stared down the street, wondering if she should have lunch somewhere. She wasn't all that hungry, but it would kill some time. A late lunch, then she could pick up something light for dinner and eat it at home in front of the TV, where she might feel like a lonely loser, but at least not look like one. She saw a promising sign and was heading toward it when a chubby girl bumped into her, laughed, and apologized. She was so friendly that Katrina couldn't help but smile. And think of Cathy.

She went back to the café's phone, pulled out the pink piece of notepaper Cathy had given her, and dialed.

"Hi, it's Katrina. I'm not interrupting your rehearsal, am I?"

"Fuck the rehearsal! The fucking dyke got mad at one of the vampire actors and threatened to lop off his dick and everyone ran for their lives. If we ever put on this goddamn play, it'll be a frigging miracle."

"So what're you doing now?"

"Crying into a beer. You?"

"I'm on Parliament . . ."

"Oh, your meeting with Windle! How'd it go?"

"Let's just say I'd be crying into my beer if I had one."

"Have one over here."

"Sorry?"

"I've got lots of beer, and the dyke's gone off to her more 'lesbian-sympathetic' friends, as she calls them. I'm not far from you, you know—I'm a Riverdale girl, too."

"You want me to pick us up some food? I'm not that hungry but—"

"I'm always hungry. Pick up lots, whatever you like. Surprise me."

"But what if you don't like something?"

"Honey, I like everything." Cathy gave Katrina directions to a warehouse in lower Riverdale which was only a quick hop on the streetcar from Katrina's house. Then Katrina turned to study the café's takeout menu and wondered whether Cathy was a fan of liverwurst.

***

They were in Cathy's kitchen, which was separated from the rest of the loft by only a long bar, where they sat on tall stools. The place was huge, open, and incredibly jammed with junk. Clothes, props, and papers were strewn everywhere. Beer cases were piled to the ceiling. The kitchen counter was loaded with dirty glasses and looked like it had hosted a party the night before. Cathy informed Katrina that was the way it always looked; she tended to have a lot of guests, invited or otherwise. They were alone now, finishing off a pepperoni pizza. None of the sandwiches at the café had appealed to Katrina, so she'd decided to go with the tried-and-true. After all, she barely knew Cathy; she didn't want to scare her off with weird food.

Katrina had gobbled down three pieces of pizza, a huge amount for her, before she was willing to stop chewing long enough to speak.

"I don't know what's happening to me," she said, wiping tomato sauce off her chin. "I usually have no appetite at all. I must be in love."

"They say that when you're in love you *can't* eat," said Cathy, noting that Katrina was finished. She grabbed the last piece before Katrina could change her mind. "I've never had that problem."

"You've never been in love?" asked Katrina.

"No, I've never not been hungry." Cathy paused in her chewing. "So tell me what happened at Windle's."

"He refused to give me Lawrence's number; said it was against the rules."

"Sorry I wasted your time."

Katrina looked at Cathy questioningly.

"Remember? I said 'fuck the rules'."

"Oh, that." Katrina waved her hand. "I'm glad you forced me to go over there anyway. I came up with another plan."

"I hope your plan isn't to go over to Lawrence's house and ask him. I'm sure the moment you left, Windle was on the phone to him, warning him that you might show up and bug him about Jonathan. You know what those old boys' networks are like."

Katrina shook her head. "Stewart was on the phone with him before that."

Cathy stared at Katrina.

"Lawrence called Stewart while I was in the office. They're getting together tomorrow afternoon."

"So?"

"So it's the perfect chance for me to go over to Lawrence's house, find his address book—"

"You mean while he's *out*!? You mean like *breaking and entering*!?"

Katrina ignored her. "Lawrence must know Jonathan since he was at the party, and if we can't get him to tell us . . ." She shrugged. "He must have an address book somewhere with all of his friends in it, or some kind of list with all the people he invited to the party."

"What do you mean, if *we* can't get him to tell us? Katrina, I really like this job. Breaking into the boss's friend's house isn't exactly the best way to keep it."

"Don't worry, Cathy, I'm not asking you. I'm going to get my roommate Stevie to help me."

"That she-male or whatever-it-was I met at your place?"

"What's wrong with Stevie?"

"Katrina, he'd be about as useful in a burglary as Liberace, for God's sake."

"What've you got against Liberace?"

Cathy pushed aside her half-finished pizza slice, reached into a wooden box on the bar, and pulled out a tightly rolled joint. She lit up, inhaled deeply, and stared at the ceiling. Katrina watched her, intrigued, and shook her head when Cathy offered her the joint.

"I think I've got a better idea," Cathy said, after finishing half the joint and stubbing out the rest for future consumption. "We go to Windle's office—while he's there, so there's no breaking and entering involved—and we steal his address book."

"But he already told me he has no idea who Jonathan is."

"And you believed him?" Cathy shook her head. "Stewart Windle. S. Windle—*Swindle*. Do you really think that man is going to tell you the truth about anything?"

"I thought you said he was hot."

"Being hot doesn't make you honest." Cathy leaned closer to Katrina and showed no effects from the joint whatsoever. Katrina figured that if she'd smoked that stuff she'd be passed out on the floor right now.

"What we do is, we go to Windle's office, you distract him—"

"Why me? You're the one who likes him."

"Because I may like *him*, but he likes *you*. You distract him, drag him out to the hallway or that other room in his office, and I look for his address book or his files or whatever the hell he's got."

"He's got a little black book. You must've seen it during your interview."

"Yeah?"

"But he keeps it in his jacket pocket. I saw him pull it out this afternoon."

"Well, he must have another book, other records—any businessman does."

"I'm not so sure," said Katrina, shaking her head. "His desk looked pretty bare." She straightened and stared at Cathy. "I like my plan better."

Cathy groaned.

"Look, it's perfect. I know exactly when Lawrence will be out, what time he's meeting Stewart. I'll be at the pool party then, but I can leave early."

"Pool party?" asked Cathy blankly.

"You're not going?"

"You mean a work thing, a Life-of-the-Party thing?"

"Sure," said Katrina, "Stewart told me about it this afternoon." Cathy looked crestfallen. Katrina felt sick. "You're not going? What am I going to do there without you? Why weren't you invited?"

Cathy grabbed for the remaining pizza and chewed it slowly, without relish, as if punishing herself. Finally, she wiped her hands with a napkin and looked up at Katrina. "I imagine Windle doesn't consider me bathing-suit material." She took a long drink of her beer. "I suppose I can't blame him."

"But Cathy . . ."

She tried for a wry grin, but it didn't quite come off. "It's okay. I'm sure he'll invite me to lots of other parties. I guess this one's more about looks than personality." She patted Katrina's hand. "No offence."

Katrina, who up till now had felt awed and belittled by Cathy's outgoingness, suddenly felt perversely better. She realized how human Cathy was. Life wasn't a total breeze just because you were an extrovert. Kind of like the way people thought it was all fun and games for her because of her looks. They had more in common than she'd thought.

Cathy looked Katrina over thoughtfully and seemed to pull herself together. "Wear the skimpiest thing you've got. A thong, if you've got one. They'll all be so busy staring at your ass you won't even have to open your mouth. I mean, if I had your packaging . . . Anyway, the point is, you'll never even notice I'm not there. You won't have time. The men will be drooling all over you so much that—"

"What a lovely image," said Katrina, feeling awkward at Cathy's dejection. She grabbed a leftover pizza crust and pretended to stuff it in her mouth. "Maybe I'll just eat the whole time so I don't have to talk to anybody."

"Don't do that or you'll look like me and you'll only get invited to full-dress parties." Cathy laughed, back to her normal self. "And you'd probably spit the food out on somebody's shoulder, and they wouldn't have a jacket to cover it this time."

"You saw that?"

Cathy nodded. Katrina burst out laughing, and so did Cathy. When Katrina subsided, she added, "But seriously, I have to find Jonathan. The moment I met him, I just knew we were soul mates."

"You were drunk," said Cathy. "You probably would've thought the TV was your soul mate if it had talked back to you."

"You're full of it," said Katrina.

"And pizza," said Cathy. "But I'm definitely not full of beer." She held up her bottle. "Another one?"

"Oh, definitely," agreed Katrina. "Just don't feed me any hard liquor."

"Oh, don't worry—I've learned *that* lesson."

24 YOU SURE THIS IS A GOOD IDEA?

Katrina was awakened by a light tapping on her door. In the darkness of her bedroom she wasn't sure whether it was day or night.

"Katrina," whispered Stevie, "you home?"

Katrina mumbled something incoherent and sat up and rubbed her eyes. It had been after seven when she got home, the beer buzzing in her brain. She remembered feeling quite proud of herself that she hadn't been nauseous at all, despite three bottles of Blue—though she had been tipsy. Cathy, by contrast, had seemed perfectly sober.

When Katrina had asked her what she was doing that night, she said she was invited to a house party, a poetry reading, and an art exhibit, but they all sounded pretty lame. The house party was at a fellow bartender's place, and she used to have the hots for the guy till he fell for the dippy hostess, a dancer weighing about 90 pounds with the brains of a retarded flea. It would just break her heart to see them making eyes at each other.

The poetry reading was an actress she'd done a play with who'd decided to expand her creative horizons. Frankly, her poems stank, and it would torture Cathy to go there and listen to them, let alone have to tell the girl later how great they were. Now *that* would be acting.

And the art exhibit—well, that guy's paintings were worse than the other girl's poetry. It was so hard, Cathy sighed, because you felt you had to be supportive of other artists' endeavours, but so many of them really were nauseatingly bad. She only hoped her artist friends didn't all feel the same way about her work.

So, instead of doing any of those things, Cathy decided she might just stay in and work on her latest play, not the vampire one but another one. When Katrina asked what it was about, Cathy replied, "Oh no, you don't. You'd probably tell me that it's been done before and get me all depressed, then send me into a bout of writer's block. And right now, the booze and the joint have me ready to roll. I only hope 15 people don't show up for an impromptu party."

"Doesn't it bug you," asked Katrina, "people just dropping in like that all the time?"

Cathy shook her head. "You gotta keep your doors open, hon—you always gotta keep your doors open."

Another light tapping brought Katrina wider awake. The door opened, and Stevie stepped in. He peered into the darkness for a second then flicked on the light switch, shutting the door behind him.

Katrina sat up, squinting. "What time is it?"

"Ten thirty. Work was dead. I got off early. Jim's downstairs. We're going out."

"Which one's Jim?"

"The tall blond guy from work. He's been into Cups a couple of times."

"The cute blond one? The gay one?"

Stevie nodded.

"I definitely remember *him*." *A date?* wondered Katrina, still groggy from her nap. Nap, hell—she'd just had half a night's sleep. After three beers. She definitely needed more practice. Maybe she could go into training with Stevie—he seemed pretty good at it.

Stevie lowered his voice. "Is Boris home?"

Katrina shrugged. "Who knows? I've been out like a light for hours."

Stevie came forward and sat on the bed. "I got your message." He glanced at the door as if Boris might be clinging to it like Spider Man. "You should be more careful about leaving phone messages. You-know-who hears them, too."

"I know, but it's not like I said anything revealing, and I just had to get the message to you."

Katrina sat up and told him her plan to go to Lawrence's.

Stevie's face was so incredulous it verged on the moronic. "You mean—*break in*?"

"How else?"

Stevie's face wasn't looking any smarter.

"I thought all guys knew how to do that stuff," said Katrina, growing impatient.

Stevie seemed to come out of his trance. "You mean like how we automatically know how to fix car engines and computers and leaky toilets?"

"I thought your fathers sat you on their knees when you were 2 and explained it all to you."

"The only thing my dad explained was how to make a great barbecue sauce and stock a cooler with beer."

"When you were 2?"

"Younger," Stevie sighed. "You sure this is a good idea? I mean, it's *illegal*." Katrina stared him down, and he sighed. "Look, I can try to help, but I can't promise you anything. All I can do is copy what I've seen in the movies."

Katrina sat up straighter. "What's that?"

"A credit card. I don't own one of those special keys they always talk about in books."

"Could you get one?"

"Oh sure—I'll just call up all my burglar friends and ask to borrow one."

"Okay, no need to get snippy. Just meet me a couple of doors down from the pool party at 6 with your credit card." She wrote down the directions, and Stevie put the paper in his pocket.

"I'd better get back to Jim."

"Where're you guys going?"

"I don't know. He probably wants to go to a gay bar. I don't—I hate those places." Stevie shuddered. "They make me feel like a fly in a spider's web. You want to come, act as my chaperone?"

"No, thanks," said Katrina, wondering why he couldn't just admit the gay thing and get it over with. She remembered Cathy's remarks earlier that day about Stevie not being gay and being in love with her. Ridiculous! "I'm starting to feel hungover, and everyone else is going to be drunk by now."

"How'd you get hungover?"

"I had three beers over at Cathy's."

"Cathy? The girl I met this morning?" Stevie scowled.

"What? You don't like her?"

"Well, you just met her. I mean, is she okay?"

"Why wouldn't she be?"

"She looked awfully cozy with you this morning, that's all," said Stevie. "In bed," he added with great disapproval.

"She's not after me, if that's what you're implying." Katrina, though offended, felt a perverse urge to giggle.

"Well, just be careful—you barely know her." Stevie paused awkwardly then added, "You sure you don't want to come out with us?"

"I'm supposed to be saving money, remember?"

"I told you not to worry about it."

"And I told you no way." Katrina saw Stevie's hurt look. "Anyway, I have to be bright-eyed and bushy-tailed for the party tomorrow. Then I should have some decent money coming in next week, and we can really get moving on things."

"All right," said Stevie, acting indignant. "You just go back to your beauty sleep and let me fend for my poor little self."

Boris, his ear to the bedroom door, quickly scampered back to his room and silently shut the door. Saturday was usually a big night for him, but since he had the pool party the next day and figured he'd score there, he'd decided to stay in and find out what Stevie and Katrina were up to. Ray, his partner, had been pissed off at him, but not as much as he usually was; he'd been seeing some chick a lot lately and was probably happy to take a Saturday night off and get laid like a normal person.

So Lawrence was going out tomorrow. Perfect. Well, not perfect. Burgling during daylight hours was never the greatest idea. But there were lots of trees and shrubs around Lawrence's house, and it was well separated from the other houses in the neighbourhood. He'd just have to boot Ray out of bed with his little tart (Ray always spent Sundays in bed, since it was the one day they usually didn't work), and they'd get over there before Katrina did. In and out—wham-bam-thank-you-man.

Boris smiled at the thought of the loot awaiting him, but his mood quickly soured. What was this "getting moving on things" that Katrina and

Stevie had been talking about? What were those two little snots up to? Boris had a suspicious feeling it had something to do with him.

25 SPEEDOS, SPEEDOS EVERYWHERE

The house was in Rosedale, a block away from Lawrence's. No gorgeous doorman this time. Katrina found the front door locked, with a sign saying to go around the side to the back. Feeling self-conscious in her sarong and bikini top, she quickly followed the cobblestoned pathway and opened a large gate. She'd barely stepped inside when a large, swarthy, hairy man in an orange Speedo wrapped her in a bear hug, his body sweat clinging to her skin.

"Hey, babe!" he cried. "Welcome to the party!" Then, whispering in her ear, "What's your name, honey?"

"Katrina," she replied, trying to escape his embrace.

"I'm Randall, but call me Randy," he whispered, holding on for dear life. "We've been seeing each other 3 months, met at a club called Wham! You're a cocktail waitress there."

"But I've never—"

"Don't worry about it. These guys never get out. They're all married with kids, for fuck's sake." Randy finally released her and turned around to face his friends.

"Katrina here, everyone!" he bellowed, as if they were all old and hard of hearing.

They weren't that old, but they weren't spring chickens, either. And they were almost all men. Ten or 12 of them. There were only two other women there, both beautiful. One topless, and Katrina knew from Windle's phone conversation yesterday that *she* was definitely a fellow PEST. Apparently this Randy guy was keeping the female contingent small so his friends might actually believe that they were all his girlfriends. Katrina shuddered at the thought.

Randy put his arm around her shoulders and led her toward the pool. Touchy guy. Katrina hated touchy guys. She gritted her teeth and tried not to squirm. She glanced around again. No sign of Jonathan. Of course, this crowd looked cruder than the men who'd been at Lawrence's party, so she wasn't surprised. Jonathan was classy; he wouldn't hang out with these greaseballs. She was disappointed, though. No Jonathan and no Cathy. How on earth was she going to get through this?

Randy sat her on a barstool and snapped his fingers at a young man who popped up from under the bar holding a couple of cans of beer. He was wearing shorts and a Hawaiian shirt, opposed to the ubiquitous Speedos of the other men, though he would've looked much better in a bathing suit than they did. Very cute, blond, surfer type. He must be a PEST. He certainly didn't fit in with the rest of the men, and Katrina couldn't see Randy letting a good-looking man in here. He wouldn't want his "girlfriends" eyeballing another guy. But why a male PEST? Maybe Stewart had sent him as a bodyguard, to keep an eye on his girls.

The bartender handed her a frozen pink concoction, complete with umbrella. It had been premade, sitting in a blender, so Katrina had no way of knowing how much liquor was in it. She'd have to take it easy, in case it was a triple. The last thing she needed was to puke in the pool. The Speedo men, who'd been openly ogling, and the two women, who'd been staring in a bored but competitive manner, finally overcame the novelty of a new arrival and continued their conversations. Katrina let out her breath. At least *that* was over.

Randy got a beer for himself, which Katrina would have preferred but was too shy to ask for, and leaned close to her. He sniffed slightly, and she wondered if he had a cold. Or maybe he was allergic to the chlorine in the pool. She'd heard of that. Though she decided, after a whiff of BO, that he hadn't been anywhere near the pool. She didn't want to look at his face, which was pitted and coarse and looked like a movie mobster's. He certainly didn't look like someone who owned a house in Riverdale, unless he'd muscled his way in. But if she didn't look at his face, she was forced to look at his body. His chest and stomach were covered in a sweaty black pelt, and below that was the Speedo, with things jiggling around that she'd rather not think about.

"Take off your clothes; make yourself comfortable," he said, and Katrina froze.

He saw her look and laughed. "*That* thing," he said, pointing at her sarong. "Don't worry, you don't have to copy her," he said, nodding at the topless girl. He leered and sniffed again. "Though you're sure as hell welcome to."

Katrina fiddled with her sarong, her fingers resisting. Reluctantly they behaved, and off it came. She now felt totally naked and vulnerable. She hadn't worn a thong, as Cathy had suggested, because she was too shy to own one. But it came close enough. She felt all eyes upon her again and wanted to grab a patio umbrella to cover herself. As she glanced toward one, wondering if it would be too heavy to pick up, she caught Randy nodding slightly at an obese bald man across the pool. The man hefted himself up and waddled into the house. Randy patted Katrina's shoulder and said, "Be right back," and followed the man inside.

Katrina sat there feeling foolish. She felt she should attempt to talk to someone, but the only person close to her was the bartender. And if he was a

PEST, she wasn't supposed to talk to him. But on the other hand, he might know Jonathan.

"Hi," she said to his back; he was bent over, filling a huge cooler with beer cans. He didn't seem to hear her.

"Hi," she repeated, louder. He finally turned around.

"You need another drink?" he asked.

"No," she said, feeling like an idiot. He raised his eyebrows. Katrina cleared her throat. "Do you know if there are any other . . ." She wanted to say PESTS, but if he wasn't one, he wouldn't have a clue what she was talking about. So she said, ". . . any other young men at this party?"

The bartender laughed. "You want young guys, I think you're in the wrong place. Besides, aren't you supposed to be Randy's girlfriend?"

Katrina ignored that. "No one at all?" she persisted.

"There's one other guy my age here, but he's in the kitchen washing dishes or something."

"Oh," said Katrina dejectedly. She took a sip of her pink sludge and crinkled her nose; it had a strange yet intriguing taste. "I just thought there might be a guy named Jonathan here."

"Jonathan," mused the bartender, then he shook his head. "Don't think so. 'Course, I don't usually get their names. They come, they get their drinks, they go."

"Oh," said Katrina, out of conversation. She turned and glanced around. "Not much mingling going on, is there?"

The bartender laughed. "I think the only mingling Randy wants is with you and those other two chicks. Me, I was told to keep my mouth shut and keep the booze flowing, and that's what I'm doing . . . or *trying* to do." He turned his back on Katrina and returned his attention to the cooler.

Katrina sighed and swiveled back toward the pool. Stewart had sure been wrong about this one: This wasn't like any beer commercial she'd ever seen. The men were all gathered at one end of the pool, sipping on what looked like scotch. They talked in low voices amongst themselves and occasionally ogled the women. No one was in the pool. No one was even lounging in a chair. Katrina felt like she was lined up against the wall at a grade-school dance, waiting for a partner.

Randall and the obese man emerged from the house, grinning. The fat man actually seemed to have a little spring to his waddle. He returned to the other greaseballs, and Randy joined Katrina at the bar, wiping his nose. He seemed a lot livelier than before. Maybe it was the retro 1980s music that had been cranked way up.

"Having a good time?" he asked so fast she could barely understand him.

"Sure," she said, trying for enthusiasm but hearing her voice fall flat.

Randy put a furry arm around her shoulders. "Have another drink, sweets."

"I haven't finished this one." Katrina stared into the pink goo. "What is this?"

"Strawberry Margarita. Isn't it strong enough? I could throw some more tequila in there." He was about to snap his fingers but Katrina interrupted.

"Maybe I should just have a beer."

"Whatever your little heart desires. I know tequila isn't for everybody. Makes me hurl myself." He snapped his fingers, but the bartender was already handing Katrina a Blue Light.

Randy nodded toward the Speedo men. "I'd introduce you to my friends, but they'd only try to steal you away. And I want *you* to myself. Maybe I'll send Honey and Ginger over." He raised his voice. "Hey, girls! Get your asses over there and schmooze with my friends!"

"Jesus," he grumbled to Katrina. "Those girls are shit. All they do is stand there and talk to each other and act like they're too good for me. What's the point of that? They're supposed to be my girlfriends, for fuck's sake." He shook his head. "I'll have to talk to Stewart about them."

As the girls sashayed to the other end of the pool, flinging their hair and thrusting out their breasts, Katrina noticed a couple more of the men get up and go inside. Was there another party going on in there that she didn't know about? Maybe they were all in there doing crack. Wasn't that supposed to have a noticeable odour, though? And decrease your appetite? No wonder there was no food at this party. At least she didn't have to worry about spitting morsels on anyone. Though she did regret not eating lunch before she came. Her usually blasé stomach was growling loudly.

"So," said Randy, thankfully removing his hairy arm from Katrina's shoulder to light a cigarette, "you like my place?"

"It's lovely," said Katrina, admiring the huge pool and the mansion towering above it.

"It's not mine," laughed Randy. "Belongs to my folks. They're traveling around Europe, left it to me to use for a few months. I couldn't afford a place like this now, not with all my alimony. Work 15 years as a stockbroker and the bitches get all my money."

Randy gulped down half his beer and sniffled again. "But enough about me. What about you?" Before Katrina could answer he said, "You know what you need? Jewelry!"

"Jewelry?" repeated Katrina, bewildered. "With a bathing suit?"

"Look at those assholes," said Randy, nodding toward his friends. "They got bathing suits on and look at the frigging gold chains. Did you notice that? They look like a bunch of pimps, for fuck's sake—or baseball players."

He looked Katrina over intently. “I could help you in the jewelry department.”

Katrina leaned back, her stomach twisting. “Oh no, that’s okay. Besides, I thought you were broke.”

“Just a little cash-poor. But I’ve got a little sideline that’s helping me in that department.”

“Oh?” said Katrina, certain he was about to tell her that he sold dead bodies to medical science or stole children for adoption.

Randy looked her over for a moment, as if deciding something. Then he said, “You want to come inside with me?”

“What for?”

“You’ll see.”

Katrina saw the two men who’d gone inside come out again in animated conversation. Randy grabbed her by the arm and practically lifted her off the bar stool.

“C’mon. Bring your beer if you want.” Katrina took a long swig, then reluctantly followed him.

They entered the house through a huge kitchen, and Katrina saw that there was food after all. A couple of trays of cold cuts and canapés, obviously put together by a catering company that was a lot cheaper than the one Lawrence had used. A man with shaggy black hair, his back to her, was bent over the sink, rinsing glasses. Definitely not Jonathan.

“Through here,” said Randy, leading her down a long hall toward the front of the house, never letting go of her arm. He directed her into a study. On the massive glass desk were several huge lines of white powder. Randy went over and held up a straw.

“Help yourself.”

Katrina just stared. She’d seen this in movies, of course, but never in real life. She’d half-suspected it was all make-believe, like the time she’d gone to Calgary with her parents and saw real cowboys and was astonished they actually existed. Now, like in the movies, she expected helicopters to thunder overheard and SWAT teams to tear down the doors.

"Oh no," she said, nearly hyperventilating. "I couldn't!"

"Of course, you can. I didn't offer any to those other bitches, 'cause they've got bad attitudes and I didn't think I could trust them, but I know you're the type who'll keep your mouth shut. I mean, you won't say anything to Stewart, will you?"

"Does he do this?" asked Katrina, shocked.

"Are you kidding? That guy's as straight as they come. Probably never stole a candy bar out of a corner store. If he found out I was selling this shit . . . well, I might not be able to use his services to hire sweet young things like you anymore. And that would be a real shame." He bent over and snorted a huge line, beaming when his head bobbed up.

"This is a hell of a lot better than the other shit I had. Got a new connection. That's why I wanted all these guys to come over today, test the new product. 'Course, I knew it wouldn't hurt to have a few 'girlfriends' here too, to impress them. They see me with chicks like you, they know I'm doing okay."

He paused for a breath and wiped his nose, but there was still a little white ring around the left nostril. "Don't tell my other friends either—you know, the other guys who use Life of the Party. You know any of them?"

"Just Lawrence, he's the only one I—"

"Fuck, especially not *him*! He's the worst, the straightest one of the bunch; definitely *don't* tell him! He's such a pathetic loser with all those Rack 'n' Roll girls and escorts and faggots."

"Escorts?" said Katrina. "Faggots?"

"I swear the guy's queer, he just won't admit it. That's why he hires escorts all the time, to make it look good. Anyway, you won't say anything to him, right?"

Katrina shook her head, afraid to offend him. She'd heard these drug fiends could get violent, and she wasn't about to set him off.

He offered the straw to her again, and she backed away as if confronted by a giant maggot.

"I can't," she muttered. "I mean, I haven't even had lunch yet. It would upset my stomach."

"No problem," said Randy, "I understand completely. It fucks up my stomach real bad sometimes, too. Get the roaring shits. I'll get the kid in the kitchen to put the food out, you eat something and then come back and snort away to your heart's content."

"Thanks," said Katrina, hoping she didn't look as panicked as she felt. "Bathroom?"

Randy pointed down the hall. "I'll go get that kid to put out the food."

They headed off in different directions. As soon as Katrina got inside the bathroom, she locked the door, leaned against it, and downed the rest of her beer. It was warm now and tasted foul, but it helped steady her nerves. She had to get a grip. She'd never been in a drug den before. Well, there was Len, but compared to this! This was the nasty stuff, hard core. People *died* from this stuff.

Katrina stood there for a good 10 minutes, thoughts racing. Should she call up Stewart right now and let him know? Sure, Randy had asked her not to, but she didn't know him from Adam. He was a hardened criminal. Stewart was the one who hired her and paid her. Should she call the police? But that would be the end of her job for sure. Randy would know it was her. He'd spread the word to all his friends who used Stewart's service that she was a fink, and she'd be cut off without a penny.

The howl of a wounded animal made her jump. Katrina wondered for a crazy second if Randy had animals caged in his basement. But when she heard an earsplitting "*FUCK!*" she realized it wasn't an animal—it was him. She rushed down the hall to the study to find Randy tossing a bureau drawer to the floor in disgust.

"My coke! Someone stole my fucking coke!"

Katrina looked from the floor to the lines still sitting on the desk. "But it's right there," she said, perplexed.

He whirled on her. "My stash, you twit! Someone came in here and stole my stash!" He whirled back to face the room. "And they rearranged my fucking furniture!"

Katrina followed his wild-eyed stare and realized that the room did indeed look different. Cozier, yet somehow more sophisticated. Like little interior decorating elves had moved the chairs and books around, creating a homey living space.

Randy took a couple of deep breaths and looked a little less likely to throttle her on the spot. "I was only gone 10 minutes, and all the guys were out by the pool with me." He turned to stare at her, looked over her tiny bikini. "Well, I know *you* don't have it."

Katrina took a step back. "Unless you hid it somewhere." He stepped forward. He looked ready to do a body search when the obese bald man trotted into the study, tits flapping.

"What's going on? I heard somebody scream."

He was followed by several other men, who all crowded into the study. Katrina saw her chance. She crept slowly backward as they surged forward, then turned and ran for the kitchen. She glanced in the opposite direction of the door to the pool, wondering if there was another exit where she wouldn't be seen by any of the guests. A door by the sink had been flung open. And a man that looked amazingly like her roommate Boris was using a shrub as a footstool to climb a 6 foot fence.

No, she thought, suddenly so dizzy she had to lean against the sink. The drinks she'd had must be playing tricks on her. That and all the criminal activity she'd just witnessed. It would make anybody imagine things. Jeez, she might as well have done the coke, she surely couldn't feel any stranger.

Taking a deep breath, she pushed herself up from the sink. And noticed the clock on the wall. It was nearly six. Time to meet Stevie and break into Lawrence's house. She fleetingly wondered if she'd get paid for this gig if she didn't say goodbye to her host. But there was no chance of that. Let the other girls be strip-searched. She had her own searching to do. For Jonathan.

26 WAITING IN THE BUSHES

When Boris had arrived at Randall's place, he could tell the guy wanted nothing to do with him. Like he was a queer or something. The other PEST, who'd arrived at just about the same time, did look queer to Boris, with his freaking Hawaiian shirt and Goldilocks hair. He got sent out to tend the bar, probably 'cause he was pretty, and Boris got assigned kitchen patrol. Which was fine by him. This way, he'd get to case the joint while everyone else was outside soaking up the rays. Like the greasy old perverts needed them—they looked like a bunch of sagging leather couches as it was. Problem was, they kept going into some room down the hall with Randall every 10 minutes, which didn't give Boris a lot of opportunity.

After about an hour, the coast had cleared for a couple of minutes, and Boris had sauntered casually down the hall, pretending to look for the bathroom. He found the door everyone had been entering, peeped in, and saw the monster lines on the desk. The dude must be selling. Which meant there had to be a lot more of that shit around. Probably in the desk. Randall wouldn't want to have to rummage around for it too long when he ran out, which he would soon, the rate these greaseballs were going.

Half an hour later, Boris had turned around just in time to see Katrina's back heading down the hall with her host. He'd never seen her in a bathing suit before; she looked damn good. A little skinny for his taste, but not bad. Good thing he hadn't turned around a second sooner. Goddamn dishes, he'd actually been getting into it. Though why he had to rinse the things when the guy had a dishwasher was beyond him. "Crystal," Randall had said. "It's fucking delicate." And why would anyone use crystal at a fucking pool party was what Boris wanted to know. But he didn't ask, didn't want to draw attention to himself. The guy was bound to remember him as it was. Good thing was, he wasn't about to call the cops when he discovered the stash stolen. He might call Windle, though, if Windle knew what he was into. But Boris could take care of that Brit dick.

Randall had returned to the kitchen a couple of minutes later, a ring of coke around his nostril, Katrina nowhere in sight. She must be powdering her nose in a different way. Randall had instructed Boris to put the food out on the bar by the pool, not too much at once; he didn't want to use it all up. *Cheap bastard*, thought Boris. *He's trying to keep the shit for himself, have it for lunch tomorrow*. The trays were pitiful looking enough as it was: skinny slices of fatty ham and frigging vegetable crackers. You'd be better off at happy hour at the pub eating pickled eggs, for fuck's sake.

Boris had taken two of the puny trays out to the bar by the pool, where Goldilocks wrinkled his nose at them, and Boris liked him a little better for that. Then he sprinted back inside. Still no sign of Katrina, and he booted it into the study. The stash was where he thought, in the desk, a chintzy lock, opened in a snap. Boris grabbed the shit, stuffed it in his socks (he'd long ago started wearing knee-highs, though they dug annoyingly into his upper calves), and did a little overhaul on the design scheme. These assholes had a lot more money than taste. What were they thinking when they decorated these rooms? It was an outrage. Then he sped back to the kitchen. Out of spite, he grabbed some hunks of cold cuts and shoved them in his jacket pockets before yanking open the door opposite the pool and heading for freedom.

Ray had dropped him off earlier up the street, and his van was still parked there, waiting. Boris jumped in, and they drove the two blocks over to Lawrence's. This neighbourhood was starting to feel familiar, almost as if he lived here. As if.

"You took long enough," bitched Ray.

Boris took the cold cuts out of his pocket and handed them to Ray, who seemed slightly placated, though there were bits of lint sticking to them here and there.

"The guy was having a frigging coke party. Everyone was in and out. It was ages before I even got a chance to get near the stuff."

"You mean you got *blow*?"

"No, I stole his TV—whaddya think?"

"Give me some."

"Not till we do this other gig. We need our wits about us." *Not that you have any to begin with*, thought Boris, but he couldn't say that now or Ray would pout and they'd never get the job done.

"C'mon, man, I haven't done blow in ages. I never have enough dough. Shit, I barely have enough money for pot these days."

"That's gonna change, my man. We're on a roll here, you'll see."

"Are we gonna go back later and steal more shit from that Randall guy?"

"I don't think so; he'll be all paranoid now. It's not worth it. And he looks like the type you wouldn't want mad at you—big and slimy."

"So we do this, and then we go back to my place and do the blow, right?"

"Sure," said Boris, wondering if there'd be any of the shit left to sell once Ray got his paws on it. "But we gotta do this fast. We don't know how much time we have, when this guy Lawrence is gonna get home."

"What about that Stevie guy—you made sure he wouldn't show up, right?"

"Stevie's taken care of," assured Boris, praying Stevie had indeed fallen for his little scheme.

***

Stevie was at that moment standing baffled at his friend Jim's door. Jim was surprised to see Stevie, since they'd just parted at four in the morning, after postpub souvlaki on the Danforth. Jim had turned off his phone and had been lying on his couch in his favourite silk kimono, relishing his solitude and sucking back root beer and cheezies to soak up last night's booze. He'd been having a great time watching a very bad kung fu movie, mostly enjoying the bad dubbing, the way the lips never matched the words, and wondering how much people got paid for doing that crap, when he was so rudely interrupted.

Stevie was panting, as if he'd run all the way over. "Why don't you answer your phone!" he cried. "Christ, are you all right? I was so worried I—" He stopped and stared at Jim's face. "What the hell?" He lifted Jim's blond bangs off his forehead and frowned. "You don't look beat up to me!"

"Beat up?" asked Jim, turning as he heard a particularly loud *ayeeee!* from the TV, hoping he hadn't missed something really good.

"You didn't get mugged!" accused Stevie.

"Don't sound so disappointed. Why the hell would you think that?"

"My roommate left a note, said you'd called, you'd been mugged, I'd better get over here right away."

Jim shook his head. "Your roommate's on crack."

"I felt so guilty, thinking how I left you alone waiting for a cab last night and—"

"Nothing happened to me!" insisted Jim, annoyed at Stevie's screeching and Drama Queen antics, his hangover increasing. Suddenly he craved a huge Bloody Caesar.

Stevie stared at Jim a few more seconds before the realization hit. He stared down at his watch. "Oh shit!" He started sweating, and he clenched his stomach.

"You need to use the washroom?" asked Jim, stepping quickly back. Hell, he'd just cleaned the toilet yesterday.

Stevie shook his head. "I was supposed to meet Katrina in Rosedale at a quarter after six. She's going to frigging kill me!"

Jim glanced at a clock on the wall. "Well, you're never going to make it now." He sighed and put an arm around Stevie's shoulders. "Come on in and have a drink, Stevie-poo. You can tell Jimsie all about it."

Katrina waited for Stevie in the bushes down the street from Randy's for 15 minutes before giving up. If she didn't leave soon, she'd risk the chance of Lawrence coming home and finding her rifling through his things. Though how she'd get in without Stevie was beyond her. She didn't have a burgling tool. She didn't have a credit card. Hell, she didn't even have a purse. She'd been afraid to bring any ID in case she dropped it in Lawrence's house and was discovered—things like that happened on TV shows all the time. It seemed moronic, of course, but she supposed people involved in criminal activities got nervous and did stupid things.

Katrina had left her sarong back at the pool during her getaway, and now she was wandering around Rosedale in her bikini, feeling butt naked. The alcohol was starting to wear off, too. Half a margarita and one light beer. Normally that would've made her drunk for hours. The last 2 nights must've made her immune. Maybe she *was* turning into a wino. 'Cause right now, she figured, if only she'd had another drink, she'd have the courage to prance around in her bikini and not give a damn, instead of dashing from tree to tree, hiding behind a shrub every time she heard a car. At this rate it would take half an hour to get to Lawrence's.

And later, she'd have to somehow get home. She'd considered stuffing a little money in her bikini for emergency purposes, but thought if she went for a swim, what would she do with it? And since she was meeting Stevie, who always took care of her and would surely have money (not to mention his lock-picking credit card), they'd share a cab home and she'd pay him back when they got there. It had never occurred to her that Stevie might stand her up.

27 A PHANTOM

Lawrence's grandmother, Gran to everyone who knew her, since anyone her own age was long since dead, was watching TV when she heard the first noises downstairs. The TV was very loud, because Gran liked to pretend she was sitting in the theatre, rather than stuck here in her little room, and the movie was some moronic chop 'n' sock thing with a bunch of Nips running around in nightgowns by the look of things. She'd change the channel if she knew how. But there were three or four of those control gadgets on the table in front of her and she could never remember which was the right one. When she heard the noises, she wanted to lower the volume, too, but couldn't remember how to do that, either. The only option was to get out of her chair and turn the volume control on the TV itself, but she was feeling awfully stiff today.

When the thumping got louder, so loud she could hear it over the bloodcurdling screams on the TV, she began to wonder: Was Lawrence having one of his parties? Maybe they were dancing down there. Lawrence had never mentioned his parties to her, which she found rather insulting, but at the same time, she didn't like to bring the subject up. Somehow, every time he had one of his shindigs, or soirees, or whatever you called them these days, she was so sleepy she couldn't bring herself to leave her bed. She hated to mention this to

Lawrence, because he'd think she was either incredibly lazy or deathly ill. Being thought lazy was bad enough, but ill was worse, for that meant a trip to the doctor, who was as useless as tits on a bull, prodding and poking her and asking her insultingly personal questions. And if he thought she wasn't doing well, it would be the hospital for her or worse—the old folks' home.

Being stuck up on the third floor of her own home was bad enough. She'd repeatedly asked Lawrence to move her down to the first floor, where she'd be close to the kitchen and easier able to get outside. Get out and smell the roses, so to speak. But ever since she'd had problems with that stupid security box in the hall, had yanked at it, and, she supposed, broken it, he'd been adamant that she stay up in her "attic," as she called it, where she couldn't get herself in much trouble. Trouble! How could she get in trouble? She could barely get down the stairs with her arthritis these days. She felt like a prisoner. These young people just didn't understand. They thought they'd be healthy forever. Hah!

But today, hearing more banging and what sounded like a crash, maybe a vase or some china hitting the floor, she thought, enough. If Lawrence wouldn't invite her to his party, she'd crash the damn thing. She was stiff, but she could make it down the stairs if she held on to the railing and went real slow. She couldn't go in her nightie, of course. Everyone else would surely be dressed up. She wondered what the young women would be wearing these days. Lord knew, the clothes they wore on television were ridiculous—barely any clothes at all, with belly buttons and God knows what sticking out all over the place. But Gran had classic clothes that withstood the test of time. As her mother used to say, it didn't matter whether it was in vogue or not, as long as it was elegant and made you look like a lady.

All her dresses were in garment bags at the back of her closet, which took some doing to wrestle free. But finally she was dressed in basic black, with a string of pearls around her neck. She stood admiring herself in the mirror for a moment and wondered why she was dressed like this. A funeral? Who had died? Oh yes! Lawrence's party. Well, she simply needed a touch of makeup, didn't she? This plain old face wouldn't do. But she hadn't worn any makeup in so long she couldn't quite remember where it was. Oh yes—the dresser. A couple of dabs of rouge, a touch of powder, and some red lipstick. Yes, definitely red, and she'd be all set. The stairs would be a trial, but perhaps once she got to the banister she could call down and Lawrence or one of his friends would come up and help. They'd be surprised, too. She could see the pleasant looks on their faces already.

When Katrina finally reached Lawrence's house, she knew entering through the front door was out of the question. Though it was well shaded by trees and shrubs, it was still likely a neighbour would spot a girl in a bikini lurking there and wouldn't soon forget. So she tiptoed around the side, up the long driveway—and was astonished when she saw the service entrance door standing ajar, as if welcoming her in. She was tentatively approaching it when she was even more astonished at the sudden screeching of tires. A few yards ahead, a van had started to reverse. It was veering directly toward her at alarming speed.

Katrina jumped out of the way, one flip-flop twisting, as the back door of the van, not properly closed, disgorged a huge television. It crashed onto the driveway. The van drove over it with a screeching sound, stopped, and a young man jumped out of the driver's seat. He slammed shut the doors, checked the lock and cursed, then jumped back in, too preoccupied to notice Katrina. On the passenger side, as the van started up again, Katrina saw a white, wooly face glaring at her. And thought, *Oh God*. She hadn't been imaging things back at Randy's place. That guy she'd seen . . . and now this one. It really *was* Boris!

So Boris was a burglar. And a bad one at that. He'd left the service door hanging open, so anyone from the street could see it and guess what happened. Anyone, including a passing cop. And no wonder he'd been so nice to her on Friday night! He'd been preparing to follow her to Lawrence's party so he could case the joint! And he followed her to Randy's place, too. He'd stolen the coke. What else had he stolen? Would they blame her?

Katrina was starting to tremble with fear; she was starting to lose it. But she pulled herself together enough to tiptoe inside and shut the door behind her. She *had* to find Lawrence's address book or party list, something to connect her to Jonathan. She'd come this far. But she didn't know how much time she had before Lawrence came home, so she'd better be quick. God, what if someone had seen Boris and his cohort, and the cops were already on their way? No, they'd been parked way back in the driveway. It was doubtful anyone would have seen them. And it was Sunday; the streets were quiet. All the people around here were probably still driving home from their big summer cottages in Muskoka.

But where should she start? She tiptoed through the kitchen and into the foyer. Without the crowds of the other night, it looked monstrously huge. And she noticed for the first time all the doors facing onto it. At least a dozen. Two stood open, probably Boris's handiwork. She peered in, unwilling to step too close for fear of feeling like an accomplice. Yep, there were gaping holes in the rooms where furniture and appliances must have been. But the one room was obviously an office, with its huge desk by the window and shelves of books all around. Katrina was heading toward it when she was stopped in her tracks by a voice from above.

"Are you here for the soiree, dear?"

A phantom leaned against the banister two stories above, a ghastly pale old woman with dabs of red on her cheeks and lips, her chalky hair askew, tentlike black velvet hanging off her scrawny frame.

“Don’t worry, dear,” she screeched again, grabbing harder at the railing. “I’ll be right down!”

The woman started hobbling toward the stairs. And Katrina thought, *Whoever this woman is, I can’t let her see me up close. She’ll tell Lawrence, and he’ll figure out who I am. And he’ll tell Stewart, and it’ll be game over.* All depending, of course, on whether the old lady could see at all. But Katrina couldn’t take the chance.

She ran.

28 SNOTTY BEHAVIOUR

Lawrence was not amused.

First he'd come home to see a smashed TV in his driveway. Then he'd discovered the servants' entrance was ajar. Cautiously entering the house, he'd reached the vestibule to discover Gran sprawled at the foot of the stairs in an evening dress, pearls jammed in her teeth, and red lipstick smeared down her chin. As if spending an hour with Windle and his annoying British pretences weren't enough, now he had to contend with *this*.

Stewart had insisted they meet at a seedy little patio pub at the corner of Sherbourne and Bloor, midway between both their homes. Though Lawrence wasn't sure where Stewart's home *was*. He knew he wasn't living with his parents, because when Stewart first reappeared 5 months ago, he'd casually (too casually, thought Lawrence) asked his friend to be vague if his parents asked about him, seeing as they still lived down the street from Lawrence. When Lawrence asked Stewart the reason for the mystery, Stewart had shrugged and sheepishly said he wanted to surprise them with the success of Life of the Party. And since it would take a few months to get it off the ground, he'd rather not see them till then. Lawrence thought this rather strange, considering Stewart had been successful at whatever he'd been doing in Montreal (he didn't like to ask, because he should've remembered—investment banking or some such thing). He was now acting like a black sheep reentering the fold. Which was the last thing Windle was.

In fact, Lawrence always thought how hopelessly straight the guy was. He'd probably never even sneaked any of Gran's cookies from the jar when he'd had the chance. God knows he'd never done drugs back in high school (though Lawrence never did either; he just talked as if he did so the others wouldn't think he was a hopeless nerd). And his snotty behaviour! As if Stewart really did consider himself an English earl or something. Maybe he'd been faking it so long he actually believed it himself.

And that pipe of his! God knows what he put in the thing. Lawrence remembered his own father smoking a pipe back when he was very small, and the tobacco had an exquisite, vanilla-like scent. Stewart's always smelled like moldy socks. Some English shit, Lawrence supposed. Probably cost a fortune.

Now, as they sat on the depressing street-side patio, Stewart with his pint of Guinness, Lawrence with his strawberry daiquiri, Lawrence coughed as several cars spewed fumes into his quivering nostrils and asked, "Why here?"

"I'd invite you to my apartment, but it's easier to meet halfway, isn't it, old chum?" said Stewart, puffing contentedly away on the evil tobacco. "And frankly, I'd rather not go to your place. There's always the risk of running into my parents, and they're so very inquisitive. They'd want to know all about my love life, my career . . . And to be honest"—here he leaned closer to Lawrence and lowered his voice—"I haven't told them about Life of the Party yet."

"But there's nothing wrong with the business," protested Lawrence.

"That's what you and I think. But my father . . ." Stewart shook his head. "He's old school, my boy. Just hearing the name, I'm sure he'd assume it was an escort service and I was a pimp."

"Well, in a way you are," said Lawrence before he could stop himself. Strangely, Windle seemed to find this remark amusing.

"Right you are. And on that note, let's get down to business, shall we?"

Lawrence was here to give Stewart some cash for the party. He'd already paid half up front, as Stewart always insisted, in case he suddenly cancelled. In which case Stewart would still have to pay his employees something, as many of them had to rearrange their schedules to be PESTS, it being a part-time night job and all.

"So you found Katrina to your liking?" asked Stewart as Lawrence reached for his wallet.

"Katrina?" asked Lawrence.

"The beautiful blonde, the new one I sent you."

"Oh yes. But I thought her name was Cathy."

"No, definitely Katrina. Does that beautiful creature look like a Cathy to you?"

"No," said Lawrence, "but . . ." He stopped, shook his head. "Funny, someone else was asking about her yesterday."

"Oh?"

Lawrence shrugged, wishing he hadn't said anything. "Just a young man who was interested," he said as if it weren't important. He raised his arm and made a fuss of signaling for another round from the bored waiter, hoping to distract Stewart.

"I'm sure there were a lot of those," said Stewart, watching Lawrence closely.

"Oh . . . yes, she's a very attractive girl." Lawrence wished Stewart would stop staring at him. He was not good at deceiving people, and he didn't want to talk about Katrina or Jonathan. For the past 24 hours, the idea had been growing in his brain that it could be Katrina who stole his money and his cuff links, and Jonathan was in it with her. After all, Jonathan had already been asking about her the night of the party, as he vaguely remembered. Had she taken off on him with the loot? And surely only a woman would rearrange his furniture like some anal decorator. And then Jonathan had run up to the bathroom yesterday, where they'd been together that night. Had he been looking for something? Fearful he'd perhaps dropped some incriminating evidence and come to look for it? Why else would he come back to the scene of the crime, implicating himself?

And if Katrina wasn't in cahoots with Jonathan, could it have been another PEST? Was it possible *Stewart* had something to do with the robbery? No, not only was Stewart too upright, it just wouldn't make sense. This was the fifth occasion Lawrence had used Life of the Party, and if Stewart was in the business to rip people off, he would've done it before now, wouldn't he?

And if Stewart had nothing to do with the theft, how did Lawrence go about explaining to him that several shoe boxes full of cash were missing from his bedroom closet? It wasn't like your average Joe had stashes like that lying around. He'd have to confess to stealing from Gran. To Stewart, the all-time straight guy. He'd probably tell his father, the criminal lawyer, and sic the cops on him. Lawrence's face flushed with shame at the very thought of it.

Stewart watched Lawrence and noticed how red he was becoming, which was curious considering his back was to the sun. It was the mention of Katrina that had done it. Maybe the old boy had a crush on her. Or maybe he'd done something ungentlemanly. The very thought made Stewart's blood boil. Katrina seemed such a sweet, innocent girl. But no, Lawrence would never do something like that. He didn't have the confidence; he was too much of a nerd. Even sitting here on the patio, sipping on his girly drink like the pansy of all time, he practically drooled like a little pup every time a halfway decent-looking woman—or man—walked by.

Frankly, it was embarrassing. Stewart remembered why he'd stopped hanging out with the fellow in high school. Though he'd been missing Gran's cookies ever since.

Well, enough of the memories. Time to attack the matter at hand, the one he'd been dreading. Stewart took a long pull on his draft and then asked, "So what did you think of Boris?"

"Boris?" said Lawrence as the waiter placed another daiquiri in front of him. He took the tiny umbrella from the rim and twirled it in his hands.

"Remember, I called on Friday and said I was sending him at the last minute. He had a . . ." Stewart coughed and tried to sound sincere ". . . uh, personal problem to attend to first."

"Boris?" asked Lawrence. He shook his head. "Doesn't ring a bell." He placed the umbrella in his empty glass and took his wallet from his pocket. "How much did you say?" Stewart told him, then Lawrence stopped and stared at him. "Boris. Dark hair? Attractive?"

"I suppose, in a shaggy-dog kind of way—very shaggy. I asked about him when I called late Friday night, but you hadn't seen him yet. I just thought he'd been delayed a little longer than I expected."

"Never introduced himself to me," said Lawrence, "though I saw someone in the kitchen fitting that description. Probably just one of the caterers, though." His eyes narrowed. "Are you *sure* he even showed up?"

"He assured me he did."

Lawrence shook his head and stopped counting his money under the table. "I don't know about this," he said.

"About what?" Stewart leaned forward, wanting to rip the wallet out of Lawrence's spindly fingers.

"This Boris character. How can I be sure he was even there?" He blushed even further, which was quite a feat. "I admit I was rather intoxicated on Friday night, but I don't like to think I'd be taken advantage of because of that." He pouted a little. "After all, it was *my* party."

Stewart sighed. "Okay, okay, pay me for one less PEST." He renegotiated the figure. Lawrence brightened and discreetly handed over the money. "And next time I'll make sure he introduces himself to his hosts, so this doesn't happen again."

Damn right, he thought, annoyed that Lawrence had agreed so readily to lowering the fee. *He could at least have halfheartedly said, "Oh no, I couldn't." And that little fucker Boris. He'd show himself next time all right, or he was out on his ass.* Did his friend Randall even know that Boris was at his party? Damn, he could lose a lot of money this way.

Still, thought Stewart, pasting a smile on his face, *Lawrence hasn't said anything about a theft. Maybe Boris chickened out. Or was planning on coming back later for a big haul. Or maybe Lawrence just didn't look in his jewelry drawers yet. No, the jerk was wearing cuff links with his suit. Shit, he must be the only man in Toronto besides me who'd wear cuff links to a pub on Sunday.*

But surely Boris must have stolen something. Even if he planned to come back later and clean Lawrence out, a little hooligan like that couldn't resist nabbing some pretty prize just for the sake of it.

Stewart sat up looking at Lawrence, still wearing a fake smile. Could it be Boris had stolen something that didn't belong to Lawrence? That Lawrence himself was a thief? Why else would Lawrence stay mum, when he no doubt suspected his chum Stewart all along? The thought was intriguing. Stewart looked at Lawrence in a different light. Maybe he wasn't the total uptight loser he seemed. Maybe he was that most interesting of all specimens—a criminal! What, thought Stewart, could he possibly do with this information?

29 A PINK-FLOWERED FLIP-FLOP

As Lawrence started walking home, he wondered if those drinks of his had been doubles. He could've sworn he just saw a blonde in a bikini getting in a cab. Lawrence knew that fashion wasn't what it used to be. Young girls wore very little these days (not that there was anything wrong with that), but really, some decorum was in order.

Maybe he should've hailed a cab himself. He'd left Gran alone longer than he normally did on weekends, when he spent time with her to make up for all the time he was away during the workweek. He'd left her a note, but she might have forgotten to put on her reading glasses to see it, or forgotten that she'd read it in the first place.

So there she was on the floor when he got home, a fine welcome. You couldn't leave the woman alone for a minute! She seemed to have passed out, but she was, unfortunately, unscathed.

But why the black dress? And the pearls? Lawrence reached down and delicately removed the necklace from Gran's mouth. She stirred, but did not wake up. Was it possible she was in a coma? *No*, he thought as she snored and turned her head. *No such luck. What's she been up to? And why's my TV on the driveway?* Lawrence turned to investigate and saw the open doors to the office and den.

A quick glance told him all he needed to know. His stereos and TVs and computers were gone. Fortunately, his paintings and sculptures were still intact. But his furniture was rearranged. Not as artfully as in his master bedroom yesterday. More like the thief had been in a hurry. Had Gran disturbed him? And was this the burglar's calling card? He supposed interior design was better than letters scrawled in blood or dismembered limbs. But it still sent a chill up Lawrence's spine. Now he knew what people meant when they said they'd been *violated.*

He considered calling the cops. But they'd wonder why Gran had fallen, why she'd been left alone in the house, how often that happened, and why wasn't someone caring for her? They'd also find out about his party 2 nights ago, and all his other parties, and the escorts, and Life of the Party. They'd think he was a fool or a pervert or both. Not to mention the money already stolen from his bedroom. What if they asked Gran questions? Like, were there any other valuables missing? She might remember her money and go searching under her bed and discover that most of it was gone. And then what? She'd no doubt squeal to the cops, and then . . . God, what a mess.

Lawrence headed back to the stairs to deal with Gran and tripped over something. A pink-flowered flip-flop sprawled there on the polished floor, looking like a surfer that had crashed a tea party. Lawrence picked it up and noticed that its strap was broken. Rather large for a woman's, but it certainly couldn't be a man's, not with that hot pink flower on it. That Cathy/Katrina girl was beginning to look more and more like the culprit. Maybe Gran would have a clue.

Lawrence shook her shoulder, and she snorted once and then opened her eyes. She looked confused for a moment, then her mind seemed to clear and she smiled up at her grandson. "How was the shindig, dear?"

"Shindig?"

"Your little soiree. I heard the noises downstairs and decided to dress up and come down and surprise you . . ." She looked around, befuddled. "Hmm, I must've fallen asleep. That seems to happen a lot when you have your parties. Not that I'm saying they're dull, dear. I'm sure they're quite fabulous."

The incredulous look on Lawrence's face spurred Gran on.

"Oh, don't worry, dear, the noise never bothered me. And I always wanted to go down and meet your friends. There must be a lot of girls, mustn't there? There seems to be a lot of squealing sometimes. But for some reason I always get so drowsy, and I keep drifting back to sleep." Gran raised herself slightly and patted Lawrence's arm. "One of these days, though, I'll force myself up, maybe even get gussied up for the occasion, and surprise you."

Gran glanced down at her velvet dress and smiled weakly. "I tried to today. I don't know what happened."

"Well, you surprised me, all right," said Lawrence, as he made a mental note to up the valium dosage for the next party. He also thanked God that Gran's room was on the other side of the house from the pool and hot tub. If she saw everyone running around half naked, she'd have a heart attack—though that wouldn't be so bad.

Gran raised herself a little more and glanced around. "I saw a blonde girl in a bikini. I wonder what happened to her?"

Lawrence's heart fluttered. A blonde in a bikini? That was too much of a coincidence.

"I suppose she was using the pool. Though I think it would have been more appropriate if she covered herself up when she came into the house." Gran gave Lawrence a reprimanding look, which told him he was responsible for the behaviour of his guests. "She looked like that James Bond girl, the one with the knife in her bathing suit."

"She had a knife?!" gasped Lawrence.

"No, no, she just looked like her, you know, Urs . . . Urs . . ."

"Ursula Andress?"

"That's the one. With Sean Connery. Now he was a handsome devil. Still is. None of the others could ever compare to him. I always thought, he—"

"Who was she with?" interrupted Lawrence.

"Who?"

"Ursula Andress."

"Who's Ursula Andress?"

"The James Bond girl, Gran."

Gran looked at Lawrence like he'd had one too many cocktails. "That's the cinema, dear. I think you're a little confused."

Lawrence sighed and wondered if he had the makings for strawberry daiquiris. If not, a straight rum would do. "Well, at least tell me what she looked like."

"Oh—the girl in the bikini. Well, she was blonde . . ."

"Yes?"

Gran shook her head. "That's all I know. Looked like she had a decent little body on her, but otherwise . . . I couldn't see well enough from the third floor to tell." She squinted at Lawrence. "How did I get down here anyway? Did you help me down?"

"Yes, Gran, I did."

"I'm awfully stiff," said Gran, trying to get up.

"Your arthritis, Gran."

"If my room was on the first floor like any caring grandson would allow . . ."

Gran babbled on as Lawrence helped her to her feet, tuning her out. If the culprit in both crimes was this Cathy/Katrina girl, was Jonathan her accomplice or someone else? The girl certainly couldn't have come in here and taken off with all those huge appliances by herself, in her bikini and her broken flip-flop. Not unless she was Wonder Woman. And Lawrence was beginning to wonder if she were.

"Let's get you a nice hot cup of tea," he told Gran, who wobbled a little when she stood.

As Lawrence led her toward the kitchen, Gran said, "It's a soiree, dear—make it a gin and tonic."

30 BURN THAT BIKINI

As soon as Katrina got home, she tore off her bikini, which she now wanted to burn, and threw on a huge, fluffy bathrobe. She felt secure for the first time in hours. No sign of Stevie, which was a mystery, or Boris, which was no surprise. He was probably off fencing his goods somewhere or snorting huge volumes of cocaine. She checked her answering machine, but no message from Stevie to explain his treason. The only message was from Cathy, asking how the pool party went and whether You-Know-Who was there and to give her a call.

Katrina felt exhausted, yet strangely wired. Even though she hadn't had a chance to find Jonathan's number, she had discovered Boris's secret, and that had to be worth something. But her mind was too fuddled at the moment to think, what with the adrenaline rush of fleeing Lawrence's and standing at a busy intersection in still-bright sunlight at 7 P.M., practically naked, all eyes upon her. She'd never heard so much giggling and hooting and cat-calling in her life.

She'd lost a flip-flop at Lawrence's. The one that had twisted on the driveway when she was nearly run over by Boris must have broken a bit, because when she was running away from the phantom upstairs, the strap fell off altogether and flopped off her foot, and she was in too much of a hurry to bend down and pick it up. The ghost woman didn't appear to be moving too fast, but for all she knew, Lawrence and/or the cops could be on the way, and she wasn't taking any chances.

Katrina ran halfway down the block, hobbling in her one flip-flop, before pausing to take it off. She considered throwing it in the bushes but thought it might be like a gun thrown by a killer. Somehow the cops could trace it back to her and accuse her of the robberies. Of course, the other one was sitting squat in the middle of Lawrence's vestibule, already pointing an accusing finger. Could they check it for DNA? Man, she was *so* busted.

Katrina ran and ran, not even daring to look back. It wasn't until she was crossing the bridge to Bloor Street that she wound down to a fast walk, catching her breath, trying to calm down. A quick glance behind. No one following. A glance ahead—why was everyone staring? Shit, she'd been so scared she'd forgotten all about the bikini. A man approaching her wore a big grin, his cell phone to his ear. Was he talking about her? *Buck up*, she told herself. *This is no time to be shy.*

Katrina took a deep breath and stepped in front of him, cutting him off. He stopped, happily surprised, and she asked to borrow his phone. He immediately forgot about his conversation and handed it to her, enjoying the view while she called her local cab company and told them to pick her up at the southeast corner of Bloor and Sherbourne. She racked her brains to think of somewhere less visible where they could pick her up. But unless she chose some back alley and hung out with the winos and the crackheads, she'd be pretty obvious in her bikini no matter where she waited.

Cathy was happy to hear from her.

"Look, I ordered Chinese a while ago. I'm just waiting for it to show up."

"Oh well," said Katrina, "another time then—"

"Shit no," said Cathy, "I'll wait till it gets here, then I'll come over with it. There's plenty for two—probably for six. The dyke's here with her musician friends, and I've gotta get out of here."

"I thought the, uh, *lesbian* was a writer," said Katrina, wanting to use the word *dyke* but unable to get it past her lips. She always wished she could use improper words or swear, but she could only do it in her head. Out loud it sounded ludicrous, like she was doing a bad imitation of a sailor. She felt as silly as the Queen using the F word, for F's sake.

"Oh, she is that, or claims to be, though I sure haven't seen any evidence of it lately. But she plays the guitar, too, much to my everlasting joy. She likes to have her fingers in a lot of pots." Cathy stopped and giggled. "That's a funny line for a lesbian, don't you think? Kind of like saying she's got fat fingers so she's well hung."

Katrina stood there feeling stupid, not sure she got it, so not saying anything.

"Anyway," continued Cathy, still giggling a little, "I can't take a punk rock session right now. I need a little peace and quiet."

"Well, that's perfect," said Katrina. "There's no one here at all."

"I thought you were with Stevie. Wasn't he in on the B&E with you?"

"Shhh! Not on the phone!"

"All right, all right, I'll be over as soon as I can, and you can tell me everything. No wiretapping worries." Cathy was about to hang up when she thought of something. "Hey, you got any beer? The dyke's drunk me dry."

"I think Stevie's got a whole case in the kitchen." Katrina's voice hardened. "And after what he did to me today, I'm ready to drink it all. I'll go in there right now and put some in the fridge."

"Thatta girl," said Cathy. "You're learning."

After Katrina and Cathy ate a good chunk of the Chinese, had a few beers, and Katrina told Cathy all about her afternoon's exploits, Cathy sat back on the couch and belched. She undid the top button on her jeans and said, "Well, it's obvious what you've gotta do now."

"What's obvious?" said Katrina. "I didn't get Jonathan's phone number, soon Lawrence will figure out who I am and think I'm a thief and probably tell Stewart and—"

"You've got to blackmail Boris."

"What!"

"Look," said Cathy, "he had one over on you with all that Glory Dog business—"

"Glory Dog?" repeated Katrina, confused. "Oh, the Glory Riders. Right. Go on."

"But now you know what he does for a living, and it's completely illegal, right?"

"So?"

"So, my little HellKat, now you've got one over on *him*." Cathy picked up her beer bottle and pointed it at Katrina. "He's a professional thief. He knows how to steal things, right?"

Katrina shrugged. "I'm not sure about that one—but I did see him in action."

"Well, he must make a living at it. You say he doesn't have another job, and I hardly think he's a trust-fund baby, so he can't be *that* bad. So what you do is, you tell him you'll rat him out to the cops unless he steals Windle's little black book for you."

"Are you nuts? He'll sic the Glory Riders on me!"

"You want my opinion? I bet he's more scared of those bikers than you are. He just pretends to have an in with them to keep you as a roommate, 'cause he's too creepy to find anyone else, and he's too shitty a crook to afford this dump by himself."

Cathy paused, thinking. "You know, I wonder how he found out about those parties in the first place—you know, Lawrence's and RandyPants."

"He was eavesdropping. I told you how he lurks around . . . and he saw Stewart's card." Katrina stopped, remembering something. "He knew his name."

"Whose name?"

"Stewart's. Boris said he knew him from Montreal."

Cathy threw up her hands. "Well, there you go! The man's a PEST!"

"A PEST?" said Katrina in disbelief. "No way. Stewart would never hire him. He's too creepy. And too ugly."

"He doesn't have bad legs," pointed out Cathy.

"Yeah, that's a *real* selling point."

"It might've helped *me* get into the pool party." Cathy drank some beer, thinking. "Maybe Boris has something on Windle."

"Like what?"

"I don't know, but why else would Windle hire Boris? He must've made Windle do it. You know, like blackmail."

"Like I'm about to do," sighed Katrina. "This is all getting awfully complicated."

Cathy lifted her beer bottle in a toast. "Welcome to the world of crime, hon—nothing simple about it."

By the time Stevie staggered home, having delayed the moment with multiple Caesars, Katrina and Cathy weren't feeling too bad themselves.

"Katrina, Katrina," he moaned, plunking down on the couch next to her, unceremoniously shoving Cathy aside. "I'm sooo sorry."

"You oughtta be," said Cathy, scowling at him. "Lucky for you she—"

Ignoring her, Stevie said, "I would've called you at the pool party if I'd had the number."

"PESTS aren't allowed to get the hosts' phone numbers," recited Katrina, as if she'd memorized one of Stewart's speeches. "Life of the Party rules, so we don't harass them or something."

"Look, Boris screwed me over. He called me and made up this whole . . ." Stevie shook his head, too tired to go on. "It's a long story."

"And a damn good one, I'm sure," said Cathy snidely.

"Dushn't matter," slurred Katrina. "It'sh all over now."

Stevie sat up and stared at Katrina. "You've been drinking!"

"And you haven't?" laughed Cathy.

"We've been making plans," said Katrina indignantly. "What've you been doing?"

"I told you, Boris made up this lame story, and I went over to Jim's, and I couldn't call you, and—"

"We're going to blackmail Boris," announced Katrina.

"What?!"

"It's a long story," said Katrina. She turned wearily to Cathy. "You tell him."

After he'd heard everything, Stevie turned to Katrina, shaking his head. "This is nuts. Ever since you've been hanging around with *her*"—he nudged a shoulder toward Cathy—"you've been drinking like a fish. And now you're burgling and blackmailing and God knows what else. Shit, pretty soon you'll be murdering people in their beds!"

"She hasn't actually burgled or blackmailed," said Cathy, laughing into her beer. "Not *yet*."

"Not to mention," said Stevie, ignoring Cathy again, "we haven't even *started* looking for an apartment together yet. That should be a little higher on your list of priorities than blackmail."

"She wants to get her soul mate's phone number," said Cathy. "That's her priority."

"Soul mate!" snorted Stevie.

"Yes, soul mate. And if you'd been there to help her today like you were supposed to, maybe she wouldn't have to resort to blackmail."

"Maybe she wouldn't have to resort to lesbianism."

"What the fuck does that mean?" Cathy jumped up, ready to fight.

"Guys! Guys!" shouted Katrina, holding her hands over her ears.

Stevie had jumped up now, too, and was ready to lunge at Cathy, when a noise at the door stopped him.

A key turned. The door opened. Boris walked in.

After talking about him for so long, it seemed strange to see him in the flesh. They all felt vaguely guilty. But not as guilty as Boris looked. He shook his mangy hair to cover his face, grunted, and sprinted up the steps. After a paralyzed moment, Stevie yelled after him.

"Hey! I wanna talk to you!"

Boris stopped reluctantly and turned.

"Jim didn't get mugged," accused Stevie.

Boris scratched his head and looked bewildered. "Who the hell's Jim? And why should I care?" He turned and continued up the stairs. Stevie turned to Katrina and threw up his hands. They both stared up the stairs after Boris in bemused awe.

Cathy stared at them. Then she exploded. "Well?!" she screamed.

They turned from looking at the stairs and gaped at her.

"Aren't you going to *do* something?! This is your opportunity. Strike while the iron's hot and all that shit. Don't just sit there quivering like sheep, for fuck's sake!"

Stevie and Katrina didn't move. Cathy shook her head in disgust and pounded up the stairs. The other two seemed to come out of their comas and followed, several steps behind. They could hear her banging on Boris's door.

"You don't know me," they could hear, "but I'm a good friend of Katrina's. My name is Cathy, and I know you're a thief! Katrina saw you leaving the scene of a crime this afternoon. If you don't want us to go to the cops, I suggest you do what we say."

Katrina and Stevie could hear some grunting from Boris but not much else. They saw Cathy take a sudden step back, heard her shout, "Don't you dare!" and then what sounded like a smack, but Cathy was leaning forward, not back, so obviously she was the smacker, not the smackee. And since it was apparent everything was in control, and they didn't want Boris to see them huddling there on the stairs, Katrina and Stevie scurried back down, as if afraid of getting caught snooping on their parents while they argued viciously about them—dying to listen, but afraid of what they might hear.

31 DRY HEAVES

Stevie always had Mondays off since the restaurant where he worked, Extreme!, was closed. Today, he'd rather be working than feeling the way he was. He meant to get up early and go to Stewart Windle's office, but after he woke up, puked, and went to lay down just for a minute, he'd fallen back asleep till three.

Stevie would have put off his mission till tomorrow, but he was sure that Boris, being blackmailed as he was, would probably try to break into Stewart's office tonight and steal his little black book. Stevie had to beat him to it. He couldn't have this Jonathan guy's phone number falling into the wrong hands.

Stevie made it over to the address listed on Windle's business card just before five. He assumed it was a regular business with regular office hours. There was nothing regular about the neighbourhood, however. Stevie was aghast. The very thought of sweet Katrina negotiating these treacherous sidewalks made him ill. More ill, in fact, than he'd felt on the streetcar ride, praying he wouldn't throw up. He nearly jumped out of his skin when one of the men from the next-door hostel started yelling. Stevie whirled around before he realized the man was shouting and spitting at the ground and not him.

He'd thought of calling ahead and making an appointment, but if Windle turned him away, and Stevie later showed up at his office, the man would be hostile. He might not even get in the door. So Stevie decided to make it a surprise and hope for the best.

Stevie opened the door at a grunt from within. The man at the desk, whose face Stevie suspected was usually peachy, was tinged green. In spite of that, he looked like a slick piece of work, what with his pricey suit and perfectly combed hair. Even his fingernails were buffed. If he spent as much money on his office as he obviously spent on himself, the place would be pretty impressive. As it was . . . well, Stevie had to wonder if poor Katrina would ever get paid. Talk about a fly-by-night operation. Not a single adornment or spare piece of furniture. No packing necessary. Just cancel the phone and go.

Stewart, who'd been about to call it a day, was less than thrilled to have a visitor. Usually he worked late and on weekends. But work today had been one long torment. From the moment he woke up this morning, his stomach had been in agony. He suspected it was caused by his poor judgment in eating at that horrendous little pub the night before after Lawrence had left. Bangers and mash, indeed! He could have sworn the sausages were Spam, molded to look like something edible. And the taste—he didn't even want to think about the taste, in case it caused more dry heaves. He would've sent the monstrosities back to the kitchen if he hadn't been so hungry and three sheets to the wind. If only, if only . . .

What was this person in front of him? Male? Female? When it opened its mouth and a high voice issued forth, Stewart was even more unsure.

"I've come to see about a job with Life of the Party," said Stevie, trying to sound stronger than he currently felt.

"Perhaps tomorrow," said Stewart dubiously, staring at the she-male. "I was just leaving for the day."

"But it has to be . . . I'd really like to see you today, if you don't mind. I have to work all day tomorrow."

Stewart sighed and sat back down. Stevie noticed Stewart's jacket was slung on the back of his chair, the infamous little black book peeping out of an inner pocket.

"You have a reference?" asked Windle, wanting to get this over with. "The ad hasn't been online for several days."

"Cathy told me about it," said Stevie, not wanting to mention Katrina, preferring this Windle character didn't know she was his roommate. Something about the guy was too perfect, too proper, which made him seem slimy in Stevie's mind.

"Cathy, the heavy girl?" asked Stewart.

The mouthy girl, Stevie wanted to say, but instead said, "Pleasantly plump, yes. Voluptuous, some might say."

"Yes," said Stewart, "some."

He realized the person was still standing and motioned it to sit, noting the way it tossed back its hair as it did. It sat like a man, though, its legs wide apart. Though Stewart supposed that didn't mean anything these days. He decided a little more digging was in order.

"This Cathy, is she a friend of yours? Girlfriend?"

"Girlfriend!" snorted Stevie. Then, realizing this attitude wouldn't ingratiate him with his interviewer, he softened his voice and said, "No, just a friend." He took a deep breath and thought, what the hell, he was already here under false pretenses, so he added, "A friend of my girlfriend's, actually."

Did that help? wondered Stewart. Not really. It could be a lesbian sitting in front of him. He leaned forward and inspected the face. A little hair here and there. And was that an Adam's apple? Perhaps, though a small one. Well, at least he thought he knew now what he was dealing with. Not that it helped the person's employment prospects any. If this was a man, he was most certainly a flamer. And Stewart didn't think that would go over so well with most of his hosts, who, like Randall, were macho wankers—though Lawrence would love the guy for sure.

Stewart decided to go through the motions anyway. He could conduct a fake interview and send the . . . err . . . whatever . . . on its way. Make a show of getting its phone number. Don't call me, I'll never call you.

"So you're available evenings?" he asked, pulling out a pen and a tiny scrap of paper from his desk. He had to pretend to be writing something.

"Oh yes," said Stevie, who worked 5 nights a week.

"Do you own a suit?" asked Stewart dubiously, unsure whether he should be asking about a cocktail dress instead.

"Of course," sniffed Stevie, wondering where this Brit got off, treating him like a moron. "I own two."

He was about to go into detail to prove his point, describing the suits, their colours, their fabric, where they'd been bought, but he was interrupted by the phone ringing on Stewart's desk, its only embellishment.

"Boris here," Stewart heard as he picked up the phone, and inwardly groaned. "I need to see you right away."

"I'm in the middle of something right now, laddie. If you could call me back—"

"I want my money," snarled Boris.

"Money?" asked Stewart, stumped.

"You know, for the two parties."

Stewart was flabbergasted. "You mean you expect to get *paid*?"

Boris's voice was huffy. "I'm an employee, *aren't* I?"

"I suppose next you'll be wanting benefits."

"Well, I wouldn't mind."

"Look here, we need to talk."

"Righto. I'll swing by right now," offered Boris.

"No, no, I'm in the middle of something," Stewart glanced dubiously at the person in front of him, who was twirling its hair in its fingertips, "and I'm heading out for dinner after this."

"You buying?" asked Boris.

"You can meet me for a drink."

"No fucking fringe benefits, eh?" snorted Boris.

"Meet me at Giovanni's on Church in an hour."

"Church? You mean Faggotville? I ain't goin' to Faggotville, man."

"Well, I am, and if you want to see me *and* keep your current position, that's where I'll be."

Stewart hung up, irritated. The last thing he wanted as he dug into a plate of pasta was Boris's surly face across the table. But the thug had to be set straight. And Stewart seriously needed food. Though he wasn't sure if those were hunger pangs or food-poisoning pangs gurgling in his stomach. But surely the worst of it was over, seeing as he hadn't eaten in almost 24 hours. And Giovanni's was a reputable place where he'd eaten many times and wouldn't be taking his life in his hands.

Stewart glanced at the person in front of him, who'd realized his phone conversation was finished and had started babbling about suits for some reason. Then he surreptitiously glanced at his watch. He didn't need an hour before meeting Boris, but he did need a couple of drinks. A couple of gin and tonics not only would make it easier to deal with that animal, but might calm his stomach, too. Didn't they used to drink tonic in India for that sort of thing? And God knows, back in the Colonial days, the food there must have been even worse than the Spam sausages at Ye Olde Pub.

Stewart was thinking these things, an occasional word about silks and worsteds registering from the person opposite and wishing that person would just go away, when his stomach contracted horribly, blitzed with another spasm. Unable to talk from the intense pain, Stewart could only grimace and hold up a finger to the stranger before he dashed into the adjoining room and its awaiting toilet.

Stevie realized he'd been babbling, but seriously, it was like talking to a wall with this guy. He really wasn't all there. Could he be some kind of drug addict? He'd sounded okay on the phone, but the moment he hung up, he'd gone all green and spaced out again. Probably jonesing for another hit.

But when Windle sprinted into the adjoining room, Stevie couldn't believe his luck. Alone with the little black book! He got a quick glimpse of the other room before Windle slammed the door. Was that a *bed* in there? Did this hoity-toity English type actually *live* in his office? He couldn't wait to tell Katrina, who practically drooled when she talked about the guy. Women were so easily fooled.

But first things first. Keeping his eye on the adjoining door, Stevie tiptoed over to Windle's jacket. He was bending over to slip his hand inside the pocket when the sounds issuing forth from the other room stopped him cold. Stevie broke into an icy sweat. His dry heaves came back and threatened to become wet. He had to take several deep breaths to steady himself. It must be heroin; the guy had to be on smack. He'd heard about how you threw up after doing it. But this guy obviously wasn't just throwing up. In fact, Stevie couldn't even think about what he was doing. He shuddered, regained control, and grabbed the little black book. If he stopped to spew now, he'd get caught in the act. He could spew on the street if he had to—those guys out there wouldn't even notice him doing it. Stevie zipped his booty into his coat pocket and darted out the door.

When Stewart staggered back into the office, weak and trembling, he noticed the prospective employee was gone. Had the horrific sounds and fumes scared him off? Or was he just another flaky flamer? No matter. Stewart was glad to be rid of him. He slipped on his jacket and turned off the lights.

Fortification awaited. A few G&T's would kill whatever bugs were swarming inside of him. And maybe a few dashes of bitters, just for good measure.

32 LITTLE BLACK BOOK

When Stevie got home, he was relieved to find himself alone in the house. Still reeling from the sounds and smells of Windle's office, he thought what the hell and cracked open a beer. Then he went up to his room, locked the door, and sat down to inspect the little black book.

There were no last names. No addresses, only phone numbers. Dates with initials beside them. Was this Windle's entire accounting system? Hell, the guy must keep everything in his head. Pretty impressive for a dope fiend.

There were two pages of J's. Stevie quickly flipped through. Jays, Jameses, Javiers, Jenns, Jims, Jodys, Joes, Joans . . . Stevie hadn't realized so many names started with a J. And then there were the Johns, and then . . . one Jonathan.

Stevie wanted to throw the entire book away, just to be on the safe side, but Katrina was expecting it. Besides, he'd be her hero when he presented it to her, no thanks to Boris. He carefully tore out the page with the Jonathan on it. He knew he should burn it in the wastebasket, like they always did in the movies, but for one, his wastebasket was full and would surely pose a fire hazard, and for another, he was curious about this Jonathan guy. Maybe he'd want to call him himself, arrange a little meeting where he could watch him from afar, just to see what he looked like.

So Stevie stuck the piece of paper with Jonathan's number inside the book he was reading, stuck the little black book in the back pocket of his jeans until he could figure out a brilliant hiding place from Boris, and went downstairs for another beer. He was feeling better already.

***

By the time Boris arrived at Giovanni's, Stewart was feeling better, too. He was on his third double gin and tonic with plenty of bitters. The taste was curiously appealing, crisp yet medicinal. His stomach had stopped contracting, and he felt he might live to see another day. Stewart decided to put off eating. Food at this point would be foolish. Let the stomach cure itself before he assaulted it anew.

Boris tried his best to swagger into the restaurant, but the lewd looks he'd received on Church Street had unnerved him. He wasn't used to feeling like a piece of meat; he was definitely on the wrong end of the kebab. If he hadn't been forced into this cruddy situation by that twat Katrina, he wouldn't have come within a mile of this place.

Last night he'd considered scoffing at her little blackmail scheme and threatening to sic the Glory Riders on her and her little friends. But that girl Cathy scared the shit out of him. He knew she'd never back down. He wondered if she was doing Katrina. She sure as hell looked like she was. Boris wondered what ole' Stevie thought about that. Must be pissing his pants in frustration.

Talk about pants. Were there any women in this joint? Boris didn't see even one. He hadn't thought Windle was queer, but then again, he hadn't thought much about it at all. And there he was, sitting at the bar, sandwiched between two suits. Two very dapper and limp-wristed suits.

When Boris thought about it, this wasn't such a bad idea. Even if he grabbed Windle all over, trying to get at his little black book, nobody would think twice about it. Except maybe Windle. And if he was hanging out here, hell, he'd probably love it.

"Boris, my man!" exclaimed Windle, as if happy to see him.

Hell, thought Boris, *the guy's sloshed*.

"Sit yourself down," said Windle, indicating a stool one of the suits was leaning against.

"Uh, that's okay . . ." began Boris, but the suit lifted his nose huffily and slid down the bar. Windle patted the seat, and Boris sat with some hesitation, wondering what kind of germs were assembled on the worn red leather.

Windle caught the bartender's eye and motioned for two more drinks.

"What's that?" asked Boris suspiciously.

"G&T. Terrific for the constitution."

"I'll just take a beer, thanks."

"As you wish." Windle placed the order and looked Boris over. "You don't have a vast wardrobe, I gather."

"I got five of everything," said Boris huffily. "It keeps it easy."

"Hmm," said Windle, raising an eyebrow. "So how was yesterday?"

"Yesterday?" repeated Boris stupidly. When he thought of yesterday, the first memory was of the coke and the two broads he and Ray had picked up with it. Boris wasn't much into coke. It didn't do a thing for him. And the chick he'd picked up didn't do a lot for him either. He left her and Ray and the other chick when it became obvious they were getting into a three-way. Just 'cause coke didn't lift him and his dick up the way they said it did wasn't his fault. Must be his genes or something. Fuck.

"The pool party?" prompted Windle, accepting his cocktail from the bartender and daintily sipping it, which he followed with a tremendous belch. "Oh, excuse me, but that did me a world of good!"

"Oh, that," said Boris, leaning away from the reek of gin. Goddamn pine needles—how did anyone drink that shit? "Yeah, the pool party was okay."

"I called your host Randall yesterday, and he said you did a fine job. Though he did sound rather angry and distracted." Windle narrowed his eyes. "Would you know anything about that?"

Boris shrugged. "The guy's a little high-strung." *But not so high now*, he thought, smirking.

"Well, I hope you said goodbye. I was told you neglected to do so on Friday night at Lawrence's party. In fact, he failed to make your acquaintance at all."

Boris drank half his beer in one gulp and eyed Windle's jacket. It was hot in here. Why hadn't he taken the damn thing off? It'd be a lot easier to grab the book that way. "I tried, man, but he was always surrounded by chicks. And he was shit-faced. Tell the truth, I was embarrassed for the guy."

"I wasn't able to charge him for your services, since he wasn't aware that you were even there."

"You mean I don't get paid?"

"You don't get paid in the first place, you twit." Windle leaned forward and lowered his voice. "You're there to burgle, are you not?"

"Did Lawrence tell you I stole stuff?"

"Oddly enough, no." Stewart leaned forward even closer, and Boris's eyes probed for the little black book, but there was no hint of it in his jacket pockets. "I'm curious. What *did* you steal?"

Boris shrugged and picked at his fingernails. "Just a little cash. And some major appliances."

"I saw Lawrence yesterday, and he didn't say anything about—"

"We did the big stuff yesterday afternoon. I did the cash Friday night."

"A lot of cash?"

"You betcha."

Stewart leaned even closer. "How much?"

Boris only grinned.

"I'll be damned." Stewart sat back and thought about this for a moment. So his earlier suspicions had been right; Lawrence *was* a criminal. Was he embezzling from his company? If so, why would he stash the cash in his house, instead of in some Bahamian or Swiss account like everyone else? The man was a fool, certainly, but still . . .

"And Randall?" he asked. "What did you get from him?"

"What am I telling you this shit for? You want a cut or what?"

"No, I just like to keep tabs on my friends. What did Randall have?"

"Drugs."

"Good Lord!" Stewart scratched his head. Now *this* was getting really interesting. Randall a drug dealer! And all this time Stewart had thought his biggest interests were booze and women.

"What kind?"

"Coke."

Well, that certainly fit, thought Stewart. Coke went with booze, and women, like pot, went with cookies and potato chips. For a moment he was excited, discovering the hidden and nefarious lives of his friends. But a second later he was worried. Here he was, trying to go straight by being employed by his so-called straight friends, and now he was finding out they were all as crooked as pretzels. Lawrence an embezzler, Randall a coke dealer . . . what might the others be?

Stewart knew many of his old high-school friends had lost a lot of money on the stock market a few years ago, having all invested in the same mineral company that went tits up, but really, hadn't they invested in anything else? And surely their wealthy families could help them out? They couldn't all be as stingy as Stewart's father, who'd never given him a dime. Not that he'd dared ask.

Oh God, thought Stewart, his stomach revolting again for the first time in an hour—what if his father got wind of any of this? He'd let slide little comments over the years indicating he was not entirely convinced that Stewart had been doing what he'd said he'd been doing, career-wise. If he found out about these criminals Stewart was doing business with, it would be game over. He'd do a background check on Stewart and find out about him, too. The only reason he probably hadn't done it before was that Stewart's mother wouldn't let him. And once old Dad found out everything . . . he'd have his lawyers tear the trust fund apart, and Stewart would be out on his ass.

Stewart's thoughts were interrupted by someone's hands on his stomach. He looked up and realized it was Boris, gently patting his midsection.

"What the . . ."

"You're in pretty good shape for an old guy, Windle," said Boris, his hands still on Stewart's abs, trying to get at the inside pockets of his jacket. "You work out?"

Stewart swiveled in his stool and puffed out his chest, his jacket falling open. "Comes naturally," he said, drunk enough not to think it out of the ordinary to have a near-stranger rubbing his belly.

Boris quickly frisked the jacket pockets, then patted the other side of Windle's belly to avert suspicion. He looked bewildered. "Hmm," he murmured.

"What?" asked Stewart, concerned. "Is one side firmer than the other?"

"No, no, nothing like that. It's just . . . impressive, is all. Hey, you wanna buy me another beer?"

Stewart waved at the bartender for another round, and Boris wondered if there were more pockets inside the guy's jacket, maybe higher up. He hadn't felt anything in the lower pockets at all. And just patting Windle's pudgy belly had made him cringe. The thought of running his fingers over the guy's man-boobs and digging around . . . Boris downed the rest of his beer, trying to give himself strength. Windle hadn't seemed to mind his groping, but then, he was blotto.

Stewart wondered briefly at Boris's sudden affection and decided he must be drunk. He was now babbling on about free weights and boxing, when it was apparent the fellow had never flexed a muscle in his life. Stewart tuned out, nodding now and then to be sociable, and let his thoughts return to Life of the Party. He was beginning to doubt he could even stay in the business. The whole thing, which had been so sparkling clean and shiny, was turning into a tarnished mess. But what else could he do? No way he could be a scam artist in this town, not with all his parents' connections. And he couldn't go back to Montreal, where everyone he'd fleeced would be only too happy to draw and quarter him. He'd have to hit another big town, and frankly, he didn't have the enthusiasm he once had. It was all just so much *work*.

But what else could he do? Get a legit job in the city? He didn't have the education or the training for anything else. What was he going to do, be a manger at Tim Horton's? Telephone soliciting? Panhandling? Maybe it was time to run. Take the earnings from Life of the Party, including the PESTS' wages, and hang out in Mexico or anywhere else cheap until it was time to collect his trust fund. Stay out of his father's way, lay low. Because if he carried on with Life of the Party, with all the criminals apparently involved, his father would be onto him in no time.

Jesus, maybe it wasn't such a bad thing that Boris had entered the picture. Otherwise, Stewart would never have known about the real, sordid lives his so-called friends had been hiding. The little weasel had ferreted out the truth. Maybe Stewart should throw in with him and get in on the burglary action, collect as much money as he could before fleeing town. Hell, maybe he should just start burgling his friends' houses on his own. But that sort of hands-on, physical theft had never really been his style. And what if he got caught? Bye-bye trust fund. Bye-bye future. Stewart had to down his G&T at the very thought of it.

He almost dropped his drink when Boris touched him again, this time on the chest.

"Nice pecs," said Boris, blushing a little, sweat beaded on his brow.

"For someone who was bloody scared to even step foot on Church Street, you're acting awfully gay, son," said Stewart, sitting up. "What is this, flamer day?"

"Man, haven't you been listening to a word I said?" exclaimed Boris, who hurriedly placed his hands in his lap, then moved them again, not wanting something that had touched Windle's body to be that close to his family jewels. "I was talkin' about working out, and I was just comparing the two of us is all." Christ, no sign of the frigging book, and now this asshole thought he was making a pass at him. "Shit, I ain't no flamer."

"There was one in my office earlier," said Windle, putting down his drink and turning to Boris. "Looking for a job. Couldn't tell whether it was male or female at first, to tell the truth, all that long hair and the high voice. Of course, he might get twice the work that way; I could send him out as either. He'd probably be fabulous on the cocktail circuit."

"Long hair?" repeated Boris. "High voice?"

"Uh-huh," nodded Stewart. "I should have asked it out on a date."

Shit, thought Boris. *That little asshole Stevie got to Windle before me. No wonder I can't find the damn book, in spite of all this groping*. How humiliating. He'd noticed the other queers along the bar watching with great amusement as he'd fondled Windle. Might as well throw on some chaps right now and get it over with.

"Uh, I gotta go," he said suddenly, rising from his bar stool.

"But you haven't finished your beer," said Stewart, amused at Boris's sudden discomfort. "And you haven't even squeezed my thighs yet." He said this loudly, to the amusement of the other customers, as they all watched Boris scurrying to the exit.

"Hey!" yelled Stewart, "I thought you wanted to hit the gay bars!"

Boris, beet red and sweating profusely now, flung open the door to a bar full of laughter and gave them all the finger.

33 BORIS ON TOP

Katrina had offered to work a bit late that night in the hopes that Boris would have the little black book by the time she got home. She was too excited and nervous to just pace around the living room waiting, and after Stevie's bender last night, he'd be in no mood for socializing. The volcanic snores erupting from his bedroom this morning had been proof of that.

Cathy called and sounded alarmed when Katrina chirped into the phone.

"Jesus, you sound like you drank the café dry! Or have you been snorting some of that Randy guy's coke on the sly?"

"I'm waiting for the blackmail scheme to pan out," whispered Katrina, glancing around to make sure she wasn't overheard.

"Ah! The little black book, compliments of Boris . . . compliments of *me*," snorted Cathy. "Well, good luck with your Prince Charming, sweets. I'm going over to Windle's tomorrow afternoon to get my pay from Lawrence's party. Can you get away for a little while and come with me?"

"I only get a coffee break tomorrow. I won't have time."

"Yeah," said Cathy. "More coffee—just what you need."

Katrina, feeling a sudden urge to pee at the mere mention of coffee, ignored that one; she'd have to cut this short. "Hey, do you think you could pick up my money while you're at it? I don't see when I'll get a chance in the next couple of days, and I don't want to wait that long."

"You're very trusting, aren't you?" teased Cathy.

"I know where you live."

Cathy laughed. "I'll see if I can find the time. Windle and I have a lot of catching up to do."

"You just met the guy."

"That's what I mean," purred Cathy.

"You really like him, don't you?"

"He has a certain wayward charm."

"Just don't get charmed out of our money," said Katrina just before hanging up. "It's been known to happen."

***

When Boris arrived home, what he really wanted was an hour-long, scalding-hot shower to wash away the germs and humiliation from Giovanni's. But he was on a mission. No sign of Stevie the thief in the living room or kitchen, so he crept up to the weasel's bedroom. The door was ajar, the lights on. He was passed out, fully clothed, on top of the covers. The guy reeked of beer. Which said something, since Boris had been drinking beer himself.

Boris considered frisking Stevie for the little black book, but he'd had enough of that for one night. He'd search the room first instead and pray his fingers wouldn't have to do the walking.

The guy wasn't exactly a master criminal. As soon as Boris picked up the book on the bedside table—*Pride and Prejudice?* Jesus, what was that?—a torn page slipped out. And whaddya know—the name *Jonathan* was written on the very top. Okay, so where was the rest of the book? Boris rifled through the table's drawers but came up empty. Then he spotted a piece of paper sticking out from under the base of the reading lamp. It wasn't what he was looking for, but it could be interesting.

The classifieds. Apartments for rent, with ads circled in red. Boris started to read, his lips moving. He was not impressed. The newspaper clenched in one hand, the page from the little black book in the other, he pounced onto the bed and straddled Stevie.

"What's this?" he shouted, and Stevie kept snoring. Boris stuck his mouth in Stevie's ear. "What the fuck is *this*?!"

Stevie's eyelids fluttered, then popped open. In a millisecond, he was aware that Boris was on top of him and he was about to be either raped or murdered. He knew the guy was a little crazed, but he hadn't suspected he was completely deranged.

Boris stuck the page with Jonathan's name in Stevie's face.

"What's this?" he asked again, quieter this time, since it was obvious Stevie was awake and paying attention. "What've you been up to?"

Stevie tried to sit up, but that brought him in closer contact with Boris, so he lay back down again. "I stole the book from Windle," he admitted.

"That was supposed to be *my* job."

"I didn't want Katrina to get Jonathan's number, so I took it before you could."

"So you got the number, I see. Where's the rest of the frigging book?"

Stevie wriggled beneath Boris, which freaked him out until he realized Stevie was reaching for the book in the back pocket of his jeans. He held it up. Boris tried to grab it from him, but Stevie held it tight. Boris considered making another grab for it, then decided to switch gears for the moment. He waved the classifieds in Stevie's nose.

"And what's *this*?"

"I . . . well . . . I was thinking of looking for a place. You know it's getting kind of crowded around here."

"Just *you*?" asked Boris. He scowled and leaned forward. "I kind of had an idea I heard you and Katrina talking about it."

"Katrina?" said Stevie innocently. "No way."

"You know Len doesn't want her moving out."

"Oh, come on. Len's in Bolivia for all we know."

"Harley isn't," said Boris ominously. "Katrina stays put."

"We were just checking things out is all," said Stevie, wishing he didn't sound so lame. "You know, seeing what the rents were like."

Boris shook his head in disgust. "Windle thinks you're a flamer, but I know better." He shook out the newspaper and began to read: "Danforth/Pape, comfy 1 bedroom, deck, laundry . . . Lower Riverdale, sunny 1 bedroom, non-smoking, no pets." He sneered at Stevie. "You're a pet, aren't you? Katrina's little pet. Funny, these are all *one* bedrooms."

Stevie looked away. "That's all we can afford."

"Trying to make a little love nest for you and your girlfriend? I see the way you look at her. Shit, it gives me the creeps. That fag act doesn't fool me."

Stevie wriggled his leg, which was starting to go numb, and Boris took a little weight off and sat back. Stevie decided to go for the offensive, even if his current prisoner-like status didn't give him much leverage.

"Look, Boris, do you really think you're in a position to keep us here?"

"What's that supposed to mean?"

"Katrina saw you taking off from Lawrence's with a van full of his property," pointed out Stevie. "We could call the cops."

"You've got no proof." Boris waved the piece of paper. "But I do. I know that you stole her boyfriend's phone number out of the book."

"He's not her boyfriend! And she won't know I ripped the number out unless you tell her. And if you even consider that, I bet there's lots of other stuff the cops could bust you for."

Boris was in a bit of a bind. At that very moment he had a whack of Randall's coke stashed in his bedroom and was wondering why he hadn't just left it in Ray's van, though he knew if he'd left it there, it would be up Ray's nose by now. If he told Katrina about Stevie tearing out the number, then Stevie would tell the cops about him. But if Katrina found out that Stevie stole the book for her, instead of Boris, then she might still go to the cops, since he hadn't done what she'd demanded.

Of course, the result was the same—she'd get the book, only without the number she was hoping for. And what if she was a stickler for a deal—you didn't do what you promised, so I'm telling. Not to mention she'd probably tell that scary friend of hers, Cathy. And even if Katrina didn't sic the cops on Boris, that bitch would for sure.

So Boris said to Stevie, "Look, I'm going to take the book and tell Katrina that I stole it."

Stevie held tightly to the black book. "No way!"

Boris held out his hand. "If I get credit for stealing it, I'll forget that I saw these classifieds with all the cute little circles, and I won't tell the Glory Riders about it."

"The Glory Riders! Shit, Boris!"

Boris reached for the book. "We got a deal?"

Stevie hesitated. "But I get to keep the page with Jonathan's number. I might want to check the guy out."

"You're so pathetic." Boris sighed. "But okay."

They quickly swapped the little black book and the torn page. Stevie squirmed. "You can get off me now."

"Like I ever wanted to be *on* you," snorted Boris, suddenly aware of his position on top of Stevie. He'd been so intent on his mission it hadn't even occurred to him. Which kind of freaked him out—how could he not be aware of sitting on top of some faux faggot? He was quickly disengaging himself when the sound of the door opening downstairs caused him to stop.

"Shit, that must be Katrina." He put a finger to his lips. "Pretend to be asleep." He grinned and looked more like a Rottweiler than a sheepdog as he waved the black book at Stevie. "I got something to give her."

Stevie shuddered and pulled the covers over his head.

34 TWO JOHNS BUT NO JONATHAN

Katrina, who was not a shrieker since it was a thing that tended to call attention to yourself, actually shrieked with excitement when Boris presented her with the little black book.

"Did you have a hard time getting it?" she asked as she began flipping through the pages.

"Piece of cake," lied Boris.

"I should tell Stevie. Is he home?"

"Don't bother; he's upstairs snoring like a hog."

"Oh," said Katrina, disappointed. She'd been mad at Stevie last night for not showing up at Lawrence's, but that was Boris's fault, not his. She'd already forgiven him. And she always like sharing things with Stevie, even if she'd been neglecting him a little lately because of her new friendship with Cathy. "Guess it'll have to wait till morning." She flipped eagerly through the book, then stopped suddenly, bewildered.

"Huh?" she grunted.

"What?"

"I don't see any Jonathans in here. Two Johns, but no Jonathan."

"Maybe Windle just calls him John."

"He didn't look like a plain old John to me." Katrina forced a smile. "But I'll give it a try."

"Yeah—anything else?"

Katrina didn't want to shake Boris's hand. The thought of touching him was too creepy, but a deal was a deal, so they shook and she said, "So we're all clear then; everything's settled?"

Boris shrugged. "Just don't blame me if you still can't find the guy. I did the best I could."

"I know, I know. I won't rat you out." Katrina hesitated. "And the Glory Riders?"

"All settled," said Boris. "Don't worry your pretty little head about it." He coughed as if something had stuck in his throat. "Look, I got stuff to do. I gotta go." He bounded up the stairs to his room.

Katrina slumped with relief, but it was short-lived. She was an accomplice to theft now, which made her an actual criminal, too. Her roommate was probably about to slink through the night burgling to his heart's content, and she wasn't lifting a finger to stop him.

She did have to lift her fingers, though, and pick up the phone. And call two strange men. A shyness attack hit her so hard she would have broken into a sweat if she were capable of it. Instead, being a natural beauty, she broke into a glow.

A drink. A drink would make her brave. Katrina peered in the fridge. Not even a single beer. Stevie had definitely been on a roll last night. She checked the cupboards over the fridge, which sometimes held something halfway palatable, and at the very back discovered a dusty bottle of Jamaican overproof rum that Stevie had brought back with him from vacation last year. He'd stashed it there when he moved in, though she wondered why, since he claimed it was undrinkable, rougher than a shot of high-test gasoline. *Well, it couldn't be that bad*, thought Katrina, *or it wouldn't be legal to drink the stuff. LEGAL.* She shouldn't even be thinking that word right now.

She crawled onto the kitchen counter and reached up and pulled down the bottle and poured a tiny bit into a rocks glass. Maybe just a touch more. Considered sniffing it but decided that wouldn't be the best idea. No sipping, either, just right down the hatch. But maybe a couple of deep breaths first, expand the lungs before she expanded her liver.

Katrina's face was green and twisted when Boris hurried through the kitchen, the coke stashed in his socks. *Damn, the bitch looks like she'd just OD'd.* He'd call 911 if he gave a shit. And if he wasn't in such a hurry to get over to the clubhouse and try to unload the coke with one of those guys. The thought scared the shit out of him, but where else could he sell the stuff? Besides, he was going to give Harley an earful about Katrina's moving plans. Little Katrina had a surprise in store for her. So he'd promised not to sic the Glory Riders on her and Stevie. He was a crook, for fuck's sake. When did a crook ever keep his word?

Katrina was too busy trying not to throw up to really notice Boris's exit. The rum was as vile as Stevie had said. Those Jamaicans must have stomachs like steel drums.

When she finally had control over her gag reflex, she picked up the phone, feeling strangely gregarious.

The first number she called was an answering machine. A man calling himself John, not Jonathan. And his voice didn't sound at all familiar. Well, sometimes people's voices did sound different on the phone than in person. Katrina barreled straight ahead.

"Hi, my name's Katrina, though I suppose you wouldn't know that when I met you at the party on Friday night. I don't think I mentioned it. I was kind of tipsy. It was at Lawrence's house, remember? The second floor. The bathroom. I'm sorry about what I did to you, I mean your poor pants . . ."

Katrina paused, thinking that probably didn't sound so good but forced herself to go on. "Anyway, if you remember me and this is you, give me a call, please." She left her number, then quickly added, "Oh, I'm the blonde one, green eyes, about 5-10, 120 pounds." Katrina hung up, then thought, how stupid was that, describing herself. How many women might Jonathan have been hanging out with in the bathroom that night?

The second number was a machine again. This time a woman's voice, claiming this was Laura and John's place. Katrina forged on before she could give herself a chance to think, basically leaving the same message as before. It wasn't until she hung up, breathless, that it occurred to her that maybe this Laura person was Jonathan's girlfriend, and if so, he was going to be in a whole lot of trouble after the message she'd just left. Not that he shouldn't be, if he'd been flirting with Katrina at a party.

"Smells like a frigging gas station in here."

Katrina whirled to see Stevie sniffing the air. He saw the rum bottle and nodded. "So you phoned the guy."

Katrina eyed him curiously. "How'd you know I got the book?"

"Well, I assumed you would. The plan was that Boris would get it for you, *or else*."

Stevie's tone was mocking, but he looked somehow guilty, and she wondered why. She picked up the book from beside the phone and showed it to him. "I guess Boris is a better thief than he looks."

Stevie snorted. "It's not like he broke into Fort Knox."

Katrina could have sworn Stevie sounded jealous. He was certainly acting strange. Too much beer, she suspected. He still reeked. Like she should talk. Light a match near her right now and the whole room would blow.

"There were only two Johns listed in the book, and neither one was home. Guess I'll just have to wait for them to call back."

"I thought the name was Jonathan."

"Yeah, but there's no Jonathan in the book."

Stevie shrugged. "Maybe Windle just calls him John."

Katrina glanced at him suspiciously. "That's what Boris just said."

"God help me, I'm thinking like that little ratshit now." Stevie picked up the rum bottle and studied its label. "Anyway, are you sure his name was Jonathan? You were pretty shit-faced."

Katrina gave Stevie a withering look. "Yes, I'm sure, as sure as I remember his face."

"Do you?" asked Stevie.

"Do I what?"

"Remember his face?"

Katrina sighed. "I'm getting a headache. I'm going to bed. I'll have to try again in the morning." She turned and started for the stairs, wondering why Stevie was being such a little snot.

"You'd better hope if they do call back, Boris doesn't answer," Stevie called after her.

Katrina turned. Stevie shrugged. "He might erase the messages."

"After the way he knows we're on to him? He wouldn't *dare*. We made a deal."

Stevie laughed. "Right—with the devil."

35 TRUST-FUND BABY

Stewart Windle had locked himself inside his office. Inside his tiny bathroom/bedroom, actually, the lights off. That way, if anyone came to his outer door, they'd think he was out. And they wouldn't be able to hear him on the phone from there, either. It was payday for the PESTS, after all.

He wished he had a real home where he could run and hide. But when he moved to Toronto to start living the clean life, he decided to keep his expenses low and save what money he could. Just in case Life of the Party was a bust. He'd had plenty of money stashed away from his Montreal days, but he'd gone crazy that one night at Casino Niagara shortly after moving here trying to impress some pretty girls with his big bets at blackjack. *Jackass* was more like it. Once he'd started losing, they'd dumped him like a dirty diaper and latched onto the next big hopeful. So much for getting laid.

Stewart had discovered his black book was missing this morning when he woke up and immediately reached inside his jacket pocket for a pack of Tums. His stomach was still protesting the Spam-and-mash from 2 days ago, and now he had a hangover to add to his woes. It was possible, of course, that the book had fallen out of his pocket at Giovanni's, or wherever he'd gone after that, but he doubted it. Stewart was certain that little wanker Boris had stolen it. So that was what all that feeling-up in the bar was all about. And here he'd been almost flattered by the attention.

But why steal the book? What was Boris planning to do with it? All the numbers of his PESTS and his hosts were in that book. No addresses, though. So if Boris planned to rob them blind, he'd have to call first and somehow find out where they lived. Frankly, Boris didn't seem that bright.

Or did Boris plan to somehow blackmail Stewart with the book? Luckily, he had an exact replica stashed under his pillow. The question was, did he even want to use it? Life of the Party seemed to be going down the tubes. It was just getting too risky, what with the lawless hosts and the felonious Boris. If Stewart's father didn't catch him cavorting with the criminal hosts, then the criminal hosts would catch him in cahoots with Boris robbing them. It was a lose-lose situation. Definitely time to pack it in.

Stewart sighed and picked up a flashlight and a Rolodex from the table beside the bed. Cot, really. To think how he'd lived in Montreal, in a penthouse suite overlooking the city. Now he was living like a bloody dog, without even a window to call his own. And all because he'd decided to go clean. Well, he'd tried, but obviously everyone was against him. Nothing more he could do about it. He would gather up all his money from Life of the Party, including the PESTS' pay, and take off to Mexico in the morning. Lay low till his thirty-fifth birthday came along, then arrive back in town in style, with trust-fund money to his name. Trust-fund baby. He did like the sound of that. Though why it couldn't have been one set up at 21 like everybody else was beyond him. Stewart cursed his grandfather for his cautious ways, then reached for the phone to call his travel agent.

The phone rang before he could pick it up.

"Windle, thank God I caught you. You have to help me!" came a breathless voice.

"And this might be . . .?"

"Andrew."

"Andrew?"

"Andrew Robertson from high school, you moron. Do you have Alzheimer's or what?"

Andrew, though the most handsome of Stewart's group of friends from high school, was hardly the most personable. He was some sort of shrink, and Stewart had to wonder if he were this rude and abrupt with his patients. The shrink thing had made Stewart nervous when he first called Andrew to tell him about Life of the Party, since he was afraid the man's shrink detector might spot him as the scam artist he was. Not so. Andrew, being a self-absorbed ass, completely accepted Stewart's tall tales of life in Montreal as an investment banker, probably because he'd barely listened to a word Stewart said.

The man had an unfortunate penchant for goatees and odd facial hair. Not to mention vests and tweed jackets with elbow patches. The shrink look, Stewart supposed. Good thing the guy had that chiseled face. Too bad about the matching personality. Andrew had a way of asking questions that made everything seem like an interrogation. Which must work for his patients, since his business thrived, but didn't go over so well with friends. Which must be why he was calling now.

"It's my engagement party tonight, and half my invitees haven't called back."

"Engagement party?" said Stewart, enjoying the man's consternation. "Aren't those things usually held on weekends?"

"Yes, but Alana—my fiancée—and I both see clients on Friday nights and Saturday afternoons. Tuesday's our only free night."

"I see," said Stewart, smirking at how like a psychiatrist he must sound.

"So can you help me?" asked Andrew impatiently.

"You should have called me earlier, old boy."

"Yes, yes, I know, but . . ."—Andrew's voice grew tight—"I was trying to do it on my own."

Stewart smirked again. He knew Andrew hated to be wrong about anything, and here he was admitting he had failed.

"So what is it you need? Family members? Friends of family? Ex-girlfriends just to piss off the fiancée?"

"I'm getting married, for God's sake!"

"Well, sometimes men have these parties in the hopes of getting out of it, you know. I've seen it happen."

"Look," said Andrew, being as polite as was possible for him, "I just want it to look like I have some friends, okay? So Alana's family doesn't think I'm a social pariah."

Stewart thought, *They must've already met you. Isn't it a bit late?* But he kept his mouth shut and waited.

"And perhaps a colleague or two. Most of them haven't called me back, either."

Surprise, surprise, thought Stewart, annoyed with the man. All the advantages in the world, and not a single social grace. Andrew had been the luckiest of all of Stewart's Rosedale friends. His parents had died while flying their seaplane to their cottage in Muskoka in dubious weather conditions when Andrew was only 20. Andrew got the house and all the money. He had a sister, but she was out in Vancouver somewhere hugging trees and being an environmentalist groupie. She wouldn't accept the money, told Andrew to donate it to Greenpeace and Save the Pigeons. He said sure, and donated it to himself.

"What time is this little soiree?" asked Stewart, pulling out his little black book from under his pillow.

"Eight, at my place."

"That is cutting it a little close," said Stewart.

"I know, I know, I'll pay you extra."

"The thing is . . ." said Stewart.

"Yeah?"

"I'm going to need the money right away."

"I'll pay you in the next couple of days."

"No, I mean today. Cash."

"Cash? Today! How the hell do you expect me to do that? I don't have any cash on me and I have two more appointments before I'm finished for the day."

"Send a courier over."

"Look, Windle, I could courier over a cheque, but I refuse to send cash. Those courier guys are maniacs. Have you seen the way they ride their bicycles? They'd probably steal the money!"

"I need cash, Andrew—now." Stewart sighed. "I hate to admit this, but I have a slight cash flow problem this month. And since this is so spur of the moment . . . well, I'm afraid it's either cash or no PESTS."

"Okay, okay. Look, this is what we'll do. You come to the party tonight, and I'll pay you cash then and there. The whole thing. I've got cash at the house."

Cash at the house. Stewart almost groaned. Surely Andrew wasn't a criminal, too? The guy was loaded, he had his parents' money, and he was the only one in Stewart's group that hadn't invested in that mineral fiasco a few years back. Well, maybe he wasn't a criminal, maybe he just liked having cash on hand for emergencies. Stewart hoped so. For as much as Stewart liked and admired criminals for their alternative lifestyles and their natural cunning, now that he no longer was one, he felt it unwise to hang out with them. A shame, really—they were so much fun to drink with.

"What do you say?" asked Andrew.

Stewart deliberated. He wasn't thrilled about the idea of going to the party himself, where his PESTS would be. For one, they'd be wanting the money they were supposed to be paid today. But what were they going to do—confront him at the party and risk losing their jobs? If any of them dared ask him, he'd assure them they'd be paid tomorrow. And tomorrow he'd be on a plane to Mexico with all of Andrew's money *and* theirs. One last little scam. What the hell. He had tried to go straight and couldn't. It wasn't his fault. Probably his parents were to blame, somehow or other. Parents usually were.

36 PEST VS. PEST

Cathy was on the Carlton streetcar headed for Windle's, trying her best to jot down notes for her latest play. It was about a werewolf cult fed up with all their hair, so they start up a beauty salon and start waxing themselves, and soon, it's a booming business. She was deliberating whether to throw in a few musical numbers and whether to call it Waxwolf or Werewax. But the asshole in front of her kept chatting on his cell phone. How annoying was that?—Having to listen to someone else's inane conversation. For some reason it was more irritating when it was someone talking on a phone, rather than two people sitting right there chatting. Why couldn't these people just turn off their phones once in a while? Cathy did. It seemed like the polite, Canadian thing to do. These streetcar conversations were always pretty much the same: "Hello, I'm on the streetcar." "Hello, I'm getting closer to you." "Hello, I'll be there in 15 minutes." Christ! Cathy was about to lean over and swat the guy on the shoulder when his words sank in and she froze.

"Just down the street from Lawrence's?" the tall, dark-haired man was saying. "Well, that's easy enough . . . This guy's new though, isn't he?" He waited, listening a moment, then laughed. "Ah, easy pickings . . . so what should I be this time, a friend or a colleague? A good PEST needs to know his motivation, after all."

Cathy suddenly realized she was practically panting in the guy's ear and slid back into her seat, though she leaned forward enough to hear the rest of the conversation.

"Look, I'm just getting off the streetcar; hold on a sec . . ." The man stood up and moved to the door. Cathy looked up and saw that they were at the corner of Gerrard and Parliament. Hurriedly she got up, too. She exited the streetcar directly behind the man on the phone, careful to stay close to him.

"I'm right by your office," the man was saying. "I'll be there in a couple of minutes to collect my pay." He stopped suddenly at the response on the other end and swore to himself, and Cathy banged right into him.

The man turned, annoyed, and a look of recognition crossed his face. As it did Cathy's. It was Jonathan! Katrina's prince from the party! He remained staring at her as he said, "But you'll have my money tomorrow, right? . . . Okay, eight o'clock, Andrew. Got it."

He closed his phone and opened his mouth to speak just as Cathy's phone rang. "Just a sec," she said, holding up a finger for him to wait.

"How would you like to attend a party tonight, luv?" boomed Windle's voice.

"Tonight? Sure. Look, I'm just down the street from your office. How 'bout I come by and get all the info when I come up for my pay?"

Jonathan had been about to turn away when his ears perked up. He turned back toward Cathy, eyeing her with interest.

"I'm afraid I don't have your pay. There's been a slight glitch. I won't have it till tomorrow."

"Well, you must have *some* money there; I'll just—"

"Honestly, luv, there's no point in coming up. I'm not even at the office, I'm calling from a restaurant. And I don't have the money because that bastard Lawrence is late paying me. Seriously, there's nothing I can do. But I assure you I'll have your money first thing tomorrow."

Cathy looked up at Jonathan and grabbed his arm, motioning him not to go anywhere.

"Well," she sighed to Windle, "I guess it's out of my hands. Give me the details, then, and I'll be there with bells on."

A minute later she disconnected and turned to Jonathan. He broke into a grin. "PEST?" he said.

"PEST!" she grinned back.

"You know, I thought maybe you were when I saw you at Lawrence's party. You didn't look like a Rack 'n' Roll girl or an escort."

"Well, thanks for the compliment," smiled Cathy.

"And you were far too friendly to be a real friend of Lawrence's." He frowned. "Well, friendly to the others, anyway. As I recall, you weren't so friendly to *me*."

"You were making rude remarks about my . . . about women." Cathy didn't want to bring up Katrina just yet. Now that she knew Katrina's "soul mate" was a PEST, she wasn't sure what to do about the whole thing.

"Was I?" said Jonathan. "That's not like me. I love women. In fact, I have three sisters."

"Yeah, I remember you mentioning it." Cathy looked him over. He was still tall, dark, and handsome, and his clothes were half-decent, if not screaming money, but he *did* ride the streetcar. She couldn't keep the disappointment out of her voice. "I thought you were some hotshot rich guy."

Jonathan laughed. "No, poor as a church mouse, I'm afraid. I don't go to those parties for the free booze and women—though I'm not sure Lawrence's women are free."

"You're creeping me out," said Cathy. "I thought it was all good clean fun."

"Nothing about Lawrence is good and clean, believe me. The man's an ass."

Cathy laughed. "So you're going to the party tonight?" Jonathan nodded. "How long have you been a PEST anyway?"

"A few months, ever since Windle started up Life of the Party."

"So you knew Windle before that?"

"God no. There was an ad in the paper, and I figured I could use the extra cash." He looked down at Cathy; he was taller than she remembered. "Are you going?"

"Oh yeah. I desperately need the money—if there *is* any money."

"This is a first, believe me. I've always been paid promptly before."

"That's almost reassuring." Cathy scowled and looked down the street. "Look, why don't we go up to Windle's office and shake him down a little? He's gotta have *some* money in there, and I'm broke."

"But he's not even there, he said he's—"

"You believe everything that guy says?"

Jonathan grinned. "You're right. Let's go."

But the office was indeed dim and dark. They thought they could hear voices inside, but figured it must be a TV or radio down the hall.

"Shit," said Cathy. "I was really hoping . . ."

"Look," said Jonathan awkwardly, "from the moment I saw you today I've been wanting to ask you . . ."

"Hmm?" said Cathy, knowing exactly what he was about to ask but not wanting to make it easy for him.

"That girl at the party, the one you said something about rescuing . . . you know her, right?"

"Which girl would that be?" asked Cathy innocently.

"The blonde one with the green eyes . . . the really beautiful one."

"Hmm, it seems to me you said something at the party about being bored by beautiful girls."

"Well, most of them, but she was different, she . . . well, when I met up with her in the bathroom—"

"The bathroom?" said Cathy, acting astonished.

"She wasn't feeling well, and I had wine on my shirt, and I talked to her, and she was so sweet, but I never got her name or her phone number and—"

"Maybe she didn't want to give them to you."

"No, she was too drunk."

"So you're hanging out in a bathroom with a strange woman who's drunk out of her head. Now I get the picture," said Cathy with a look of disgust.

"I wasn't trying to do anything. I . . ." Jonathan stopped and realized Cathy was playing with him. "Look, can't you give me her name and number?"

Cathy debated. How did she know this guy was just a simple PEST? What was the "easy pickings" remark to Windle about? Maybe he was a burglar like Boris for all she knew, or somehow in cahoots with Windle. She couldn't give Katrina's number to just anyone. She felt strangely protective of the girl. So Cathy said, "Sorry, afraid not."

"Why not?" Jonathan gave her a pleading look. "It's not like I'm asking you where she lives."

"You could be some nutcase, for all I know."

"I'm starting to think *you* are."

Cathy laughed. She was starting to like this guy in spite of her earlier doubts. "Okay, tell you what I'll do. You give me your number, and I'll pass it on. You'll have to work your own magic from there."

"Oh, that's terrific! My name's Jonathan, by the way." He gave Cathy his number, and she punched it into her phone.

"Cathy."

"Cathy?" repeated Jonathan. "I think that might be her name, too."

"Really?" said Cathy, amused.

"Well, that's what Lawrence said, but he was half in the bag that night. Can't you just tell me her name?"

Cathy smiled. "Now that would ruin the mystery, wouldn't it?"

Jonathan shook his head. "You *are* stubborn, aren't you?" Then he brightened as he mused, "Maybe she's a friend of this Andrew guy. Maybe she'll be at the party tonight."

"Anything's possible," Cathy said, glad she hadn't given him Katrina's number. Jonathan probably thought Katrina was rich, and Katrina thought *he* was. Let them meet at the party and figure it out for themselves. That way, Cathy wouldn't be the harbinger of bad news. If Katrina still loved him in spite of his poverty . . . well, that made her stupid, but there was no accounting for taste.

37 TAKE A MESSAGE

When Katrina got home, she was thrilled to see the message light blinking on her answering machine. She'd even left work early, claiming a nasty headache, because she couldn't stand the tension of wondering if one of the Johns had called her back. She supposed she could've checked her messages from work, but she could never remember how to do that, and anyway, it wouldn't feel right doing it that way. She had to be right there, by her own phone, to hear it. After all, how often did your soul mate call for the very first time?

"Windle here," boomed the voice, and Katrina slumped onto the kitchen chair, wishing she'd brought a latte home with her from work. She could use a boost right now. "I tried calling you at Cups, but you'd already left. Hope you get this. There's a last-minute party tonight at my friend Andrew's. It's near Lawrence's and Randall's. I'll have a taxi pick you up at 7:45. A cocktail dress should suffice—nothing too immodest, though; it's an engagement party and you're not an evil ex. Say you're a friend of his sister's. Nobody there will know her. Her name's . . . Marjorie, that's it. Lives in B.C., likes the environment and all that nonsense. You met her . . . let's see . . . at one of those god-awful travel slide shows, Machu Picchu or some such thing. That should do it. Call me back if you can't make it. Ta-ta for now!"

Katrina let out a long sigh. She wanted to cry at the fact the message wasn't from Jonathan, but on the other hand, the party might be good for her. She could certainly use the money for her and Stevie's new apartment. And there was always the slight chance Jonathan would be there, even though Stewart had insisted he didn't know the man—the swine. At the very least, it would keep her busy and keep her mind off the Jonathan thing. Otherwise, she'd just sit by the phone all night waiting for a call. Or worse, keep calling the two numbers in her book till they were so pissed off they never called her back. And if Stevie showed up before she left, she could ask him how to check her messages from the party—maybe she'd write the instructions down this time, just to be sure.

The phone rang as Katrina sat there pondering, and she jumped. Maybe she didn't need that latte after all. Could it be her prince? She was suddenly terrified.

"Katrina!" boomed Cathy's voice. *Did everyone have to yell over the phone?* "You going to the party tonight?"

"Andrew's?"

"The groom-to-be."

"Yeah, I guess—it'll keep my mind off you-know-who."

"No callbacks yet, huh?"

"No," sighed Katrina, "just Windle. Hey, did you get my money?"

"No, he wasn't there. I'll have to try again tomorrow." Cathy paused. "Look, wear something spectacular tonight. I've got a good feeling about this."

"Oh, sure—you know how much I like parties."

"You'll like them after this, believe me." And on that mysterious note, Cathy hung up.

Katrina dragged herself up the stairs to have a shower. In spite of her little pep talk to herself, the last thing she felt like doing tonight was going to a party. She glanced at Boris's room. The door was closed as always, and she wondered if he was in there. She shivered. She was passing Stevie's room. The door was open, and Stevie was nowhere in sight when the phone rang again.

Stevie's phone was closer than hers, so she ran into his room and lunged for it.

"Katrina?" came a strange voice, and Katrina flopped onto the bed, trying to catch her breath.

"Yes?"

"I got a call from you yesterday. My name's John. I—"

"John? Not Jonathan?"

"Well, you can call me that if you like, though I always thought it was kind of stuffy. The thing is, I don't have a clue what your phone call was about, that whole party thing, but it sounded awfully interesting." He laughed lewdly. "Especially the part about the pants. So I was thinking, if you'd be interested in getting together . . ."

Katrina had been staring blankly at Stevie's bedside table with distaste, wondering where this guy got off, and about to say as much, when she noticed a piece of paper sticking out from under the lamp. She idly pulled it out and looked at it as her phone suitor rambled on.

". . . I've always liked tall blondes and green eyes . . . whew, you sound like my kind of girl, so what do you say . . ."

It was a piece of paper torn from a small book, and at the top was clearly written "Jonathan" with a phone number. Katrina gaped at it and slowly removed the phone from her ear. The last words she heard were "start with a couple of martinis and . . ." before she hung up.

What on earth was this page doing in Stevie's room? What was it doing anywhere but in the little black book where it belonged? Boris was the one who'd stolen the book, not Stevie. So why . . .?

Katrina pushed the niggling little thoughts aside. They didn't matter right now: She had the number, dammit. And this time, she didn't need a shot of overproof rum. She was fueled by annoyance at that dumb John and fury at Boris and Stevie, or whichever one was to blame. She picked up the phone again and dialed.

A woman answered, and Katrina inwardly groaned.

"Jonathan?" the woman replied, no malice in her voice. Maybe she wasn't a girlfriend or a wife. "Sorry, he's not home right now. Who's calling?"

"My name's Katrina. I met him at a party last week, and I really have to get in touch with him. I—"

"Last Friday?"

"Yeah, it was at—"

"Hey, you're not tall and blonde and green-eyed, are you? Jonathan's been going on and on about you for days."

"You're not his wife, are you?"

The woman laughed. "Yeah, like I'd be talking to you like this. No, I'm his roommate, and I'm sick of him moping around like a lovesick hound. Give me your number and I'll call his cell right now and give it to him. He's gonna love this!"

"That's okay, I could just call him myself and—"

"He's going to another party tonight, in Rosedale. Isn't that where the last one was? You guys sure have a sweet deal."

Sweet deal? thought Katrina. What was that supposed to mean? The roommate must think she was rich, too. And another party in Rosedale? Surely that was too much of a coincidence. Where else could Jonathan be going tonight but to Andrew's? He *had* to be a friend of Windle's, but Windle was keeping him to himself for whatever reason.

"Look," she tried again, "I don't mind calling him, just give me—"

But the roommate would have none of it. She took Katrina's number and said, "The name's Cathy, right?" and before Katrina had a chance to correct her, the woman hung up.

Katrina slumped against Stevie's pillows and stared at the piece of paper in her hand. She read Jonathan's number over and over again, memorizing it; someone certainly didn't want her to have it. Eventually she glanced back at the table and noticed the top drawer was slightly ajar. She leaned over to close it and saw a page torn from the classifieds. Several ads were circled in red. She scanned a few. Odd. They were all listings for rentals—but one-bedroom rentals. Hadn't she and Stevie discussed this? That was why she was working at Life of the Party in the first place, to earn extra cash so they could get a decent-sized apartment. Why would he be looking at one bedrooms? Unless he was planning on moving out on his own. But why would Stevie do that? They were best friends.

Katrina heard the squeaky front door open. It had to be Stevie. Boris wouldn't be out at this time of day, and anyway, he always used the side door. She jumped, feeling somehow guilty. Which was ridiculous. *She* wasn't the thief here. Though at this point, she wasn't sure who was. But whoever it was had stolen Jonathan's number from her after stealing the book from Windle, and that was double theft. But what if Stevie had nothing to do with it? What if Boris had planted the phone page in Stevie's room for some reason, to implicate him . . . for what? To make it look like Stevie was trying to keep Jonathan away from her? Why? That made no sense at all. And what about this whole ad thing? It was all too much. Katrina's head was starting to throb.

Well, there was nothing to do but go downstairs and talk to Stevie. Boris had to be behind it all; maybe Stevie could explain it.

She was halfway down the stairs when the phone rang. She heard Stevie's footsteps in the kitchen, then his voice on the phone.

"Katrina? No, sorry, she's not home right now. Who's calling? Sorry, who? John? Sure I'll take a message, just let me get a pen . . ."

At the name John, Katrina was ready to leap down the remaining steps. But something stopped her. She hesitated, then gingerly descended two stairs until she could peer into the kitchen and see Stevie beside the phone. He wasn't writing down anything; he didn't even have a pen. He said "Uh-huh" a couple of times with a self-satisfied grin. Then a goodbye and hung up the phone, a whistle on his lips. Surely he wasn't . . . no, that was impossible.

Katrina took a deep breath and forced herself not to charge down the stairs. She descended slowly and deliberately, her head high, blood rushing to her face. She could almost feel steam erupting from her flaring nostrils. Stevie, sensing her, suddenly whirled around. The whistle trickled and died.

"Shit, you scared me, Katrina. What's up?"

"Who was that?" she asked, as casually as possible.

"Hmm? Oh, I don't know, they wouldn't say; they just hung up." He offered a feeble grin. "You're home early."

"I was upstairs. I could hear you on the phone, something about me not being home."

"I didn't know you were."

"And how would you know that if you didn't bother to find out?"

"It's a bit early, Katrina, you're not usually home at—"

"You could've called up the stairs to find out."

"Katrina, now you're being silly. Is it the Jonathan thing? Hasn't he called back? You've been through a lot lately. Your nerves must be shot." Stevie stepped toward her, but she nudged him aside and stared down at the table.

"Where's the message?"

Stevie looked trapped. "What are you talking about?"

"I heard you say you'd take a message. And you said you'd get a pen." Katrina glanced around the table, her voice steely. "I don't see a pen. I don't see a message."

"Katrina, you were upstairs. What is it with that bionic hearing of yours? You're imagining things. I'm telling you, there was no—"

Katrina raised the torn page with Jonathan's number and waved it in Stevie's face. "What's *this*?"

Stevie recoiled and looked as if he might cry. Katrina resumed her attack. She waved the classified pages with the red circles in his face.

"And *this*?"

"Classifieds?" said Stevie stupidly.

"Sure they're classifieds—all one-bedroom ads. Didn't we go over this? What are you up to, Stevie? Are you planning on moving out on me? Slithering out in the middle of the night?"

"No, Katrina! Those ads are for both of us!"

"One bedrooms," sneered Katrina. "*Right*."

"I was only trying to save you some money. I was only . . ." Stevie stopped, his voice quavering. "I was only trying to save you, Katrina."

"Save me from what?"

"From Boris, from that Jonathan guy . . . you don't know what men can be like; you're so innocent, so naïve. I mean, you went out with Len, for God's sake! It's obvious you don't have a clue!"

"Shouldn't I be able to decide for myself?"

"You need someone to look after you, Katrina."

"Oh—and that would be you?"

"I love you, Katrina." Stevie made a feeble attempt at wrapping his scrawny arms around her, but she easily pushed him away.

"Don't pull that shit on me now, Stevie."

Stevie looked like a pup on display at the Humane Society. "No, Katrina—I mean I *love* you." His voice was a whimper. "I'm in *love* with you."

Katrina stared at him, incredulous and horrified. "So *you've* been erasing my messages all along and blaming Boris? And you were planning to rent a little apartment for the two of us to use as a love nest? Did you ever plan on telling *me* any of this? Or were you just going to rearrange my whole life to suit you?"

Katrina shook her head. Her whole body was shaking. "You're unbelievable! You're *worse* than Boris! At least he's up front about being an asshole."

"Katrina, I never meant any harm. I was only trying to look after you."

"Look, I know that was Jonathan on the phone. I just called him, and his roommate told me she'd have him call me right back—"

"Katrina, don't do this to yourself! You don't even know this guy. What's so great about him?"

Katrina considered telling Stevie how she'd felt when she met Jonathan: how he saw inside of her, not just her outsides like every other guy. How he was her soul mate. But Stevie would scoff at that. So instead, she flippantly said, "Why, he's tall, dark, and handsome, of course."

"Katrina . . ." Stevie was practically on his knees now. Katrina felt a twinge of mercy, but after what he'd done, she had to force herself to be hard, no matter how pretty his hair looked in the afternoon light.

"There's a party tonight, and he's going to be there, and I'm going to see him again, and you can't stop me! He could be a wife-beating alcoholic crackhead for all I know, but I'd kind of like to find out for myself."

"Katrina . . ."

She started to turn, then thought of something and looked at Stevie with total disdain. "And I thought you were gay!"

"*Gay*?" shrieked Stevie, his wrists flapping. "What the hell gave you *that* idea?!"

38 WRONG NUMBER

Jonathan was on the subway when his roommate tried to call him with Katrina's message, and the call wouldn't go through. He hadn't intended going home from the office tonight; he'd planned to go straight to the party. But an insane model had kept him late at work.

Her best friend ("that fucking twat!") had just been signed by another agency for a high-end cosmetics campaign she'd been hoping to catch herself. She was despondent; she was in tears. Jonathan tried to comfort her. He didn't have the heart to tell the girl that he'd advised his sister to either completely sever contact with her or at least slowly drop her. She was, frankly, nuts. A couple of weeks ago, she'd stripped naked in Jonathan's office and thrown herself at him, claiming he reminded her of her baby brother. And now she'd done it again, taking his cooing consolations as a come-on. She'd started to strip, he'd shaken his head, then she'd flown into a rage. Next, she started tearing his office apart.

Unfortunately, part of that office was his suit for the party that night, hanging freshly dry cleaned on a rack. She'd torn off the plastic wrap, reached into her bag, and grabbed some of the cosmetics from the company she'd been hoping to model for. Then she'd proceeded to scrawl very unladylike words all over his jacket and pants. Jonathan had somehow managed to get her out of there without calling the police (she'd eventually run out of lipstick and rage) and had written a threatening memo to his sister: "Either she goes or I go," and headed home for another suit, one not streaked with "Tahitian Peach" and "Scarlet Sensation." For the millionth time, he wondered why beautiful women were so unbalanced—and where his beautiful Cinderella from the party was. He felt certain she was normal—she just had to be. He prayed she'd be at the party tonight; he would find out then.

***

Stevie stayed in the kitchen and waited till he heard Katrina turn on the shower upstairs. Then he played back the messages until he found the one from Windle about tonight's party. Damn, no address. Windle had a cab picking Katrina up. He supposed he could always call another cab and have it wait in the shadows, then follow her there. But she might spot him. No, there had to be an easier way. Well, there was always Boris, but that wasn't exactly easier. He would've listened to Windle's message for sure and found out where the party was through whatever resources a thug like him had.

Shit, he *had* to go to that party tonight. If that guy Jonathan was actually going to be there, Stevie had to keep him away from Katrina. But how? An idea crept into Stevie's brain. Devious, yes, but definitely workable. Of course, he had to find out what the guy looked like, and he had to get into the party in the first place. Stevie sighed. Boris seemed to be the only answer. What an ugly answer it was.

Stevie coughed hard a few times to roughen his throat, then called work and told them he couldn't come in tonight. He thought he was coming down with the flu. Satisfied, he hung up and took a deep breath and waited till he heard the shower stop upstairs. A moment later, the door to Katrina's room shut. Then he tiptoed up the steps and knocked lightly on Boris's door. Before Boris had time to answer, which Katrina would certainly hear, Stevie slipped inside.

Boris nearly dropped the pastrami on rye he'd been chewing. Stevie nearly toppled over. He couldn't believe it. Boris was earnestly watching a home decorating show as he lay on his bed atop a satin spread, surrounded by velvet curtains and luxurious rugs. Hell, there was even a fur throw. Stevie had never been in here before, but he'd always figured it for Frat Boy décor at best.

"I had no idea . . ." he muttered in awe.

Boris shrugged. "Yeah, well, it's a hobby of mine."

"Why didn't you tell us? You could've helped us decorate the house."

"You didn't ask, did you?" Boris sulked. "And besides, all you've been doing is planning to ditch me and get outta here. Just 'cause I'm a burglar doesn't mean I ain't got feelings, you know."

Stevie glanced toward the door then back to Boris. "Look, can you turn up the TV?"

"Why?"

"Because I don't want Katrina hearing us."

"What're you doing in here anyway?" Boris's voice was surly, but he hit the button on the remote and turned up the volume as requested. "What is this, the frigging train station?"

"I need to know where the party is tonight."

"What for?"

Stevie pulled over an ecru silk ottoman and sat down.

"Careful with that," warned Boris. "I paid an arm and a leg for it, and it took me forever to find just the right colour."

"Oh sure," said Stevie, adjusting his butt so he wouldn't stretch the fabric. "The thing is, I think Katrina's making a big mistake, going after this Jonathan guy, and I hear he's supposed to be at the party tonight."

"Tell the truth, Stevie boy, it's none of your fucking business, so why should I help?"

"I'll give you twenty bucks if you tell me where the party is."

"Make it thirty and you got a deal."

"How about a ride there?" asked Stevie.

"What am I, a fucking taxi service?" Boris stared at his celadon velvet drapes and considered. "Make it forty and we're on."

"But how do I get in?" ventured Stevie.

"Fifty bucks and I'll get you in. But after that, you're on your own. I don't know this jerk-off Jonathan, and I don't wanna know."

"But didn't you see him with Katrina at the party?"

Boris just shrugged. "You'll have to find him on your own. And I don't know what you plan to do with the guy once you find him, but I don't want nothin' to do with it."

"I just want to talk to him is all," said Stevie innocently.

"Uh-huh," said Boris.

Stevie rose awkwardly from the ottoman and glanced around the room again. He flung back his hair and placed his hands on his hips. "You obviously have good taste. Tell me—what do you think I should wear tonight?"

By the time Jonathan finally got home, his roommate had gone out. A message was scrawled by the phone. "Your girlfriend from the party called" with a number, and underneath in brackets, "Cathy."

Was that the number of Cathy from this afternoon, or had she given his mystery girl his number and she'd actually called? And was her name Cathy, too? Damn his roommate—she was the absolute worst with messages. It would help if he had a clue who he was calling. But what the hell. It was worth a try. Jonathan picked up the phone.

It was just before eight when Stevie followed Boris and his partner Ray out the kitchen door. He stopped as the phone rang. There was no question of not answering it. It could be Jonathan, and there was no way he'd give that guy a chance to leave a message. Stevie motioned Boris to wait and picked up the phone.

"Hello, may I please speak to Cathy?"

"There's no Cathy here. You must have the wrong number." Stevie started to hang up.

"Wait! My roommate could have gotten the name wrong. Can I leave a message anyway?"

"It's your coin," snapped Stevie.

"My name's Jonathan."

"Jonathan? Oh, yeah, I got your last message."

Jonathan sounded bewildered. "I never left a message."

"Whatever you say. What's the message this time?"

"I tell you, I didn't *leave* a message before. I just got this number."

"And I think you've got the wrong number. I'm telling you, there's no Cathy here."

"Is there a woman living there at least?"

"You're sounding pretty desperate, mister."

"A blonde, green-eyed, beautiful woman?" said Jonathan, becoming annoyed.

"Believe it or not, this is not a dating service."

"Well, at least take down my phone number and let her decide if she wants to call me."

"Who? The Cathy who doesn't live here?"

"Could you at least do that?"

Stevie paused, making the guy sweat. Finally he said, "I could . . ." Then he started to laugh. "But I won't."

He hung up and followed Boris and Ray out to the van.

39 A BUNDLE OF BILLS

At eight o'clock, Katrina found herself inside yet another massive Rosedale home, a smile glued to her face, a shyness attack shaking her bones. There were a lot of gorgeous women here, but the men were few and far between and left a lot to be desired. There was a lot of gregarious chit-chat, and Katrina figured Stewart must have pulled out all the stops. She wanted to be gregarious, too, and she was looking around hopefully for a waiter passing a tray of champagne when a voice from behind startled her.

"Fancy meeting you here."

Cathy was in dress-up mode again, stunning in a long black evening dress with eye-popping cleavage.

"Stewart said not to wear anything immodest," chided Katrina.

"Funny, I didn't hear him say that." Cathy smiled at a few guests that passed, and kept her voice lowered. "Aside from the obvious PESTS, they're all a bunch of pretentious bores if you ask me."

"Have you seen Jonathan?"

"I'm not sure I even know who he is, remember? What did you say he looks like again?"

"Tall, dark, and handsome."

"Well, there aren't many of those here, I can tell you right now." Cathy smiled at a couple of geeky men who were torn between staring at her bosom and staring at Katrina. "The host isn't bad, but he looks like a total prick. And anyway, he's about to get married." She laughed. "Not like *that* ever stopped me."

"Cathy!" Katrina caught sight of a nearby waiter and waved him over. She grabbed two glasses of champagne off his tray, thought it over, then grabbed one more.

"You're not doing that again, are you?" asked Cathy with an upraised brow.

"One's for you."

"How kind of you," laughed Cathy. She sobered as she took the glass. "How many of these people do you think are PESTS?"

"No idea," said Katrina, not really interested. She was busy scanning the room for Jonathan and gulping down champagne.

"Do you think the other PESTS are on the up and up?"

"What do you mean?"

Cathy shrugged. "Maybe they're all crooks like Boris for all we know."

"That's impossible! If they were, the hosts would've reported Stewart to the cops long ago."

"Not necessarily. Not if they're criminals, too, like that Randall guy with his coke." Cathy leaned closer to Katrina. "This whole Life of the Party thing could be under surveillance by the cops. Shit, we could end up in jail."

"For what? We haven't done anything."

"I don't know, I just have a bad feeling about tonight."

Katrina rolled her eyes. "When you called before, you said you were expecting great things." She sighed. "I could use something great right about now."

Cathy turned in concern. "What do you mean?"

"Remember how I thought my roommate Boris was erasing all my phone calls?"

Cathy nodded.

"Turns out it was Stevie, not Boris."

"Stevie!"

"Apparently he's in love with me."

"I could've told you that. In fact, I think I did."

"I guess I should've listened."

Cathy shook her head. "What a jerk. I guess he didn't want any other man getting his paws on you."

"If I weren't so mad, I'd almost feel sorry for him."

"Forget that—be mad! *After* you find your prince, of course." Cathy scanned the room again, as if hoping Jonathan might suddenly emerge. Then she turned and stared at Katrina. "Look, I know you want money so you can start up your own salon some day, but other than that—how much does it really matter to you?"

"Not that much, I guess. I mean, as long as I have enough and don't have to worry about it."

Cathy patted Katrina's hand. "That's all I needed to know."

Katrina was about to ask Cathy what the hell she was talking about when Cathy suddenly said, "There's our host. He'd better not see us talking together—scatter!" and she slipped away, her bosom plowing through the crowd.

The man who held out his hand and introduced himself as Andrew would have had a stunning face if it weren't for the wispy goatee and the stringy sideburns. Not to mention the velvet vest. His grin was a little frightening, too, like a barracuda looking for lunch. Katrina introduced herself, then gulped down the rest of her champagne and set down the glass before taking his hand, hoping her terrified shaking had stopped. She immediately had to burp. She turned away and covered her mouth, but there was nothing quiet about it. Luckily, her host looked amused.

"You really should sip that stuff," he said with a more human smile. "If you want to knock it back, go for the hard stuff. No bubbles. I have some very fine scotch at the bar if you like."

"Oh no, I don't really drink," said Katrina, starting on her second glass.

"I can see that." Andrew glanced around and lowered his voice. "I'm Andrew, your host. And who might you be?"

Katrina felt confused; she'd just told him her name. He caught her look and added, "Stewart sent over so many PESTS tonight I'm having trouble keeping the names and backgrounds straight."

"Oh, I'm—"

"Oh, there you are, sweetheart," came a shrill voice, and Katrina glanced up to see a very tall, very gaunt woman in a skintight red dress that made her look like a licorice stick. She linked her arm possessively around Andrew's and grinned at Katrina very much the way Andrew had earlier. Katrina felt like food floating atop a fish bowl, helplessly awaiting her doom.

"I'm Alana, Andrew's fiancée. And who might you be?"

"This is Katrina," said Andrew, slightly embarrassed, as if he'd been caught in some sordid act. "She's . . ." He trailed off, since he had no idea what she was. Katrina stood there stupidly for a moment before she realized he was waiting for her to fill in the blanks.

"Oh, sorry," she said, blushing. The licorice stick's gaze was unwavering and very unnerving. Katrina tried desperately to remember her background story. What had Stewart said? "I'm a friend of Alan's—"

"Andrew," corrected Andrew.

"Sorry," said Katrina, holding up her glass with a wobbly smile as if in explanation. "I'm a friend of Andrew's sister, Margaret."

Alana glanced curiously at Andrew. "I thought your sister's name was Marjorie?"

"It's . . . it's an old nickname, one of those silly childhood things."

"I see," said Alana. "And is she still out in Utah with the Mormons?"

"B.C. with the environmentalists," said Katrina, remembering in the nick of time and realizing this bitch was trying to catch her up. She'd better escape before she really put her foot in it.

"Oh!" she cried, glancing across the room. "There's someone I know. I should go say hello." She flashed Alana a saccharine smile. "Nice meeting you. I'll talk to you later." She nodded to Andrew, who was staring at her a little too hard, especially in all the wrong places. She turned her back to them. As soon as she was safely ensconced in the crowd, she downed her second glass of champagne and went frantically in search of another.

The doorman, Andrew's doughy teenage nephew, didn't give Boris any trouble when he arrived on the stoop and whispered, "Life of the Party, this guy's with me. Check with Windle if you want." So many complete strangers had already arrived that the nephew had long since abandoned his list and was letting in anyone who was interested. Shit, he was only getting thirty bucks for this gig, plus whatever leftovers he could nab from the kitchen. He hoped there was lots of roast beef. He didn't want any of that smoked salmon or pate shit.

Boris had left Ray waiting in the van down the street, ready for a quick getaway. He was ready now for a quick getaway from Stevie. As soon as they were inside the massive foyer, he said, "I've done my share—now scat," and started to move away.

"But look at all the people here," exclaimed Stevie, grabbing Boris's sleeve. "How am I going to find the guy?"

"Didn't you say he was tall, dark, and handsome?" asked Boris.

"Yeah," said Stevie doubtfully. "That's what Katrina said."

"So start there." Boris scanned the room. "From the looks of this crowd, there's not a helluva lot to choose from."

Stewart Windle, arriving at the party a fashionable 15 minutes late, immediately sought out his host. Well, immediately after having a glass filled with single malt at the bar. "Andrew!" he said, shaking his hand, trying not to frown at the man's elbow patches, "How fabulous to see you again!"

"I suppose you want your money now," said Andrew under his breath, glancing around to make sure Alana and her relatives weren't nearby. He nodded to a closed door a few feet away. "Come to my study."

Windle gulped down half his scotch, hoping to make his old classmate more likeable, and followed him into an oaky room. Andrew slid aside a painting and opened a safe.

"Kind of clichéd, that, don't you think?" asked Windle.

Andrew shrugged. "It works. There are a lot of strangers here tonight, after all—no reflection on you, of course."

"Of course," smiled Windle. He accepted the bundle of bills Andrew handed him, counted quickly, and nodded. "Excellent."

"You can keep it in my safe till the party's over if you like," said Andrew.

Windle, who had a six A.M. flight to Puerto Vallarta, had no intention of staying till the end of the party. He shook his head and separated the bills into two piles, then put one pile into either side of his jacket.

"Makes you look a little hefty," said Andrew, studying him. The jacket wouldn't close, and Windle's paunch was sticking out. The money was sticking out a little, too.

"Damn," said Windle.

"You sure you don't want to use the safe?" asked Andrew.

"No, I don't trust those things," said Windle, thinking of all the people he knew in Montreal who could've opened that little baby in a matter of seconds. "I'll think of something."

"As you wish," shrugged Andrew. "I'd better get back out there."

He left, and Stewart glanced around. He had to stash the money somewhere until he left. Otherwise, all the PESTS he owed money to, the ones he hadn't paid this afternoon as promised, would spot the wad on him and be all over him like flies on shit. He removed the bills from his pockets and walked slowly around the room, considering.

Boris saw Andrew leaving the study and smiled to himself. He hadn't seen anyone else in there; it had to be off limits to the crowd. Perfect. There might be some goodies worth stealing later. Probably nothing small he could nab right now; the guy wouldn't be likely to leave stuff like that on the ground floor with a party going on. Boris would have to sneak upstairs for that.

He'd just slid in and shut the door, unaware of Windle standing by the curtains, when the door opened and Stevie entered.

"I don't see anyone out there who matches Jonathan's description. Come on, Boris, you were there that night. Are you sure you didn't see him?"

Windle, who'd been about to stash the money behind the curtains, cursed and stepped behind them himself. He'd forgotten about that little bugger Boris. Was nothing sacred? How was he going to hide the money he was stealing from his PESTS with that little thief around? He'd have to think of something less obvious, somewhere the wanker wouldn't look.

Something about the voice stirred a memory. Windle peeked around the edge of the drape and recognized the long-haired whatever talking to Boris. It was the flamer who'd showed up at his office looking for a job! What was she-he doing here now? How did it know Boris? And why was it asking about Jonathan?

"Stevie," said Boris, fed up, "is it really that important to you?"

"It's a matter of life and death," breathed Stevie.

"I doubt it," muttered Boris, "but come on." He nodded to Stevie, and they both left the room. Windle stepped out from behind the curtains with a sigh of relief and continued his search for a clever hiding spot. It would be a helluva lot easier to just go home with the money right now, of course, but he was kind of looking forward to seeing his PESTS. Aside from the grim fact that they'd be all over him for the money he owed them, he did want to see them one last time, see them in action, appreciate the fine team he'd put together, enjoy his handiwork. For after tomorrow, it would all be gone, never to return. When he came back in 3 years, a trust-fund baby, Life of the Party would be a mere memory. He wouldn't very well be able to start it up again, not after ripping off his employees. Even with all his scam artist charm, Windle couldn't get away with *that*.

Boris scanned the foyer he and Stevie were in and couldn't find anyone who looked right, so they went into the humongous living room. He had better things to do than babysit Stevie—he wanted to get on with his burgling. So the second he saw Andrew, who was tall, dark, and handsome in a creepy, strange-whiskered way, he pointed at him.

"That's the guy," he said, already slipping away.

"Are you sure?" called Stevie after him.

Boris took a menacing step back toward Stevie. "That's him, satisfied? Now leave me the fuck alone."

At that moment Katrina surfaced through the crowd, and the man Boris had pointed at was sucked toward her like a magnet. Stevie saw the man talk to Katrina, saw him place a possessive hand on her shoulder, and saw her blush. Was that a blush of pleasure? Was that really him, Jonathan—her soul mate? He looked a little mean to Stevie, but he'd been expecting as much. It was time for action. But not with Katrina around. She couldn't see Stevie there, not yet. She'd be furious.

Then another man showed up, a pudgy man with buffed, pink skin. It took Stevie a moment to realize it was Stewart Windle, whose little black book he had robbed. Katrina seemed surprised to see him. Jonathan seemed pissed-off to be interrupted. Just then, an extremely tall, thin man with quivering nostrils and a bad comb-over arrived on the scene. As he spoke to Jonathan, Windle nodded a greeting then drew Katrina aside. They were quickly swallowed up in the crowd.

A big, oily, hairy man slithered up and spoke to the comb-over victim. Stevie moved cautiously toward Jonathan, wondering how he could get close without drawing their attention. So much for that idea; they all turned to stare at him.

"Do I know you?" asked Jonathan, setting his drink on a nearby table. He lowered his voice. "Are you with Life of the Party?"

The two men with him shook their heads, looking Stevie up and down.

"Never seen him . . . her? before," said Comb-Over.

"Would've remembered *that*," said Oily.

"Windle sent me," whispered Stevie.

"You have a cover?" asked Jonathan dubiously, staring at his long hair. "I really don't think—"

"Oh, there you are!" exclaimed Alana, sliding up to Jonathan. She glanced at Stevie, trying to decide whether to be jealous or not. "Your brother wants a word, something about the caterers, the wrong kind of Bordeaux or something."

"Christ," muttered Jonathan. He motioned to the men with him, immediately forgetting Stevie. "Alana, have you met Lawrence and Randall?"

Stevie took the opportunity to slide behind the biggest fellow, Randall. He reached into his pants pocket, which he'd carefully packed before leaving, and withdrew two Fiorinals. Quickly he popped off the caps and slid the contents into Jonathan's drink on the table. Stevie stirred it with his finger, with which he'd earlier picked his nose, then slipped back into the crowd.

The introductions over, Jonathan picked up his drink and followed Alana toward the kitchen. Lawrence and Randall turned away to check out the strange PEST, but he was gone.

"What the hell do you think that was?" asked Randall, sniffing a little from the huge line he'd done before leaving for the party.

"I think it was a woman," said Lawrence with some hesitation.

"I would've said a man . . . a very gay man." Randall shook his head. "Stewart could've at least warned Andrew about that one. Shit, he's actually charging for *that*?"

Lawrence laughed. "Maybe it's pretending to be Andrew's sister."

"Marjorie the Eco-Humper?" Randall joined in the laughter. "Well, that wouldn't be far off."

40 EASY PICKINGS

When Jonathan finally arrived at Andrew's party, pissed off from the asshole who'd answered Cathy's phone, pissed off at the model who'd made him late, and generally pissed off at the world, he was in no mood for schmoozing. So he went directly to the bar to sharpen his social skills, and asked everyone within hearing distance if they knew of a Cathy that was here. The first four people said no, but the fifth, a man with the face of a disappointed beagle, pointed through the crowd. "Over there. Great tits," he sighed, and returned to leaning against the bar and moping into his drink.

Jonathan picked up his Manhattan and followed the beagle's lead. No sign of towering blonde locks, so he wasn't surprised when he came face-to-face with Cathy from this afternoon.

"Well, we meet again," he said, interrupting her conversation with a short man whose eyes were glued to—and level with—her cleavage. "Though you're not the person I'm looking for."

"What a lovely thing to hear," said Cathy, turning away from the little man as if he were a piece of furniture—a short stool, perhaps. "You are incredibly tactful, you know that?"

"Come on," said Jonathan with a grin, "we've been through this."

"Yeah," sighed Cathy, "we have." She looked him over. "You know, you're not bad in an obnoxious sort of way. You sure you're absolutely stuck on this girl?"

"Uh-huh. And I get the feeling you know where she is."

"I didn't know you *had* feelings," said Cathy, biding her time. "Just a lot of very strong opinions." She stared up at him, suddenly more serious. "I heard you on the phone with Windle today. Tell me, what did you mean when you said this party would be easy pickings?"

"Easy pickings?" repeated Jonathan, bewildered. He glanced around, as if the crowd might give him a clue. "You got me."

Cathy glanced around, too, to be sure they weren't overheard. She lowered her voice. "You wouldn't be something more than you're pretending to be, *would* you?"

"Have you been watching too many spy movies?" asked Jonathan, totally baffled. He leaned forward. "Something more like *what*?"

"Like . . . a thief," blurted Cathy, louder than she'd meant. She and Jonathan both quickly glanced around, then she lowered her voice and tossed back her hair. "There, I said it."

"A thief!" Jonathan started to laugh. "Ah, now I get it. Look, when I said easy pickings I just meant the people at this party." He lowered his voice again, and Cathy had to lean forward to hear him. "I meant they'd be easy to fool, they'd never suspect there were PESTS in their midst, because they're all such self-absorbed, pretentious assholes. Not a thought for anyone but themselves." He grinned at Cathy. "Satisfied?"

Cathy surveyed the people around her with a slight scowl. "I see what you mean." She grinned now herself and spread out her arms. "Okay, I give. *Katrina* is the girl you want. It just so happens she's at this very party. Shit, I'll even introduce you to her."

Jonathan gave her a scolding look. “You could have made this easier, you know.”

Cathy shrugged. “I wasn’t sure about you.”

“You’re right—I could be lying.”

“You could be a lot of things, Jonathan . . .” Cathy smiled and took his elbow. “But Katrina will have to take her chances.” Arm-in-arm, they went in search of Cinderella.

Stevie, who’d just emerged from the bar where he had ordered a hefty Margarita with which to enjoy his home-made entertainment (namely, the drugging of The Villain), stopped short when he saw Cathy a few feet away. He stopped even shorter when he saw she was talking to a tall, dark, and handsome man. And his brakes almost sparked when he heard her call him Jonathan.

Holy shit, he’d put the Fiorinal in the wrong goddamn drink! Boris had led him astray! Next time he saw that little asshole . . . But this wasn’t the time to be thinking of his thieving roommate. Something had to be done to fix the situation. Luckily, Stevie had brought extra Fiorinal. He had to keep his wits about him and figure out this situation. He downed his Margarita, all the better to think.

“Cathy!” he cried, approaching her like a long-lost friend. “What are you doing here?”

Cathy was so shocked she dropped Jonathan’s arm. “What am *I* doing here?” She loomed forward, breasts leading, and Stevie cringed, afraid she might heave them at him. “What are *you* doing here? Shouldn’t you be at home, manning the phones? Erasing any stray messages that might turn your girlfriend against you?”

She turned to Jonathan. "Jonathan, this is Stevie, Katrina's roommate and your main competition. He's in love with Katrina, and he's been very busy keeping the two of you apart."

"Apart . . ." The light dawned. Jonathan stepped forward. Thankfully, he didn't have huge breasts for weapons, but he was a lot taller than Stevie. "*You're* the asshole I talked to on the phone earlier! You told me I had the wrong number."

"I told you that no Cathy lived there."

"Cathy, Katrina, big deal. You knew exactly what you were doing, you little worm!"

Jonathan set down his drink on a nearby table and grabbed Stevie's arm. "I think we should have a little talk. Outside."

Stevie lunged away and muttered, "I'm not feeling well," and suddenly bent over, as if about to throw up. With his back to Cathy and Jonathan, he took the Fiorinals from his pocket, uncapped them, and poured the contents into Jonathan's drink, all the while moaning and writhing.

"Coward!" shouted Cathy. "I know you're faking it!"

Stevie groaned hideously once more for good measure, then ran off like the chicken he was. He wasn't hurt by the name-calling, even though he suspected it was true. After all, his mission was accomplished.

Jonathan watched him, shaking his head in disgust. He picked up his drink. "What a jerk."

"No kidding," said Cathy. "I'll take care of him later."

"I'll help," said Jonathan. "I just hope your left hook's better than mine."

"A big strapping fella like you?" Cathy fluttered her lashes. "Of course, it is."

Randall had excused himself to go to the bathroom—he did that a lot, maybe he had some sort of bladder problem, thought Lawrence as he studied the crowd, thinking how much more fun his parties were. Though, of course, this was an engagement party, so you couldn't expect it to be too lively—right up there with a baby shower. The lack of attractive, big-breasted women was also a sore point. That woman with Stewart had been quite beautiful, though not in the Rack 'n' Roll league (at least the rack part) by any means . . .

Lawrence's eyes stopped swiveling at the women around him as he reconsidered the blonde with Stewart. He'd seen her somewhere before, and recently. A party, wasn't it? Then it hit him: It had been at *his* house. She was the one Jonathan had asked about the day after his party, the one who supposedly was in the master bathroom with him. Was *she* the one who stole his money and rearranged his bedroom furniture?

Lawrence had wondered before why Jonathan would come back to the scene of the crime, asking about her, if he was in cahoots with her. That would just implicate himself. No, she had to have another partner, some other PEST perhaps. Could that PEST be here now? Lawrence was dying to find both of them and shake them down. Get his money back, or at least beat the shit out of the little creeps. His anger was starting to fester. Not that it hadn't been festering for a long time. But it was bubbling to the surface now, and Lawrence was about to lose it, big time.

Stewart had excused himself from Katrina to get them both drinks at the bar. At least that was his excuse. In reality, he'd seen a couple of his PESTS making a beeline for him and decided he wasn't yet ready for the attack.

Katrina had moved closer to the wall, to feel less conspicuous, and her eyes caught someone at the foot of the stairs a few feet away. Boris! Yesterday she would have cringed at the sight of him and let him go on his merry thieving way, but today, she felt a need to apologize. She hurried toward him.

"Boris!" Katrina called, and he froze, as if caught with his fingers in a safe. Slowly he turned, and his expression wasn't exactly one of joy at the sight of her.

"What the fuck you want?" he whispered. "I'm workin' here."

"I have to talk to you."

"We been livin' together for months, and you never wanted to talk to me before. You got great timing, I gotta say."

"I just found out something I didn't know before." Katrina took two steps toward Boris, and he didn't back away. That was a good sign. "Look, I've been blaming you all along for erasing the messages on the answering machine, and—"

"What!"

"And now I know it was Stevie, and I just wanted to apologize for blaming you."

"Stevie's been erasing your messages?" Boris sneered. "That little toad!" He paused, thinking it over. "Though I always figured he had the hots for you."

"You did?"

"Why'd you think I never hung out with you guys? Three's a crowd, you know?"

"You couldn't have seriously thought—"

"I got feelings, too, you know. You guys always shut me out, and then when I found out you were planning on moving out and ditching me . . . It hurts"—Boris pounded his chest—"right here."

"Boris, I'm so sorry! If I'd known what Stevie was up to earlier, I might have . . ." Katrina hung her head. "I might have been nicer to you." She put her hand on his arm, and he looked at it forlornly. "Can you ever forgive me?"

"Shit!" cried Boris, "I wish I'd known all this yesterday."

Suddenly he jerked her hand away and looked at his watch. He broke into a sweat and twitched, and Katrina wondered if he'd dipped into the coke he'd stolen from Randy.

"I gotta go," he said, pushing Katrina aside. She grabbed his arm, an uncharacteristically aggressive gesture spurred by two and a half glasses of champagne.

"But Boris—we need to talk!"

Boris had almost shaken her off when a grotesquely fat man stepped in his path, a huge stein of beer in his hand. Boris, a step above the man, peered desperately over him, but no way could he get around him.

Randall returned from the bathroom, sniffling, and Lawrence wondered if he had allergies as well as a bladder problem. The guy should see a doctor. He looked awfully flushed. Probably had high blood pressure, too.

"It's too fucking crowded here," said Randall, talking fast. "I feel like I'm being groped all over, and not by the right type of groper." He grabbed Lawrence's arm. "Let's move over there by the wall, where it's not so touchy-feely."

Lawrence followed Randall, then stopped and stared. A few feet away, on the stairs, stood the blonde, Cathy. And she was talking to someone else who looked vaguely familiar.

"The women here all suck," Randall was saying. "Nothing like the ones you get at your parties. These ones all look like frigging morticians or librarians, for fuck's sake, and even if they took off their glasses and let down their hair, I doubt it would help. None of them have any damn tits!"

Lawrence nodded absently, still focused on the man that the woman Cathy was talking to. *That was it!* He'd been at Lawrence's party last Friday, but Lawrence had only seen him briefly, hadn't known who he was. He had assumed he was one of the caterers.

But that shaggy hair . . . what was it Stewart had said? He'd mentioned one of his PESTS being kind of attractive in a shaggy-dog kind of way. Well, he was way off on the attractive part, but . . .

Lawrence tapped Randall's shoulder and whispered, "That guy over there, the one with the black shaggy hair . . . you know him?"

Randall, who'd been staring overtly at a brunette who'd just passed by with magnificent melons, though the rest of her was unfortunately proportionately large, dragged his eyes away and followed Lawrence's gaze.

"Yeah, that guy worked my last party, but he just stayed in the kitchen the whole time. You know him?"

"Yes," said Lawrence with a scowl. "He was at my last party, too." He turned meaningfully to Randall. "And there were things missing afterward."

"Things?" asked Randall, astonished. "You mean like drugs?"

"Good Lord, no!" said Lawrence with disgust. "Just some cash . . . a little cash . . . petty cash really."

"Fuck!" exclaimed Randall. "I had some . . . uh, *cash* missing, too."

They both turned to stare accusingly at the shaggy-haired man, and the woman talking to him turned to set down her empty glass.

"Cathy!" said Lawrence with disdain. "She was at my last party, too."

"No kidding? Mine, too!" exclaimed Randall. "And here they are, chatting away like best buds." His eyes narrowed. "Kind of coincidental, don't you think?"

"I'll say."

"Probably casing the joint."

"Quite possibly."

"I think we should have a little chat with these hooligans," said Randall.

"Most definitely," agreed Lawrence, and they started forward.

41 A COLLECTIVE GASP

Stewart was returning with the drinks for Katrina and himself when he heard a familiar voice loudly saying, "and then I actually saw a girl prancing down the street in a bikini! Not something you'd expect in Rosedale, is it?"

"Now dear," said another familiar voice, "how many times do you plan on telling that story this evening?"

Stewart nearly dropped the champagne. There, a few feet away, stood his mother and father, chatting cozily with Randall and Lawrence. And if that weren't bad enough, a couple of feet away stood Katrina and Boris! Katrina looked pale and ill, as if she'd just popped a bad oyster. Stewart hadn't been anywhere near an oyster, but he knew exactly how she felt.

This had to be stopped! Of all the people at this party, how could his father have bee-lined to this crew? Was it the criminal lawyer in him, some sort of special antenna? Randall and Lawrence—a coke dealer and a God-knows-what. And Boris, a blackmailer and burglar. All of them connected to Life of the Party, and all of them probably plenty boozed up enough to blab about it.

Stewart had no idea Andrew still kept in touch with his parents. He must've been pretty desperate for guests to have invited them. Stewart felt pretty desperate himself by now. He'd just escaped two lovely PESTS at the bar and had to work all his considerable charm to convince them he had no money right now, but he would, of course, have it for them first thing in the morning if they'd come round to his office. If they came round to the airport was more like it.

And now this. He was trying to back up through the crowd without spilling his drinks or stepping on any toes to call attention to himself when his father spotted him. He didn't exactly beam with pleasure, but he put on his best paternal smile for the surrounding witnesses. Though there was no hiding the accusation in his voice when he said, "I heard you were in town."

"Well . . . er, uh . . . yes," managed Stewart, wondering how much lying was possible here. Sure he was in town, he'd been in town for 5 months. It wasn't the sort of thing you told your parents and they took lightly.

"A phone call would have been nice," said his father.

"Well . . . I've been busy," said Stewart weakly. He flashed a fake smile at his father and stepped toward his mother and kissed her on the cheek. "Lovely to see you, mother, dear."

"You too, Junior," said his mother, grasping his hand. Stewart heard the snickers of his friends. They'd always made fun of the "Junior." As if the names Larry and Randy were any better; they sounded like the Two Stooges.

"But why on earth haven't you been in touch with us? What have you been doing? Where are you staying? How long have you been here?"

It was just as Stewart had feared: The Inquisition. He prayed for a diversion: a trap door falling beneath his feet, a drive-by shooting, or better yet, an Act of God. A nice little cyclone would do the trick. Anything to stop the piercing questions in his parents' eyes.

And then, suddenly, his prayers came true.

Andrew had been in the kitchen with Alana, wondering if an inferior Bordeaux would be noticed by his guests, and hoping they'd ingested enough alcohol to let it slip by their snobby and knowledgeable tongues, when the Fiorinals kicked in. Suddenly, he had in insatiable urge to test *all* the wine, check each bottle before it was sent to the dining room. He could feel Alana's anxious eyes on him, knew he was acting strangely, since he usually drank in only very small doses, yet he couldn't seem to stop himself. He felt giddy and light-headed and wanted to keep it that way.

While he was in the process of opening a fifth bottle for testing, with the catering crew giving him amused sidelong glances that he couldn't care less about, though he usually would, Alana suggested they go into the living room and tell everyone it was time for dinner. She, in fact, started to drag him in that direction. Enough was enough. Andrew turned to her, eyes goggling, and shouted, "I can handle it! Do you think I'm an imbecile?"

Her lips quivering, a twitch in her left eye, Alana backed off. She told Andrew that the living room was up to him; she would inform the guests in the other areas of the house that dinner was imminent.

Andrew reluctantly left the kitchen and all its Bordeaux bounty and staggered into the living room. He was crafty enough to know there were not only trays of champagne to be had there, but a full bar.

"I'm here to make an announcement!" he shouted at the top of his lungs. All conversation stopped. All eyes turned toward him.

Andrew giggled. "But damned if I remember what it was!"

"Dinner, perhaps?" suggested Windle Sr., who'd been starving since he got here and couldn't stand the sight of another scrawny little canapé smothered in seafood. God, he hated seafood.

"Didn't we already have dinner?" replied Andrew, and people exchanged uncertain glances, wondering if this were a joke. Were they supposed to laugh? Andrew looked down at his hand and saw that he was holding a full glass of red wine. He downed it in one gulp and frowned. This really was awful plonk. His guests would never come to another one of his parties. Oh well, their loss, his financial gain. The thought made him giggle again, which gave him a very strange look, since he had a red wine moustache which didn't at all match the wispy dark bits of hair on his chin.

He looked up from his empty glass, wondering how it had gotten that way and how he could remedy the situation, and his eyes locked on Katrina.

"Holy Mother of God!" he shouted, stunning the still-bewildered guests. He stumbled toward her. "You are the most beautiful fucking woman I have ever seen!"

Katrina, horrified at the man's crazed behaviour and the attention it was eliciting, tried to take a step back, but her heel twisted on a step and she lurched forward instead into the fat man. His beer stein went flying, and the man lunged after it. Katrina would have ended up on the floor, but Boris caught her just in the nick of time.

Andrew, oblivious to all around him, fell to his knees before Katrina and grabbed her hand. "Marry me," he pleaded.

Someone tapped him on the shoulder. His head jerked up. Alana was glaring down at him from an Amazonian height. "You're engaged to *me*, Andrew."

A collective gasp swept the room. All eyes turned to Alana. She squared her shoulders and tried to control the twitch in her eye. "If this is your idea of a joke, Andrew, I am not amused. Get off your knees, now, and away from that woman!"

All eyes turned to Andrew, who was attempting to get up. His balance was way off, and he staggered into Katrina. He clutched onto the hem of her dress for support. It ripped with a loud rending sound, and several inches of fabric were suddenly in Andrew's hands and no longer covering

Katrina's legs. All eyes turn to her legs. Then her face, which had turned from ashen to red in less than a second.

"The wedding's off!" screamed Alana, who'd finally dropped all pretense of cool. It was obvious she wanted to slap Andrew, but his ass was on the floor, and he'd done enough lowering for both of them. She stomped off, her parents at her side, throwing killer glances at the no-longer-future-son-in-law.

Katrina stood like stone for a moment, unsure whether to faint or flee. She decided to flee. She ran in the opposite direction of Alana, her eyes tearing, which thankfully kept her from seeing the faces all around her. Boris was tempted to follow her, but he had something far more important to do. He started shoving his way slowly through the crowd, cursing as he went.

Windle Sr. glanced around and asked, of no one in particular, "Does this mean we don't get dinner?"

Cathy and Jonathan had headed for the dining room after being told by Alana that dinner was about to be served. Jonathan had wanted to continue his search for Katrina, but Cathy pointed out that all the guests would be assembled in the dining room for the toasts and speeches, and he would see her there. They were passing the entrance to the living room when they heard loud voices. They tried to see what was going on, but the door was blocked by other curious onlookers.

"Whatever it is, it can't be that exciting," said Cathy. "You saw the engagement couple, didn't you?"

Jonathan laughed, then suddenly hunched over as his face turned green. "Oh fuck!" he grunted, as if he'd just encountered a mutilated body on the floor.

"What!?" asked Cathy, alarmed.

"I think I'm going to be sick."

"Was it something you ate? It wasn't the escargot, was it? God, I hate puking. What about the arctic char? Did you eat that?"

Jonathan couldn't respond. This was no time to be civil. He shoved his way through the crowd at the door and dashed through the living room, oblivious to the drama unfolding. He finally found a bathroom at the end of a hellishly long hall, but the door was closed. He pounded on it.

"Leave me alone," came a weak voice.

"Please," croaked Jonathan, unable to speak, afraid that more than words would come out. *"Please."*

Still no response, so he tried the door handle. It wasn't locked, so he barged in.

A woman was standing in front of the mirror, blocking the toilet. Of all the times to be preening; didn't women ever stop? This one looked very beautiful by what he could see in the second before he lunged toward the toilet. He fell about 2 feet short of his goal. He couldn't hold it any more. He projectiled all over the woman's dress, which seemed ridiculously short, and partially on her legs, which were ridiculously long. Then he didn't remember anything more for a while because he passed out at her feet, which seemed strangely large. Just before he lost consciousness, she looked down at her Fiorinal-and-Manhattan-covered legs in shock and repulsion, and he recognized the lovely face. His princess, his soul mate, his Cinderella.

Katrina.

42 DAMN THE TORPEDOES

Once Alana and Katrina were gone and Andrew had slunk away, the living room was strangely silent. Everyone just stood around, staring at each other. What now? Did the party continue? Did they pretend nothing had happened and go in to dinner as planned? Or quietly shuffle out and leave the hosts to their misery? The etiquette books never covered territory like this. And they should. Everyone knew where to find their salad fork. Who the hell knew what to do about a busted engagement party?

"Oh, there you are!" trilled a voice in the crowd, and all eyes turned, glad for a diversion.

"I was beginning to wonder if there was anyone here I knew at all! And that would be a pity, since it's so long since I've been out!"

All the partygoers who weren't acquainted with the speaker looked amused at the sight of the elderly lady in her full-length mink and leather gloves on a summer evening. Everyone who knew Gran looked as if they'd seen a ghost. Most of them, frankly, had forgotten she was still alive. Stashed away on the third floor of Lawrence's house, she hadn't been seen in years. Yet amazingly, tonight, she'd somehow escaped.

"Don't look so shocked, Larry," admonished Gran, wondering why his jaw seemed to have fallen hopelessly open. She reached over to shut it, but it wouldn't move. "I heard you on the phone speaking to Andrew, and I, of course, knew that he would have invited me as well, if he'd had a chance to speak with me, and I was about to say something, but you hung up so abruptly . . ."

Lawrence pulled himself together enough to rearrange his jaw and coldly said, "Do you *always* listen in on my phone calls, Gran?"

"I was just picking up the phone to call the pharmacy, dear, now, why all the fuss?" She glanced around, smiling only vaguely at Randall and the Windles, all of whom she knew (or had known, in ancient history) quite well. "Where is the young rascal, anyway?"

"Andrew?" asked Lawrence stupidly. "He, uh, he had to go out for a few minutes, Gran."

"At his own party? How rude! Well, are there any gin and tonics floating about? I'm parched. I had to walk all the way here, you know."

"You walked, dear? By yourself?" said Mrs. Windle, aghast. "Surely Lawrence—"

"Lawrence!" scoffed Gran. "He probably wouldn't have let me come if I'd told him. But after I heard about the party, I thought, damn the torpedoes, I deserve to get out of the house. So I got dressed, and then I realized I had better take a taxi. I live four houses down the road, you know. But I couldn't quite remember where I'd put my purse—"

"Gran," interrupted Lawrence, "do you really think everyone wants to hear—"

Gran kicked Lawrence in the shin, and he shut up immediately. ". . . so I reached under my bed where I keep my spare cash, and as God is my witness, there was almost nothing there!"

Gran turned to stare at everyone watching her, then Lawrence in particular, who looked like he was ready to join Jonathan hugging the porcelain in the washroom down the hall.

There was complete silence—until Boris, who'd been blocked at the other side of the room by the fat man again, this time holding two steins of beer (how could anyone so huge move so fast?), couldn't resist turning and shouting, "Holy shit!" before he burst out laughing.

"What's so damn funny?" demanded Randall, who suddenly remembered his and Lawrence's mission to confront the guy before Stewart's parents had imprisoned them in conversation. "You know something about that?"

Boris stopped midlaugh and turned desperately back toward the fat man, who still hadn't budged. Randall took a step toward him, then thought of something and turned to Stewart.

"Hey, this little twerp works for you, Windle, and he's a thief! Kind of a coincidence, don't you think?"

"What's this all about?" asked Windle Sr., turning to his son. "Thieves? Working for you? I demand an explanation!"

Stewart, who thought he'd been saved when Andrew started ranting like some crazed meth-head, knew he was in deep shit. So Lawrence had stolen from Gran, and Boris had stolen from Lawrence. No wonder Lawrence hadn't mentioned anything. Stealing from his own grandmother! And after all those delightful cookies she used to make. Of course, *she* was the one who had Stewart in hot water now. No matter how good they used to be, her cookies didn't make up for *this*.

Lawrence, seeing a way out of his predicament, turned on Stewart, too. "That's right, Windle. That kid worked one of my parties, too, and as Gran just testified, *money is missing*!"

Several of the PESTS who'd been milling nearby overheard this exchange and approached. "Money missing? You're not missing *our* money, are you, Stewart? You're paying us tomorrow, *right*?" They were suddenly surrounding him. "First thing, *right*?"

Boris, seeing all eyes on somebody else for a change, took his opportunity and shoved aside the fat man, grabbing one of his beers while he was at it. He chugged the brew as he ran and glanced at his watch. Christ! They'd be here any minute! The way things were going at this party, his plan was definitely overkill.

Katrina stared down at herself in utter dismay. Not only was her dress torn and just barely covering her crotch, now it was covered in spew, as were her legs. Who was this animal? With him lying there like that, she couldn't even take off her dress to clean it. Would he *ever* move?

She nudged his head with her toe. No movement. Surely he wasn't dead? Maybe people would think she'd killed him. No, that was ridiculous. She obviously wasn't thinking straight. But she had to get him out of here so she could clean herself up and get back to the party. Or rather, *out* of the party. What a disaster. She hadn't even had too much to drink this time, but that jerk Andrew obviously had. What the hell had he been drinking? The man obviously had a problem. And his poor fiancée, even though she seemed like a real bitch. Even a bitch didn't deserve that.

Katrina stared down at the man again and sighed. He was tall and probably heavy. She certainly couldn't lug him out of here by herself. Maybe some cold water on his face would do the trick. Revive him enough to kick him out. She went over to the sink and looked for a water glass. No luck. Well, she'd have to use her hands. She cupped them together, then shook the water over the man. Nothing. She repeated this action three times until suddenly he moaned and turned his head. About time. Katrina stood over him, ready to give him the boot when he lifted his head and she gasped.

"Jonathan!?"

No, it couldn't be! Here she'd been looking for him for days, and when he finally does show up, she doesn't recognize him and wants to get rid of him. And what was it, some weird karmic thing, his showing up and puking on her like this? Katrina started laughing so hard that *she* almost puked, then she kneeled over him, a big mistake because she got more spew on her knees, and she shook him and looked into his half-shut eyes.

"Jonathan?"

He groaned.

"It's me, Katrina."

He squinted up at her, then his eyes widened. "Is it *really* you?"

Katrina nodded.

"You never told me your name. It might've saved me some time."

"I never gave you my number, either. Not that it would've helped."

"It didn't, believe me."

"You mean Stevie? . . . How on earth did you get my number?"

Jonathan tried to lift up his head, but it refused to cooperate. He groaned and shut his eyes to stop the swirling. "Long story."

"We do meet in the strangest places," said Katrina.

"Yeah," grunted Jonathan. "We must be puke mates."

"I've been looking all over for you," confessed Katrina. "I was desperate. I did some very bad things."

"I'd love to hear all about it," said Jonathan, "but . . ." Katrina leaned closer to hear him, but all she heard was a gentle snore.

Once Cathy heard through the grapevine about the breakup of the engagement couple, she wasted no time heading for the dining room. Damned if she wasn't getting her fill. With all the shit breaking loose, the catering crew was likely to break up the buffet soon. She wasn't taking any chances.

Glancing around, she saw that the huge French doors to the patio were open and tables were set out there, too, to make it one large dining room. Linens and candles and real silver. Real nice, if you cared about that sort of thing. Cathy only cared about the food. As she approached the buffet, she saw she had an accomplice, the doughy teenage doorman who'd apparently abandoned his post when he heard the news. He'd abandoned any pretense at manners, too; he was gnawing on a giant slice of roast beef with his bare hands.

"You think this food is safe?" asked Cathy, sidling up beside him.

"Why wouldn't it be?"

"My friend just got sick. I think it might've been those little canapés."

"That shit would make anybody sick," scoffed the nephew. He waved the roast beef in his hand. "Stick to the meat, I always say."

"What about the couple having the party tonight?" asked Cathy, always eager to know the scoop. "What do you think happened there?"

"To Andrew?" DoughBoy laughed. "He's my uncle. I'm not surprised. He always was a knob."

"Oh," said Cathy, disappointed, hoping for more.

"But I heard he took LSD and maybe some kind of horse tranquilizer."

"Really?!" said Cathy, reaching for the roast beef.

Katrina had taken off her dress in the bathroom, and when Jonathan came to (sort of), she shyly insisted that he look away while she washed herself and put on a towel over her underwear. Looking away was no problem for Jonathan; his head was still spinning from the Fiorinal-Manhattan cocktail, and he was still slightly nauseous. He lay back down on the bathroom carpet, rolled several feet away from the multicoloured puddle, and closed his eyes. Not that he didn't want to see Katrina with her clothes off. But he wouldn't have been able to properly focus, anyway.

Katrina washed and wrung out her dress with the hand soap beside the sink, then found a hairdryer in a cupboard. The dress was polyester and should dry quickly. She hoped so. All she wanted was to escape from all these crazies and be alone with Jonathan.

The cord on the hairdryer looked dubious, and she wondered if the thing even worked. But she couldn't find another one anywhere, and she certainly wasn't going to start searching the house. God knows who she might run into. If the hairdryer didn't work, she'd just have to leave in her towel. She'd run around town in her bikini, hadn't she? A towel was a parka in comparison.

The blow dryer started off with an even hum, and Katrina felt encouraged. She went from holding the dress 8 inches away to 2 to expedite the process. She was starting to hum happily to herself, glancing down fondly at Jonathan half-asleep, when a giant spark leapt out of the end of the hairdryer and on to her dress. Immediately the fabric was on fire. Katrina, in shock, flung the dress at the wall and the dryer to the floor. It fell in the puddle of puke, sparked a few times, then died. The dress was livelier. It collided with the drapes over the window, which immediately burst into flame.

Katrina screamed and yelled out Jonathan's name just as the smoke alarms in the hallway started to shriek.

Then an equally high-pitched voice squealed, "So there you are!"

Katrina glanced up to see Stevie in the doorway, leering at her. He glanced down at Jonathan and said, "So how do you like him now?"

"Stevie," cried Katrina, "this whole place is going to go up in flames! You have to help me get him out of here!"

"A drunk like him?" sneered Stevie. "I don't think so."

Jonathan groaned and stirred and opened his eyes. “You!” he gasped.

“Yes, me,” grinned Stevie. He turned to Katrina. “You’re too good for him, you know.”

“How would you know?” said Katrina. “You don’t even know him!”

“Neither do you. For all you know, he’s another PEST like you.”

Katrina’s eyes widened, and she knelt down by Jonathan. “I never even thought of that! Is it true? Are you?”

Jonathan feebly nodded his head. Katrina laughed. “That’s wonderful! Here I thought you were probably some big-shot rich guy, but it turns out you’re normal just like me!” She leaned over and kissed him. Stevie grunted in disbelief.

“You’d rather have normal than rich? The guy’s probably as poor as you and me.”

“He may not be rich, but I still think he’s a big shot.”

Stevie snorted and glanced down at Jonathan. “Look at him. He can’t even take care of himself. How’s he going to take care of you? You need looking after. You’re too frigging shy to make it on your own.”

Katrina’s emerald eyes flashed, and white knuckles clasped her towel. “I can work on my shyness, Stevie. But you’re a devious, manipulative bastard, and there’s *nothing* you can do about that!”

Stevie flinched, but flipped his hair in a show of bravado. “It was all for your own good, Katrina. You need me.”

“You know what I need, Stevie? A normal relationship with someone who cares for me, not a madman like you who slinks around behind my back pretending to be my friend.”

Katrina took a deep breath and nearly lost her towel. “I may be scared, and I may be shy, but I don’t need you, Stevie, and I *never* will!”

43 ONE HELLUVA PARTY

When the smoke alarms in the hallway were overshadowed by an institutionally loud fire alarm, Cathy, in the dining room, dropped her food (which was promptly caught by DoughBoy) and dashed away from the buffet in search of Katrina.

Everyone else was running in the opposite direction, to the safety of the patio and the great outdoors. Cathy fought her way past them and heard the sound of approaching engines—motorcycles, she thought—a great roar as if a whole gang were descending upon the house. Strange. She should be hearing sirens, not motorcycles. Those daiquiris must've been stronger than she thought. She shook her head. Whatever. She had to find Katrina. And the most likely place, considering the last party they'd attended together, was a bathroom.

The third one she searched revealed Katrina in a towel, trying to stop Stevie from kicking a prone Jonathan. Which was difficult because she had one hand holding together her towel and the other grabbing Stevie's shirt collar. Jonathan was trying to roll away from the kicks and was covered in some slimy substance that made Cathy want to hurl. The air around them was thick with smoke, the drapes over the windows flaring fiercely.

"What are you idiots doing?" screamed Cathy. "Can't you see this place is about to burn down! We have to get out of here, *now*!"

Stevie put his foot down for a moment to glance up at Cathy. "Fuck you! I don't take orders from Katrina's lesbo friend."

Cathy stepped forward and leaned over Stevie. "You know, I've had about enough of you!" She pulled back her fist as far as it would go and punched Stevie in the nose.

He toppled backward, just missing Jonathan, his nose streaming blood. Cathy surveyed her handiwork with pride, then said, "Always did have a good left hook."

She motioned to Katrina to help her, and they started to lift Jonathan up. With Stevie no longer kicking him and the Fiorinal and Manhattans slowly wearing off, he almost managed to sit up by himself.

"Man," said Cathy, "I'm sure glad I didn't eat what you did."

"That little maggot slipped something in my drink," grunted Jonathan. "Must've thought I was his date."

"He must've thought Andrew was, too," said Katrina. She was tempted to kick Stevie where he lay, crying, but he looked too pathetic with his mushy nose bleeding into his puke-strewn hair.

"Come on," said Cathy, nudging Stevie's head with her shoe. "Get up."

Stevie just cried and shook his head.

"Then stay here for all I care. You'll make a very pretty piece of barbecue."

Suddenly the room got much brighter and hotter, and they turned to see that the drapes had caught on a towel hanging on a rack, which, in turn, was threatening to heat up the nearby beauty products on the shelves. They might blast off at any moment. Adrenaline cleared the last fumes from Jonathan's head, and he used Cathy and Katrina as a ladder to drag himself up, dislodging Katrina's towel. It slipped to the floor, and she started to pick it up, but Cathy stopped her.

"No time!" she screamed, and she shoved them all through the door. Stevie suddenly realized his plight and forgot his bloody nose long enough to jump up after them. But he still cried like a little girl.

When Boris had implored the Glory Riders the night before to crash Andrew's party, they'd agreed reluctantly. Boris was nothing more to them than Len's former two-bit burglar roommate and Harley's little spy. But they *had* ripped off Boris pretty damn good on the coke he'd just sold them and were going to make a bundle on it. So they were in the mood for a party. And there was nothing they liked better than ruining someone else's.

They were astonished when they roared onto Andrew's patio and were greeted by a terrified Boris, frantically waving his arms, a beer stein in one hand.

"Shit, guys, this was all a mistake! I'm sorry, I don't need you here after all!"

"But you invited us!" yelled Harley, dressed in full biker regalia, even more resplendent than the rest of the gang. "Too late to call us off now!" He laughed maniacally and waved to the rest of the Glory Riders to start circling the patio.

"But I just wanted to scare her a little!" yelled Boris. "I've changed my mind."

Harley ignored him and drove through the open patio doors, straight into the dining room. Tables and chairs went flying.

"Oh my God!" cried Boris, tearing at his shaggy hair. "Do you have any idea how much that stuff is worth?"

As he watched, hordes of panicked guests streamed into the dining room, escaping the imminent fire, only to come to an abrupt halt at the sight of

Harley. Many guests toppled into the ones before them. Others avoided that mistake and sidestepped the fallen, only to be chased by the other Glory Riders, who'd driven inside, yelping war cries with unabashed glee.

Boris glanced around desperately. Randall and Lawrence and Stewart could be right behind the rest of the crowd. And when they saw him . . . Boris gulped down the last of his beer and flung the stein in the bushes, then jumped in after it.

Harley spotted him and roared after him, but the bushes were too thick and his hog too precious to go in after Boris. "That's it, Burglar Boy!" he yelled. "Start a riot, then shit your pants! Len would be proud of ya!"

Harley backed up and turned around, chasing after a few people fleeing toward the open gates that led to freedom. In his absence, a few other guests followed Boris's lead and lunged into the shrubbery.

Andrew, who'd run immediately to the dining room after his debacle with Alana, knowing the wine would be open and ready for the guests, now stood there, stunned. He chugged from a bottle of wine, tears in his eyes, and laughed hysterically as one of the bikers swooped down to pluck a wine bottle from the table beside him.

Gran, who'd been swept up by a strange fat man and deposited near Andrew, stood clutching a gin and tonic, slowly going round in circles, watching the roaring bikers. They reminded her of a rodeo show she'd seen long ago. Certainly the hollering was the same; only the animals were different.

"I had no ideas these parties were so lively," she said to a stunned Lawrence, who suddenly appeared beside her.

Randall, who arrived on Lawrence's heels, gaped in awe at the devastation around him, then abandoning all pretense, pulled a coke vial from his pocket and snorted a big spoonful. A passing biker grabbed the vial from his hand, howling like a banshee.

"Fuck!" yelled Randall.

"Mind your mouth, son," admonished Gran.

"This is amazing," said Lawrence, in awe. Gran squinted at him. "It's just like a sixties movie; it's like *Breakfast at Tiffany's* or something; it's fucking phenomenal!"

"Mind your—"

"Fuck you, Gran," said Lawrence, and he grabbed a bottle of Bordeaux off one of the few surviving tables and started chugging, absently spitting out a cigarette butt that one of the bikers had tossed in. After a couple of swigs, he stepped onto a chair, then onto the table, and began to dance the twist.

Stewart arrived late to the chaos, having spent several minutes convincing all the PESTS who were after him for money that now was not the time. They might not live to see it if they didn't get their asses out of here.

He flagged down one of the Glory Riders like a passing cab and offered a generous sum to get him the hell out. He'd stashed a lot of money in Andrew's study, but, being a prudent fellow, he'd kept some on his person. He'd have to let the rest go or risk getting involved in this brouhaha and lose his trust fund altogether. It wasn't a difficult choice. He'd heard one could live very cheaply in Mexico.

He had just swung a leg over the Harley and wrapped his arms around his driver when he spotted Katrina and Cathy, supporting a dazed-looking Jonathan, followed by that thieving flamer, who was blubbering like a lost puppy.

"Wait a minute!" said Stewart to the driver. "I have to talk to somebody." He took a hundred-dollar bill from his pocket, tore it in half, and said, "Stay put. You'll get the other half when I get back." The driver took the torn bill and shrugged. Stewart clambered off the bike.

"Ahoy there!" he shouted over the noise of the bikes and the fire alarm and the screaming crowd.

"Stewart!" cried Cathy and Katrina in unison. "What on earth is going on?"

"I've no idea," beamed Stewart, glancing around. "But it's one helluva party. I had no idea Andrew had it in him."

Katrina glanced over at Andrew, who now clutched three bottles of wine, whether for weapons or libations she couldn't tell. "Neither did he."

Stewart grinned at Katrina and nodded at Jonathan. "So you found him? Good girl. I always thought you might."

"You knew all along who he was!" exclaimed Katrina.

"Of course, dear. Jonathan is one of my favourite PESTS."

"I don't see why you couldn't have just told us," said Katrina.

"I told you from the start there were rules. And I think you ladies broke one or two—sending a thief to steal my little black book, for instance." He nodded toward Stevie, who'd stopped crying and was now picking at his bloody nose and looking at the smears on his fingertips as if wondering where they'd come from.

"Okay, okay, I guess we're even," said Cathy. A Glory Rider roared past her swinging a giant turkey leg, and sirens howled in the distance. "Looks like chit-chat time's just about over."

"You're right about that," conceded Stewart. "But you know, I have a soft spot for you two ladies. You're my true idea of what Life of the Party is all about."

"Even me?" said Katrina. "I'm not exactly—"

"Oh, but you are." Stewart grinned. "And besides, you two and Jonathan are the only PESTS who haven't pestered me about money all night. And for that reason, I'm going to tell you a little secret."

He put his lips to Katrina's ear and told her where he had stashed the money Andrew had paid him earlier. Katrina gasped. "But it's yours! Why don't you go get it? Why don't—"

"No time," said Stewart, jumping back on the bike. "I'm not as young or fast as you, and I can't afford to get caught by the cops and spend the night in jail. I have plans tomorrow."

"But we can't just take your money!" said Katrina as the bike's engine revved. She could barely hear Stewart's reply.

"I can always find myself more money," he laughed. "Now go get yours, before it's burnt to a crisp." The bike roared through the patio gates, and the sound of the sirens got closer.

"We've got to get out of here!" yelled Katrina. She grabbed Cathy's and Jonathan's arms and turned them in the other direction.

"But what about me?" whined Stevie. "You can't leave me here with them!" The Glory Riders roared menacingly around him, taunting his pale, skinny frame and long, limp hair. He sniffed with some difficulty. "Where are you going?"

"Where you're not," yelled Cathy. "Go on, get outta here!" She pushed Stevie toward the patio, where some of the bikers, eager to escape before the arrival of the police, had left a gap. The guests were rushing toward it like a herd of crazed cattle, threatening a very sloppy stampede.

As Katrina, Cathy, and Jonathan ran toward the study where Stewart had left the money, they heard Andrew yelling after Stewart. "I want my goddamn money back, you limey prick! Look what your PESTS have done! I'm not paying for this mess!"

Windle Senior, standing at the buffet table next to DoughBoy, his wife trying to drag him away from the food without success, dropped a leg of lamb when he spotted Katrina in her underwear running by.

"There she is again!" he yelled. He turned to his wife. "I *told* you I wasn't making it up!"

Lawrence, still dancing on the table, raised his wine bottle in a toast and howled at the ceiling. His howl was suddenly superseded by the whining of sirens.

Katrina, still trying, along with Cathy, to half-carry a still-slow Jonathan, looked up at him and shook her head. "We're going to have to let you go."

"But I just found you."

Katrina kissed his forehead. "Not forever, silly. Just long enough for us to get the money. We'll never get out of here in time, dragging you this way." She nodded to the left. "Look, there's a servants' entrance over there, away from the patio. Go outside and wait for us. We'll be quick." Katrina and Cathy were already sprinting toward the study as Jonathan staggered toward the entrance.

The flames were approaching, and the smoke was getting thick. Luckily, the money was right under the rug where Stewart had told them it would be. "Simple and obvious," he'd said. "Works every time."

"Wow!" cried Cathy. "Look at this wad!"

"Yeah," said Katrina, grabbing her. "Now let's go."

"We can't just run out of the house carrying all this cash. Someone might find it a little suspicious." Cathy looked over Katrina's underwear. "You don't exactly have a lot of hiding spots there."

Katrina shook her head. Cathy sighed. "Oh well. I get to play the Fat Lady again. Nothing new, really." And she started stuffing the cash down her dress, running as she went.

Jonathan was waiting by the servants' entrance as promised, sitting on a little bench. "Where's the money?" he asked, still a little stunned. "Couldn't you find it?"

"Thanks a lot," said Cathy, whacking him lightly on the head. "I just came out of there 20 pounds fatter, and you didn't even notice." She hauled him up with more force than necessary, and Katrina grabbed his other side, and they hobbled down a cobbled path, far from the cops and the fire trucks.

"Wow," said Katrina. "Do you suppose Len sicced those bikers on us?"

"Naw," said Cathy. "I don't think you're ever gonna see him again. I bet it was Boris, that little thug."

"Boris? Seriously? And I was starting to think he might be an okay guy," mused Katrina.

"You've got a weird definition of *okay*," said Cathy.

"Who's Boris?" asked Jonathan.

"My roommate," said Katrina.

"Jesus," said Jonathan. "You know how to pick 'em."

"It's a long story," said Katrina.

"And I want to hear every single word of it," said Jonathan, and he stopped Katrina and kissed her hard and long on the lips.

"Hellooo," said Cathy, stepping between them and dragging them apart. "In case you hadn't noticed, there's cop cars and fire trucks all over the frigging place. Not to mention Glory Riders. We get out of here in one piece, and I'll pay for your motel." She jiggled her ample breasts and some bills peepcd out from her cleavage.

"But Cathy, we have to give that money back to Stewart!" exclaimed Katrina.

"I hate to break the news, hon, but we won't be seeing Swindle any time soon." She sighed. "He *was* awfully cute." She turned to Katrina with a grin. "Besides, the money's already spent."

"What!?"

"On your *dream*, Katrina—something about a hair salon?"

Jonathan grabbed their shoulders and propelled them forward. "I hate to break up the conversation, but if you have any intention of keeping that money, we really should get the hell out of here."

Katrina beamed at him as the fire flared behind them and the sirens howled closer.

"You're right. Who wants to spend the night in jail?" She leaned close and brushed a promising finger over his lips.

"We have much better things to do."

Looking for more from Katrina?

Check out the second in the series,

Friends of the Deceased,

written by Dale J. Moore

(over)

Friends of the Deceased

a Trials of Katrina Novel

Dale J. Moore

How does a small town girl end up investigating crime at a funeral home in Toronto? Drop-dead gorgeous Katrina is trying to run her new salon and take her relationship to a new level. The unexpected death of a client and struggles with her salon lead her to the Shady Rest funeral home.

As she stumbles her way through the personal problems that plague her world, Katrina ends up immersed in the world of preparing people for the next world. With the help of a ruggedly handsome police detective, some old friends, and a few new ones, will she get to the bottom of what's going on, or end up buried by it? One thing is certain; when Katrina gets involved, chaos and comedy will ensue.

www.northernamusements.com